MW01138550

The Legacy of

MAXIMILLIAN BAUER

~ A TOM HALL MYSTERY ~

Arthur Norby

Copyright © 2019 Arthur Norby
Revised June 2019

A Kart Press Publication

All rights reserved.

Printed in the United States of America

All rights reserved. Except as permitted under the U.S. Copyright Act of 1976, no part of this publication may be reproduced, distributed, or transmitted in any form or by any means, or stored in a database or retrieval system, without the prior written permission of the publisher.

* * * * *

Cover photo by Kari L. Barchenger

Interior formatting by Debora Lewis deboraklewis@yahoo.com

* * * * *

Disclaimer
This is a work of fiction, a product of the author's imagination. Any resemblance or similarity to any actual events or persons, living or dead, is purely coincidental. Although the author and publisher have made every effort to ensure there are no errors, inaccuracies, omissions, or inconsistencies herein, any slights or people, places, or organizations are unintentional.

ISBN-13: 9781091302983

Acknowledgments

In writing *The Legacy of Maximillian Bauer* I have missed the enthusiastic support of my wife Kathryn, who passed away in 2016. I thank my daughter Kari Barchenger for stepping in to help me through my battle with computers. Also, my nephew Scott Eastvold, the consummate genealogist, for a wealth of historical information. And—of course—I want to thank my family, friends and art collectors for making me believe writing another mystery is a great idea

Foreward

WHEN BEAUTIFUL BUT promiscuous Roberta Swan is brutally murdered in her bed, local jurist John Chamberlin calls on Tom Hall to solve the mystery of her death. The judge believes the woman's murder is connected to another unsolved death from a year earlier and may be just the most recent act of vengeance against descendants of the early Minnesota pioneer Iverson family.

Tom's search for Roberta's killer traces a complex chain of events as pioneers cross the Atlantic Ocean, then continue across the American prairie to find new homes, lives, and loves. As Tom tries to sort the uncounted pieces of the mysterious puzzle laid before him he learns of the challenges that were faced by one small group of immigrants who have become the subjects of this story.

They journeyed across the Atlantic Ocean, then across wilderness that seemed to have no end. They were welcomed in some places, vilified in others. They came with no guarantee they would survive, let alone thrive. And, just as in this story... well, I think you'll get the picture.

From the time the Iversons of this story embarked on their journey, to the conclusion of Tom Hall's mystery, every day and every mile they travelled was an experience we can only pretend to understand. The Heinrichs, the MacGregors, and every family depicted in Chippewa County crossed the State of Minnesota and the vast American frontier before that. The good and the valiant—as well as the degenerate man or woman who has no chance for redemption—might have been the one who challenges the same mysteries you and I find in our dreams or in our nightmares.

If some of the characters seem familiar, please just enjoy the comparisons. As Max Bauer plunders his way across the wilderness, and as Boyd fights demons only he recognizes, look carefully at the woodlands and the muddy rivers they challenged. When the MacGregors, the Iversons and the Heinrichs followed game trails—not paved roads—perhaps to become the first white people to see the Minnesota River or to be the first person to set a plow in native prairie, they may have been challenged by dark complexioned natives. Or, accosted by travelers who looked just like themselves.

But, let's not forget the other experiences hidden in our various histories. As always, in addition to hate and violence, there was lust and love. Sometimes the lust was violent and cruel, but I can imagine the vulnerable hope felt by Alice Bevins. Think of the surprise Tom and Mary experienced when their true feelings were discovered.

One

WHEN I FIRST came to Chippewa County and to the county seat of Montevideo in the autumn of 1938, I had no idea my family would be the focus of a very unusual murder investigation. I was just looking for information about my ancestors. It was mid-October— that in-between month on the northern prairie. Small grains such as oats, barley, wheat and flax had been harvested, but the corn was just on the cusp of maturity. Another week, maybe two, and the fields would be filled with horse-drawn pickers. Picking corn was slow and tedious process. Two rows at a time, or four rows at a time if you were a richer custodian of the land. Back and forth across the fields, stripping the cobs of corn from the stalks.

The mechanical pickers were faster than picking by hand, which had been the only option not so long before. When the corn harvest was complete the cows could be turned out into the stubble fields. In many cases, especially if the winter was mild, the cows would graze there for the entire winter. It was a win-win option. The cows were conveniently fed, using corn remnants which the mechanical picker had left behind. All the cows had to do was wander across the stubble, nudge away a little snow, grind corn from the left-behind cobs and ruminate to their heart's content.

Alternating fields, which earlier had been filled with crops of oats, wheat, or barley, would now be host to stacks of hay reaching two stories high. Round mounds of hay or straw, blown into existence as the harvested grain-shocks were fed into the huge threshing machines, now provided roughage and protein for free-ranging cattle and horses. As the mechanical threshing machines blew hay or straw into mounds, they also blew the oats, wheat, and barley grains into waiting grain wagons. The wagons ultimately delivered their cargo to a convenient granary somewhere on the farm site.

But this was not the month of harvest, and I had not come to drive a team of horses or pitch bundles of grain. I've been an amateur genealogist for a long time and was looking for my ancestors. I might have just been trying to validate my own identity by recording some family history, but I was interested in knowing the history of my grandparents, their parents, and their parents, and so on, hoping to go back to their country of origin. Who could tell; maybe I was related to a king or a queen somewhere. So, I decided to make the Journey to Chippewa County, where four generations of my ancestors are buried, and where, it seemed, I could begin to trace them to their exotic and far away origins. The possibilities seemed endless and I was excited to start my new adventure.

I got side-tracked long before finding royalty, however. What I found in Chippewa County was a mystery playing out over nearly one hundred years. Although I was to be little more than an observer, I was to be a ring-side observer as the puzzle which was Maximillian Bauer's legacy of hate was put together one small piece at a time. Pieces of the puzzle would complete a picture nearly half a continent wide and nearly a hundred years deep. One man's anger and jealousy created a legacy of hate and violence.

A puzzle is at first a jumble of small pieces, seemingly unconnected, and gathered in a pile after being dumped without ceremony from the box. The first pieces of this puzzle showed a family of emigrants preparing for the journey of their lifetime. During the year of 1843, nearly sixteen hundred Norwegian citizens would immigrate to America, leaving behind the comforts of home and family. For many of them there was little to leave behind. In the manner of the times, only the oldest son in a family could expect to inherit land, and therefore, inherit the hope of prosperity. Even though that son stayed on the land there would be little prosperity for him and his family, but rather a life filled with hard labor and privation. So, for the three-hundred men, women and children gathered here, there was hope for a better life across the Atlantic Ocean.

Among the travelers waiting to board ship was three-year-old Hans Iverson, his two brothers Halvor and Ole, their parents Hans II and Anne, as well as grandfather Hans Iverson. Also among the three-hundred-one passengers was an unkempt red-haired German youth named Maximillian Bauer. Bauer was unknown to the Iverson family, but the violent ship-board skirmish that was soon to take place was between Bauer and a member of the Iverson family. Those two men would meet on the American prairie one more time, in 1853. The anger and violence from their first meeting would affect the lives of others for nearly one-hundred years.

The history of the Iverson family in America, the trail they followed, and the tale of their ultimate settling in Minnesota's Chippewa County, began like hundreds of other families. Those families left the safety, if not comfort, of earlier lives, hoping to improve their conditions. The Iverson's journey began on a crisp morning in May of 1843. The rain had not yet started but was expected soon. When that happened the day would not be pleasant; the spring breeze would become harsh, and the anxious crowd would wish for even a little respite, a little protection from the weather. For the past week hopeful travelers had been arriving from all parts of Norway. For another week they would fill the streets and alleyways of Havre as the waited for the arrival of the Argo. Like so many before them, the Iversons had nervously made the journey from their native Norway to Havre, France. From there they would sail to the United States of America. In spite of the day's cold spring rain the crowds were in high spirit and there was excitement in the air.

The three generations of Iversons huddled together in the lea of a large gray building, finding what shelter they could from the freshening wind. "It's quite simple, Anne." Hans explained once again why it was so important to uproot their family, "Anne, there is nothing left for us here. If we stay we will never be more than laborers on the Iverson farm. We can never own our own land here.

At least, when we get to America, we will have a chance to build a home for our children. In America we can give them hope, which we can never do if we stay here." Hans Rui Iverson, at the age of thirty-eight, knew the only future for him, his wife, and three children, lay in the trip they would soon make, and although they had discussed their journey many times, Anne just needed a little encouragement.

Hans Rui Iverson, his wife Guru Osland Rui, and their three sons: Olav, age fifteen; Halvor, age nine; and Hans II, who was three years old, were not really leaving *everything* behind in the truest sense; Hans' father Olav Kiettelsson Rui, already an old man at sixty-seven, would join them. "It is a sad thing for me, Hans," he had said. "My whole life I shared with Lorna, and now she is gone from me." Lorna Marie Karlsdodtter Rui had been buried only weeks before. When Olav looked at the meager possessions he had acquired over a lifetime he too was preparing to make the journey to America. "Without my dear wife I shall have nothing here to live for when you and your children have gone."

In only a few days, depending on the tides and the impending weather, three hundred-one excited and anxious people from the milling crowd would board the Argo and sail for America. Among them were some twenty-eight related members of the Rui and Osland family, who would eventually settle on the untamed prairies of Minnesota. In addition to the Rui's and Oslands, and in the tradition of the times, there were Kilens, Bukaasens, Nykasses, Jordgrafs and others, who, as tenant farmers, had taken first the Rui and then the Iverson farm names.

In order to pay their passage, each of those who would board the Argo would have saved from their meager earnings or would have sold something of personal value. For every passenger: man, woman or child, it would take five dollars of that savings to get to Havre, France, and for the final passage to an American port, another eight dollars.

In their excitement to find a new life, and with an unexplainable optimism for what may lie ahead, most left their families and undertook their journey with only hope. Many of those in the crowded streets would be turned back before boarding when the ship's captain found they actually didn't have the fare, or even when they did, if it was discovered the hopeful emigrant did not have enough money to sustain him or herself on the dangerous journey ahead.

The sailing vessel Argo, a three-mast-barque of one hundred sixty-one feet, left Havre, France May 16, 1843 and arrived in the United States after six uneventful weeks at sea. The journey could be considered uneventful if you disregard frequent passenger bouts of sea sickness and a fight which took place below-decks the last day at sea. When the Argo, with its fifteen-man crew, finally set sail, there would be three-hundred-one hopeful passengers collected for the trip

From Havre, the ship sailed around the south coast of England before setting a course which would end on America's coast and the city of New York. For most passengers there was no such thing as a private cabin. For a select few who could afford the luxury there was a between decks area which gave semi-private lodging. Only a few passengers could afford the pure luxury afforded by private cabins above deck. Most of the three-hundred-one men, women and children shared the cavernous space below decks. In spite of the conservative and pious lives these pioneers had led, there was little opportunity for modesty or privacy; at best, a blanket or quilt separated family groups.

The passengers on this trip had been merchants, farmers and laborer, not seamen. For most of the voyage there was misery throughout the ship. In stormy seas the stench below deck became unbearable. Being seasick was the norm rather than the exception. The ship frequently tacked into the westerly wind and when it did, adults and children alike braced themselves against the roll and pitch caused by the choppy seas that threatened to throw them to the deck. Parents, children, and grandparents huddled together and offered each other encouragement. Good days, days when the sea was friendly, passengers found short intervals at the rails, hoping to be the first to spot land while marveling at the seemingly endless ocean they were crossing.

On this arduous journey to America friendships were made that would last a lifetime. There would also be angry moments. Enemies would also be made, which needed to be avenged.

Two

FOR THE IVERSONS, the ocean journey from Havre, France to the United States of America was a relatively short trip. The hardy Iverson family ate, slept and prayed together. Hans continued to extoll the virtue of hard work and Godliness to his sons while Anne mothered them as she spoke of God, laughed with them as she had them read to her, ensuring her sons would be as well-educated as she could make possible.

As the journey neared its end, Hans would encourage Anne by reminding her "Our journey is nearly over, Anne. I am told we will be in America tomorrow, or the following day, at the latest. Then we can find a home for our children." Hans Iverson had no way of knowing that it would take them more than ten years to cross the vast spaces of America. Before they would reach their final destination the Iverson family would exchange their labors for sustenance on several occasions. A winter's protection from the elements would be paid for with a winter of animal husbandry by husband, wife and children, given to strangers in a strange country. An autumn of cutting timber for another emigrant's home would allow them to stave off hunger for a season. The naive and excited immigrants would travel across Lake Erie and Lake Ontario by barge. Sometimes travelling by themselves and sometimes with groups of like-minded pioneers. They would learn that the cost of their journey was not to be measured in dollars, but in loneliness and fatigue, or dangerous encounters with those who wanted to steal their meager belongings, or who would threaten their lives.

On their last day at sea, and only a day after encouraging Anne that their voyage was almost over, the Iverson family came perilously close to calamity. Hans had been on deck with other men, excitedly discussing their impending arrival. The Iverson children had joined those from other families and were playing in the open cabin near the center of the ship, leaving Anne time to mend a pair of torn trousers for one of the boys.

As he descended below-deck Hans had come around a cluster of barrels which held drinking water and found Anne struggling to free herself from an unkempt and smelly red-haired young man. As she had been sitting on a soft pile of bedding she had been suddenly grabbed from behind. She was roughly thrown to the deck as the red-haired man pounced on her. Somehow, it was one of those rare times there were no other passengers in the area. She kicked violently at her attacker but could not scream with his hand tight against her mouth. In spite of her panic and fear Anne continued to thrash at her attacker, refusing to submit to his evil intent.

With a hand over Anne's mouth, he was pawing and tearing at her dress. Anne's eyes were wide with fright as she kicked and struggled to free herself. Although she thrashed her arms and legs as she tried to break free she was no match for her assailant and felt herself beginning to lose the battle.

Seeing his wife being assaulted, Hans jumped forward and in a violent rush he grabbed the man by his hair, yanking him away from Anne. Nearly scalping the attacker as he violently threw the stranger to the deck, Hans yelled "My God, man, what are you trying to do?"

One screaming in Norwegian and one in German, the two men snarled at each other as they threw themselves into battle and into a nearby stack of barrels. Hans pummeled the man who had attacked his wife. Now, it was not Anne but Hans who had the attacker's attention. The attacker could not just slink away; he needed to subdue the man who had intruded on his lustful attack. The red-haired German was younger than Hans by many years, but after hard years of farming Hans was no easy victim, and he was intent on subduing the man who attacked Anne. They rolled across the deck, throwing each other against the crates, barrels, and trunks containing the life's possessions of the passengers; each man was bent on hammering the other into submission. Then, as Hans charged the other man, he slipped on the wet deck of the steerage hold and lost his footing.

Sensing victory, the German pulled a sharp short-bladed knife from the sheaf on his belt and lunged at Hans. Passengers now crowded close to the combatants, cheering, without knowing the cause of the fight, but intent on seeing someone—anyone—brought to submission. The anxieties and tensions built up during the arduous trip surfaced and many in the crowd just wanted to see violent emotions released. In one moment Hans threw his legs up and caught his attacker square in the chest. The knife sailed out of sight, leaving the red-haired man unarmed and now looking for a way to escape. In the semi-darkness of the steerage hold the younger man sent a crushing blow of his elbow into Hans's temple. Then the stranger thrust himself through the crowd, and in another instant he became invisible.

Although Hans wanted desperately to pursue his wife's attacker his first concern now was for Anne. All this time Anne had knelt near the ladder leading to the next deck, trying desperately to cover herself while clutching three-year old Hans to her side. Somewhere in the dark steerage hold her other two sons heard the yelling, but they were unaware of the drama taking place just a short distance away.

After comforting his wife, Hans spent the rest of the day searching for her attacker, but even aboard the small ship, it was to no avail. Hans knew if he had found him that he would have driven the red-haired man's own knife deep into his chest, but when the hold finally became too dark to investigate further he discontinued his search. On the following day Hans's attentions were given to Anne and their three sons. Nothing was more important now than getting them safely from the ship and started on their journey to Minnesota Territory and their new life.

The Iversons joined hundreds of immigrant families as they sought new homes. Across the state of New York, through Lake Ontario, then across Lake Erie before travelling across the untamed prairie to the lush forested lands of Illinois and Wisconsin. It was a journey filled with new and exciting sights. The family crossed the northern plains using whatever transportation they could achieve. It would be nearly ten years before they found their first home in Minnesota. In the hilly country of Fillmore County they would establish their first homestead. There, they would challenge the land to give up its first-ever crops to a white man. In Fillmore County, Hans Iverson would meet the red-Haired German for the second time.

Before settling in Fillmore County, the family found refuge in the Skoponing community of Wisconsin for a short time. It was there they would bury the grandfather and celebrate the birth of a daughter they named Laura. Then, the family crossed the river into wilderness that someday would be called Iowa. With other Norwegian families, they gathered together for safety and a feeling of community while they planned for their next move.

In 1852, Hans joined a dozen other men who ventured further north into land that had seldom seen white men. These were the first white men to settle their farmlands in the Minnesota Territory.

Men of similar backgrounds, they were immigrants seeking a better life for their families as they gathered together. Earlier hardships they had faced just to reach this remote land brought them close. Safety in numbers from the native Indians, who still claimed the land as their birthright, kept them on watch for each other. They shared labors to build a hut, dig a home out of a hillside, hunted wild game, which would be shared by one and all as they strove toward a common goal. The frigid winter was spent huddled together with little protection from wind and snow. Some were protected only by the canvas covering of their wagon. They foraged singly, or in small groups, to find whatever wild game to feed them. Although the deer were plentiful, getting a carcass a half mile to their encampment through two or three feet of snow would drive more than one man to his knees. On a rare day a bison, called buffalo by those who had travelled further into the wilderness but never seen by them in Norway, would be killed. The huge beast would feed them for weeks, with the hide going to the man fortunate enough to have made the killing shot.

After a hard year without his family, fighting cold and snow in a nearly unbearable winter and a month of heat, flies, mosquitos and loneliness in the summer, Hans had managed to dig from the ground a home for his family of six. Into a south-facing hillside he flattened the dirt, then, by cutting sections of sod from the prairie, he did what many others had done and would still do in the future. He built a fourteen foot by eighteen-foot sod dugout home into the hillside and covered the roof's sapling frame with more sod to keep out the weather. The Iverson family now had a home in America.

In the summer of 1854, tired to the bone, Hans travelled back to Iowa. His shirt, trousers and shoes were worn nearly past the point of repair. His bones ached from the frigid winter. There had been many days he questioned whether he should have taken his family from their poor but safe home in Norway. When his family came into view he thrust those thoughts aside. Here, here in America he had created a humble home for his family. It would always be theirs, he told himself.

Reunited, the family packed their meager treasures and set out for Minnesota Territory. Small settlements were now being established where only months before there had been only virgin prairie. They spent a week following an occasional trail in a land where two years earlier the ground had never been touched by a wagon wheel. The hordes of flies and mosquitos which had tormented Hans when he had worked to claim the land seemed to not exist as the family laughed and luxuriated in their excitement as they found their way north.

Hans immediately began the task of turning the prairie into farmable land. Using nearly all his savings, he bought a sound horse and a single bottom John Deere Prairie Queen plow, adding these to his possession of one ox, one cow and a pregnant hog. The ox that had pulled his wagon with the family's meager belongings on the final leg of their journey now pulled the plow. Hans spent seemingly endless day after endless day turning the native prairie sod into a cultivated field, one furrow at a time. Even as he collapsed in fatigue at the end of the day he could smile. This was all his. It belonged to him and his family. They had never before known such richness.

The Iversons knew there was no going to town for frivolous purchases. The nearest town, such as it was, was Rushford. Along with a few other fledgling businesses, the little village contained a general store for basic goods and a blacksmith for those lucky enough to own a horse but without the proper equipment to shoe it. For those without the equipment or skills needed to accomplish the repairs, the blacksmith provided the service for a nominal fee. Near the edge of the village was a small church for souls in need of saving or soothing. And, of course, as in many settlements on the edge of that great wilderness, there was a saloon.

Twelve years had passed since the Iversons had reached America, and now, in the summer of 1856, Hans and the red-haired German would meet again. At sunrise on a Thursday morning Hans and his eldest son had left the farmstead, going to Rushford for flour and the other miscellaneous household items Anne needed and could no longer do without. It was a full day's journey into Rushford and back.

The horse picked its way around rocks and through small gullies still running with water. There were no roads between the Iverson farm and Rushford. From time to time they could pick out tracks made by an earlier traveler. Occasionally, they would spot a clearing or a building jutting from the trees in one of the valleys they passed. The horse chose its own path with only an occasional correction by Hans as he tugged a rein or clucked encouragement as they crested a hill. It was a good time for a father and son to talk of the crops and to plan for the next year. And, it was a good time for father and son to grow closer without the overburden of hard farm work.

Father and son spent an hour wandering from business to business. Hans greeted everyone with a smile, and proudly introduced the younger Hans with praise for his son's natural talent for farm chores and his natural ability to adapt to their new home. It seemed to take no time at all to accomplish their tasks. Finally, Hans sent his son to the buckboard with a sweet treat for himself and one for each of his siblings.

It was just after mid-day as they finished their tasks. The lunch Anne had prepared was safely stored under the wagon seat, and both father and son were looking forward to sandwiches put together on fresh baked bread and a jar of milk. The milk had been stored in the water tank near the house and was now wrapped in two thicknesses of dish towels from Anne's linen cupboard to keep it reasonably cool for their journey. They would enjoy their lunch as they made the long trip home.

A few riders on horseback plied their way along the muddy street of Rushford, as did occasional buggies and wagons drawn by horses or oxen, which were prevalent in the area. It had rained on Tuesday night and most of Wednesday, making Thursday a good day for the trip to Rushford. A cold wind had begun to blow as they arrived in Rushford, and now the sky to the south looked like it might bring rain again. Hans hoped he and his son would stay dry for the trip home.

In 1856, Rushford was a hardscrabble collection of buildings along the shore of the Root River. Limestone cliffs to the north of the river gave a meager promise of protection from prairie winds. The dirt street undulated through the protected valley, following the natural lay of the land. It was dusty most of the summer, but after this week's rain, it was muddy and rut-filled by the passing traffic. A boardwalk of rough timber connected the buildings fronting on Main Street. In places two broad planks eased the step from the boardwalk to the muddy street.

As the younger Hans sat in the buckboard, holding the horse steady, his father brought the last of the supplies from the general store. He had added a bag of salt, five pounds of nails needed to finish enclosing the livestock shed and, for Anne, a special treat of three yards of gingham cloth.

The saloon, which stood next to the general store, was little more than a canvas-sided shelter from the elements. Its owner prayed he would be able to put the slab-siding around the building before winter set in. It was from the saloon the red-haired man appeared once again. Hans was burdened with two large sacks containing flour and was concentrating on the boardwalk with its uneven steps as he maneuvered his way to the buckboard. He did notice the approaching man until the moment they collided.

The red-haired man lurched from the saloon with a large mug of beer in his hand, shouting profanities at the world as he stumbled across the boardwalk. The muscular teenager from aboard ship had become a man. A decade of prairie life had turned him into a six-foot tall, two-hundred-pound tyrant. Hard labor, when absolutely necessary, and hard drinking whenever he could, had made him a force to be wary of. His companions were not the peers of the community, but the scourge of the territory, and he relished in their adulation. As he stumbled through the saloon door he spun around, trying to maintain his balance as he shouted an obscene expletive to his companions who were still in the tavern. He connected solidly with Hans, who was burdened with his sacks of flour and was knocked to his knees.

In a rage, the drunken German lashed out at Hans, kicking him viscously in the side before finally losing his own balance and crashing to the ground. Hans looked up to see the distorted features of his assailant. Even after twelve years Hans recognized his attacker. The man was older, of course; he weighed perhaps forty pounds more than as a teenager aboard the ship, but the mean look in his bloodshot eyes was the same, if unfocused now because of the liquor. But, it was without question the same man, with a week of unshaven beard and grimy hair which fell past the collar of his filthy shirt.

This time Hans swore to himself that he would not let the red-haired stranger get away. Anne deserved retribution for the attack she had suffered aboard ship. He rose to one knee, thrusting aside the heavy bags which trapped him on the boardwalk. A mild-mannered man by temperament, Hans was now intent on striking out with all his ability at the man whose memory he had quietly carried for so many years.

The last thing he remembered however, as he tried to regain his footing, was the guttural laugh directed toward him. The red-haired man slammed his beer stein into the side of Hans's head, sending Hans into the muddy street, thereby ending the confrontation. In spite of his good intentions, Hans was once more unable to exact retribution.

Later, as Hans was slowly regaining consciousness, blood oozing from his cheek as the storekeeper wiped his face with a rag, he could only query, "Where is the man who attacked me?" None of the strangers gathered around him knew where the attacker had gone. Whether they did not know where the man had gone, or were afraid for their own safety, no one could identify Hans's attacker or the direction he had taken. It seemed he had disappeared again. It was as if he never existed. All that remained for Hans was the fleeting moment when he recognized the man who had attacked Anne aboard ship all those years before.

Three

I WOULD LIKE to take credit for solving the mystery, and with it the several deaths connecting the arrival of my ancestors to the shores of the United States. Here was a mystery involving my own family, living peacefully in the farming community surrounding the towns of Montevideo, Milan, Watson, Appleton, Big Bend and Lac Qui Parle, Minnesota. But it would be Tom Hall who would assemble the pieces.

Tom Hall was in Montevideo for the second time. His first visit to Montevideo had been in 1936. He had come to recover the body of his elder brother, who had been murdered while laboring on a huge Public Works Project. During the following eighteen months there were two seemingly unrelated deaths in the county. There were no apparent suspects and no clues relating to either death. Tom had been asked to return to Montevideo by retired judge John Chamberlin. The judge believed Tom's experience in the U.S. Naval Investigative Service, and his success in tying together the series of deaths which included his brother eighteen months before, were just what was needed to end the mystery of those two recent deaths. Judge Chamberlin also believed the recent deaths were part of a greater mystery.

I walked the three blocks from the train depot to the Riverside Hotel. Montevideo's Main Street runs north to south, paralleling a branch of the Chippewa River just a hundred yards away. The downtown district had been carved from the valley's steep eastern hillside and was on a slight terrace above the river. Even the trip from the depot to the hotel was slightly uphill, levelling off from time to time, yet on enough of an incline for me to feel the exertion of my walk. With the hot summer weather, my topcoat was slung over my arm. I easily carried my one suitcase as I made my way up the street; surely enough baggage for my limited visit, I thought.

I walked into the Riverside Hotel through mahogany-framed glass doors and stepped into a room with plush carpets and smelling of good housekeeping. It was a grand interior that lived up to the promise I had been given. It occupied nearly a half block at the upper end of Montevideo's main street. The lobby was carpeted and richly trimmed in well-polished mahogany. A huge chandelier hung over a leather couch and side chair that looked as if a visitor would just sink out of sight should he choose to sit in either one. A short hall to the side of the registration desk led to another set of doors. Through the doors I could see a dozen round dining tables, each with a large bouquet of flowers in crystal vases. The chairs, six at some tables and eight at others, had backs and seats covered in burgundy velveteen.

For some reason, I was surprised to find such lush appointments in a rural prairie hotel. My urban upbringing left me believing small towns on the prairie were made up of unpainted and dilapidated buildings, occupied by plain people just trudging through their colorless lives. Perhaps I felt a little condescending. Yet, here on the prairie I saw freshly painted storefronts and showroom windows polished and clear to show local residents they could trust to find only the best here to fill their needs, whatever they may be. The hotel could compete with those in Chicago or Kansas City.

That autumn and winter in Montevideo gave me an education I will not forget. I would discover that in the evening I could hear the pleasant murmuring of water over the tiny waterfall just below the hotel. I would learn that even on the prairie I could find excellent dining, and I soon discovered that small communities on the prairie were far more complex than I anticipated. I was also going to learn that even pristine little towns on the prairie could have dark secrets.

I was expecting to check in and eventually enjoy a quiet dinner, a shower, and a good night's sleep after my travels. Instead, I found a Tom Hall speaking to a large crowd which was gathered in the hotel lobby. He was just wrapping up his explanation of events. "…and when a murder is committed in a small town like Montevideo, then for whatever reason is left solved, it is a sad thing. When that death remains unsolved, the details fade. Before long, life goes on somewhat normally, and eventually, almost no one thinks there might be a deeper connection between that death and the history of the community.

"Some of you may remember that I was here about a year and half ago, when my brother was murdered. I certainly didn't expect to be back again, especially under the current circumstances. A few weeks ago, Judge Chamberlin asked me to return to Montevideo. He asked me to investigate the death of Roberta Swan. I must admit that I had no idea how complex the story of her murder would turn out to be.

"We know that although the web of this mystery is nearly invisible, her death was not an isolated case. It appears there might be a connection to another recent and unsolved death. Beside the death of Roberta Swan another local man many of you knew—Arne Thorson—died under mysterious circumstances last year. His death was never explained, and that investigation just languished. There didn't appear to be any connection to Mrs. Swan's death; and again, no suspects. I am not suggesting that every unsolved or unusual death in Chippewa County is connected. Nevertheless, I have been asked to dig deep, look at circumstances from the perspective of an outsider, and hope to bring justice where it might otherwise slip away."

As Tom Hall spoke to the crowd gathered at the hotel, he was joined not just by Judge John Chamberlin, but law enforcement representatives and reporters from radio and newspapers, who had come from St. Paul, Minneapolis, Owatonna, New Ulm, as well as the several small towns near Montevideo. There were also shop keepers, farmers, and local residents who had come to hear the update on Tom's investigation.

It was not a gathering Tom had requested. Word had spread, incorrectly as it turned out, that a famous detective had uncovered clues regarding the recent murder of Roberta Swan. In fact, there would be no clues of any substance for several more weeks, and Tom spent a great deal of time apologizing for the premature news conference. The gathering had evolved abruptly, when a news reporter for the Minneapolis Star Tribune, on his way home from Watertown, South Dakota had spent a night in Montevideo. He heard a hastily put together tale of murder and investigations, and with too much enthusiasm, called his scoop in to the news desk at the Tribune. His report mistakenly suggested there was to be a news conference held forty-eight hours later. When that news was published there was no turning back.

Tom's first visit to Montevideo had begun on a frigid February day in 1936. He was expecting to retrieve the body of his older brother Ernie. At the time of his arrival in this small rural community it was believed that Ernie had been the victim of a malicious hit and run driver who, while drunk, had intentionally struck Ernie and left him to die in the middle of a winter blizzard. It had been a bizarre winter, a deadly winter, as it turned out. Before Tom left, there had been several other connected murders, which Tom had been instrumental in solving.

Now, he was back in Minnesota to give new perspective into the recent death of Roberta Swan. Or so Tom thought. A day after his arrival, Tom would be given information of another mysterious death, and within a few more days he would learn that Judge Chamberlin thought there might be a conspiracy reaching into the shadowy past of the county.

As Tom spoke to the attentive crowd that gathered, I gazed around the hotel lobby. Young and old, men and women alike, were captivated as Tom told his tale, sketchy as it was. I quietly introduced myself to a young woman who was also staying in the background. Her lapel badge showed she was Mary Collins, the railway depot agent. We intermittently carried on a quiet conversation. She filled me in on the basics of what Tom was talking about. She also told me, with a slight blush, that she and Tom Hall were sort an "*item*."

I soon realized the magnitude of the whole situation by the intensity of the dialogue in the room as Tom finished speaking. I decided this was not going to be the best moment to introduce myself, nor to begin asking Tom for information related to my own quest, and I left the lobby after Mary promised she would tell Tom of my interests. Before long, I would be brought into the many conversations raging around the county. I would get snippets of gossip, short interpretations of the unusual history that connected modern day Montevideo and the surrounding county to the emigration of my ancestors and their eventual arrival in Chippewa County. And I would learn of the unusual connection my family had to the legacy of murder in Chippewa County.

Four

NEARLY EVERYONE LIKES to hear a little gossip, especially if it's about indiscretion or infidelity; unless that gossip is about themselves, that is. Even before her death there was a lot of gossip about Roberta Swan, but especially after her naked body was found in one of the tourists cabins she and her husband operated on the edge of town. Those who hoped their names would not be connected to her death that July day were certain that, in their minds, they could see Roberta, known to most as just Bobbie, as she lay back on her pillow. Discretion would keep them from sharing how their hearts raced, how their pulses pounded, and who—without exception— hoped their own connection to Roberta Swan would disappear without being discovered by Bobbie's husband.

On the afternoon of her final indiscretion, her last day on earth, Bobbie sank languidly into the wrinkled, clammy sheet beneath her. Bobbie's luscious body was bathed in her own sweat, her face flushed as she began to relax, and as she recovered from the last moments of the passionate sex which, for a short time, had consumed her every being. On the small round table near the window an oscillating fan breathed just a hint of a draft, but it did not come close to cooling the darkened room. It was July and nothing would cool the little tourist cabin until the approaching storm drenched the valley later in the day.

This was not the first time Bobbie had shared this bedroom with a friend, or with a stranger. It was not even the second, or third, or fifth time. When her diary was discovered later, it would recall that for months she had found comfort in this room. Although she tried to be discrete with her rendezvous, she had been brave enough to save the memories of the days or nights when she found passions somehow not shared with her husband. Many men who were saddened by her death were extremely relieved that she had at least been discrete enough to never mention names as she filled the pages of her diary.

As she lay back, she could hear her latest companion in the shower. For just a moment she enjoyed the pleasant memory of his strong body as he had wrapped his arms around her and thrust himself into her welcoming flesh. The afternoon tryst had happened unexpectedly. The forty-ish year old salesman had stopped for directions, information about how far it was to Watertown, South Dakota, and how long it might take to get there. Bobbie couldn't help herself. He was good looking, looked muscular as he stood there in his slightly wrinkled suit. His white shirt showed a day of hot travel and his necktie was loose at the open shirt-neck. His smile was just a little rakish. And he was going to be gone long before her boring husband came home.

Bobbie wasn't sure how she ever got married to Darrel Swan. Actually, she did remember, just chose to try forget whenever she could—like right now. It had been a pleasant if somewhat rushed afternoon. She did not seem worried, but the travelling salesman, well, he wanted to be travelling. When Bobbie had leaned seductively across the counter, exposing the ample swell of her breasts, and with a look that could melt glass, she suggested they explore an afternoon escapade before he travelled on, he was caught between an ego rush and mild—although fleeting—panic.

Now, their moment of recreational sex was coming to an end. If not for the whirring of the fan, the pattering water from the shower, and the rustling of the bed sheet as she turned over, Bobbie might have heard the slight rasping motion of the cabin door being pushed slowly open as another person entered the room. She may even have heard the throaty click as the gun's hammer was pulled back, and finally, that last click as the trigger was pulled. In the moment her life was ended.

The door closed again, quickly and quietly. From the shower the pistol shot had been heard, but loud as it was, it was muffled by the running water and unrecognized by a man who could not have imagined such an event was taking place. Bobbie's most recent admirer called to her with a romantic but slightly lewd comment. The man in the shower gave no thought to Bobbie's silence. He was still thinking of the great afternoon he and Bobbie had spent, writhing, lurching, moaning out their pleasure. He was thinking that maybe there was time for just one more hot sweaty tumble before he headed for his appointments in Watertown. He leisurely stepped onto the tile floor and grabbed a huge monogrammed towel from its resting place before striding confidently back into the bedroom.

In the next seconds his confidence and his rising masculinity both disappeared as he saw Bobbie's dead body. Now, instead of the ravishing auburn-haired seductress with the ample breasts and hips which had brought him to such a heated climax, he looked down on her grotesque corpse. Her flaming hair was already caked with matted blood,. A small hole just above her left ear was precise and neat. The right side of Bobbie's head no longer existed; fragments of skull, skin and hair showered across the pillow before creating a horrible pattern on the bed sheet and the headboard.

For a fleeting moment, Bobbie's afternoon lover considered calling the police, or anyone who could be brought in to save him from this horrible scene. After that moment of consideration, he thought better, and decided that he would rather run, just become invisible. He would just get the hell out of town. No one knew he was even in town. Had just stopped on the spur of the moment to get directions, expecting to be far down the highway by now, instead of looking down at the bloody scene before him.

In a panic, he threw on his clothes, and with sox in hand, shirt open and stuffed into his slacks, hat and pocket clutter clutched in his hand, he ran for his car. Without looking back, the stranger sent his car rocketing west across the bridge spanning the Chippewa River and on his way to Watertown. On the floor by the bed and covered by a corner of the bloody sheet was a Zippo cigarette lighter with the engraved initials *BG*. It would soon be missed by the fleeing man.

Later, it would become part of the mystery surrounding Bobbie's death. What might have become the grandest tale he could have shared with his pals at the golf course, became instead, a frightful tale he would have to keep secret forever.

Five

SEVERAL DAYS AFTER my arrival I was able to meet Tom Hall. In the first few minutes we shared, I explained my reason for coming to Montevideo, and in exchange, Tom gave me snippets of the mystery he had become responsible for unraveling. I could not help but put myself in Tom's place, to imagine the strange experience into which he had been called.

"Once again, into the den of the bear," Tom Hall thought, half aloud, upon his arrival. Then, for a few moments more, Tom stood silently on the depot platform. The morning Milwaukee Railroad passenger train moved slowly off to the west, on its way to Aberdeen, South Dakota. Just eighteen months before, Tom had stood on this same worn deck. How different that winter day was from this August morning.

That previous day had been in February, 1936, and Tom had come to Montevideo, Minnesota for the first time, to retrieve the body of his brother Ernie. According to the telegram that brought Tom here, Ernie had been killed by a drunken hit and run driver. During a snow storm, according to Chippewa County Sheriff Carl Brown, and in a drunken stupor, a young rowdy had killed Ernie and driven off without looking back. When Tom arrived in Montevideo that day all of southwestern Minnesota was shivering from the bone chilling cold as it struggled through another of the many winter storms the locals had come to expect. He had arrived alone, made his way along snow covered streets to see Carl Brown, and abruptly found himself caught up in local intrigue. Over the next weeks there would there would be three additional deaths in Chippewa County — including the murder of the sheriff.

But, this was not 1936 and it was definitely not February. It was 1938, and once again Tom had not been met at the depot. This August morning was already on its way to becoming a blistering hot day. It was the kind of day that made the corn grow, and the oats, wheat, flax, and barley explode in vibrant shades of gold. It would only be a few days before the entire county came alive with the frenzy of harvest. At 7:45 in the morning, it was already seventy-five degrees in the shade—if you could find shade. By late afternoon, the radio announcer from WCCO in Minneapolis said it would be in the high nineties. It was going to be way too hot for anyone except the kids who would flood the swimming beach just on the edge of Montevideo's Main Street.

A whirlwind of dust blasted at Tom as he turned toward the depot waiting room. In the few minutes since Tom had stepped off the train he was already drenched with sweat. Leaving the scorching depot platform, Tom stepped into an even hotter waiting room. Even with all the windows open the depot was stifling. The occasional gusts of wind brought only hot air to the room. On his previous trip Tom had expected to be in Montevideo for only a day or two and had brought just a simple travel bag. Today however, he had no idea how long he would be here and travelled with two suitcases, which he now wanted to retrieve. As he pushed against the depot door Tom was dreading the next few minutes. The start of his last visit to Montevideo began by listening to a cryptic and prejudiced tale from the depot agent. He shuddered as he considered a repeat of the experience.

The woman who greeted him from behind the counter, however, proved to be the new depot agent. Tom gave an almost perceptible sigh of relief. He would be spared another encounter with last year's unpleasant depot agent. He noticed that when she smiled and greeted him she was more than "barely attractive." In fact, Mary Collins, although less "pretty" in that cute little Gibson Girl way, was more than just attractive. More accurately described as handsome and with surprisingly precocious dimples creasing her cheeks, she smiled her hello at Tom. He guessed her to be somewhere around thirty, tall, maybe five feet-eight or nine. Although she was dressed conservatively, he could see she had an attractive figure.

"I guess you'd be Tom," she bubbled, and her cheeks flushed red as she greeted Tom, who thought her blush was a perfect accent to her auburn hair. "Judge Chamberlin said I should expect you this morning, and swore he'd paddle my butt if I wasn't good to you."

"Wow," Tom thought. *What a difference a year makes! No snow and no wind, no nasty lying sheriff, and no hypocritical station agent."* Tom had arrived in Montevideo, the little farm community in southwestern Minnesota, at the express request of John Chamberlin, who was not just *"judge,"* but a retired Senator and State Supreme Court justice. Judge Chamberlin and Tom had formed a long-distance relationship after Tom had brought his brother back to Ohio to be buried. A little over a week ago Tom had received another telegram, this time from Judge Chamberlin, asking Tom's help in solving another unusual death.

As if reading his mind, Mary produced Tom's bags and offered "We still don't have taxis in Monte," as the town was known to the locals, "but the judge has arranged a car for you. I t's that little Ford coupe across the street. The keys are in it."

Six

A FEW MINUTES later Tom was seated across from Judge Chamberlin in the judge's spacious office. His Honor John Chamberlin, now in his late seventies, might have been considered by strangers as past his prime. In fact, His Honor, as he was known by nearly everyone in Chippewa County, was a man with unlimited enthusiasm and with physical stamina of many men much his junior. In his younger career he had been an energetic attorney, then an outstanding—if sometimes outspoken—activist in the Minnesota legislature, before being appointed to the Minnesota Supreme Court. Instead of occupying that seat until his death, he had opted to retire at the age of seventy-two, to return to Chippewa County and once again become active in guiding the affairs of Montevideo, which was the county seat.

It seemed natural and comfortable that the judge's office would be at the upper end of Main Street. His inner sanctum looked out a large picture window with a view of the entire Chippewa River valley. Just below the office there was a small dam in the river. Below the dam the river flowed over small rocks for twenty yards before it settled into an easy series of deep pools, and then followed a course parallel to Montevideo's Main Street. A mile south of town the Chippewa River disappeared, as it joined the larger Minnesota River, which in turn coursed across southern Minnesota. Its fish-hook course traversed the entire state of Minnesota, connecting Montevideo to Mankato, New Ulm, and Saint Peter, and to the civilized world downstream. This was the river which brought immigrants, trappers, and traders from Saint Paul, where it joined the mighty Mississippi River on its journey to the Gulf of Mexico.

Before the incursion of white settlers, and before Montevideo had even been a small town on the prairie, the Ojibway and Dakota Indians had called this valley home. For three hundred years, or more, they had fought each other for possession of the valley where they had hunted, fished, and intermarried. A hundred years ago the valley was home to nearly three thousand dark-complexioned natives. Now, it was instead home to a similar number of European immigrants, and now, in the spring, white men hovered over the exposed rocks in the river to snare or spear a fish for dinner. In the languid days of summer, it was now the white settlers who brought their sons and daughters here. It was here, they taught them where the fish might pause to find their meal, or to just let the children throw a fishing line weighted with a lead sinker, or a metal washer, into the current and wait expectantly for the sudden tightening of the line when a walleye or a bullhead grabbed the offered bait and headed for a quiet pool to enjoy its dinner.

Above the dam was the large lagoon that in the summer was the town's swimming beach. During the winter it was the gathering spot for ice skating. At the far end of the lagoon, just visible from the judge's office, was a stone building that served as warming house for skaters in winter and as bath house for swimmers during the summer.

At the eastern edge of the swimming beach stood a huge wood-framed structure. It resembled a ski jump platform, but of course that could not be. It was a slide-tower, rising up more than fifty feet over the sand and reaching nearly one hundred feet out over the river. Brave men—and sometimes women—toted a small toboggan-like platform up the ladder and placed it on a track. The daring man or woman then sat on the little platform and plunged at break-neck speed downward until being catapulted into space from ten feet above the river. The trick, everyone knew, was to stay seated on the toboggan and keep it balanced until they hit the water. If they stayed in place they would race across the lagoon. If not, it was a hard landing in the river, and maybe a follow-up bang on the head from the toboggan.

A dirt and gravel road disappearing into the woods behind the beach was little more than a primitive trail which led to the ski and toboggan hills of Windom College. The scene played out for Tom like an image from the popular Currier and Ives calendars which could be purchased around town.

It was all visible from the judge's office. Tranquility, peace, the romance of a good life in a small town on the prairie;. It all unfolded below the office—even if the truth was very different from the view. The judge's office was a quiet and sumptuous retreat from the world outside and the two men were immediately at ease in each other's company. It seemed to Tom that only days had passed since he and the judge had seen each other. Even though it was mid-day, the judge had poured a snifter of brandy for himself and Tom, then began to lay out his unusual tale and the reason he had called upon Tom.

"There are seven generations of the Iverson-Osland clan living in Minnesota – that we know of," said Judge Chamberlin. "They first showed up in Fillmore County, the Iversons that is, in 1852 or 1853, before moving on the Chippewa County some years later. Of course, they've married into other families, and the daughters became Swensons, Bloms, Halvorsons, Clausons, mostly here in the county. And, who can count the possibilities? I guess there are still some Iverson descendants down in Fillmore county as well. Considering that this family started moving into Chippewa county right after the big Sioux battles in 1862, the family was pretty well established throughout the area before the turn of the century.

"Based on what I know about the size of the earlier families and taking into my account that more recent generations have had smaller families, my best guess is that that, by themselves, that early pioneer couple are responsible for some ten thousand Minnesotans, living or dead, since they first arrived in Minnesota!" The judge was obviously enjoying this line of conjecture and he smiled at his personal thoughts. He became more serious, as he continued. "The problem I am faced with is that it seems to me, somewhere along the way, someone gave birth to a killer, or to a family of killers, that might have ties to this family. It might be that it was just some individual, or a couple, or perhaps even an entire family still living in Chippewa County; or Lord knows where they might have relocated. But… well, Tom, I'd like you to see if you can't figure out what has been happening around here."

Tom and the judge were having a wide-ranging conversation as the judge explained his theory. Outside the picture window, the Chippewa River could be heard cascading over the small dam. The afternoon sun was now casting longer shadows across the nearby park, but Tom spent little time enjoying the summer view. "You might wonder why I am concerned by the size of that family, Tom. Here is my problem. The Iversons are a respected family, among the earliest pioneers in the county. Over the past seventy-odd years they've married into so many other pioneer families I really can't even guess how many of our residents are related. By now, it really is in the thousands. Of course," he chuckled, "some of them may not have done their duty in propagating; that leaves some holes in this whole mathematical game of mine."

"Add into the equation that the total population of our county today is only somewhere around twelve thousand souls. That means that there is a possibility, truly slight however, that nearly everyone born in Chippewa County and living here today is related in some way, and that just this couple alone… well, you can see why I am intrigued, and at the same time can hardly keep from laughing out loud."

As much as Tom enjoyed the judge's genealogical tale, he couldn't quite see what the Iverson-Osland family history had to do with his urgent call to return to Montevideo and to the mystery of Roberta Swan's death. Just as he was about to ask, the judge dropped his bomb.

"What I did not share with you when I asked you to come back to Montevideo, and of course there are many things I haven't shared, is that over a period of the past thirty odd years, since the turn of the century actually, there have been a number of unaccounted deaths in or around Chippewa County. I don't have any concrete evidence. Its just a gut-feeling. I've been around a long time and my gut is telling me there's some reason to believe someone is specifically targeting this large family. The most recent death happened just at the beginning of summer, with the death of Roberta Swan. But, there has been other unresolved violence in the area, and I think there may be some connection between those events. There are no obvious suspects in any of those deaths. So far, our investigations have led us nowhere, which is why I have called on you.

"I'd like you to take an outsider's look at that whole history, Tom. I have arranged finances for your stay here, and of course you already have the car I made available for your use. See which—if any—of those deaths might be connected. I'll fill you in on some other names and events as we get started. And try not to get everyone in the county riled up and thinking we're trying to destroy a family's reputation. You might think that in a small community made up of farmers and small-time merchants it would be easy to find a killer. I think we have an angry or deranged citizen who has been exacting revenge on our little prairie community."

There was a light knock on the study door, which was then opened by the judge's assistant. "Pastor Sherman is here to see you, Judge. I know, you said you didn't want to be disturbed, but I thought you might make an exception for the pastor. He said it has something to do with the Roberta Swan murder."

The judge made his introductions in the same straight forward manner he did with everything. Just get the facts out there, and let the details come as they would. Of Tom, he just said, "Tom helped us with all that mess that happened the winter of '36. It was Tom's brother Ernie who was killed on the road by Buster's." At this, Pastor Vernon paled a bit, but was silent as the judge continued.

"I think if not for Tom we might not have connected all the pieces that winter. Who would ever believe that we would have three separate murders, with no apparent connection, in less than a month? No one in the whole county gave a second thought when it looked like Tom's brother was the victim of a hit and run. Partly, I suppose, because Ernie was just a transient worker, here for a while, then he would just have moved on as so many have done since the depression. In an unspoken voice, the community just said, 'Ernie Hall was an outsider. He's not one of us, so why worry about him?' As you may recall, the sheriff hauled Warren Marshall in and had the community convinced that Warren was the killer. Then, while young Marshall was out on bail, Timmy Coyle was brutally murdered. It appeared Marshall had gone berserk and beat him to death with a tire iron.

"We might just have let things progress without any more thought, if Tom here had not gone to the transient camp across from Buster's and found that even more shenanigans had taken place. It seems that the sheriff and Ollie Martin, who was another transient on the project, got into a spat. The sheriff had found evidence it might have been Ollie, not Warren, who had committed the two murders, and went to the camp to confront him. Well, before that episode was over, the sheriff and Ollie got into a big fight. Ollie ended up dead in the river. When his body was sucked under the ice, Carl just thought 'good riddance,' and would have let Warren go to trial for the death of Ernie Hall.

"Now, of course, we know that we had three different killers; the murders were connected in a convoluted manner. But, back then, the picture laid out before us by the sheriff looked altogether different. I guess you could just say greed, lust, and prejudice, caught up to each of them. It sounds like a perfect subject for one of your Sunday sermons, Bill," he chuckled as he looked at the pastor. "However that may be, it was Tom here who put the pieces together. That's all history now. I'm hoping that Tom can shed some light on this other mess we have here in Monte."

Bill Sherman blushed just a little as the judge joked with him. William Tecumseh Sherman, pastor of the county's only Baptist Church, was not one to make light of such sins as lust, greed, or prejudice. Pastor Sherman, as he was known to his flock, not Bill, nor

B.T., as some would speak of him behind his back, was the guiding light to the small Baptist congregation. A good Baptist clergyman, he always looked as if he were on his way to the little white church up near the court house, the protective chapel where, on Sundays, he could be at his best. On Wednesday evenings he would explain the true meaning of bible verses to those blessed souls who looked to him for guidance in their meager lives.

Bill Sherman would never be found in a tavern, or in a dance hall. Never would you see him flirting with the women of his parish; single or married, they were held at arms' length. In his sermons, he frequently spoke of female virtues and how it was the responsibility of all his parish to revere them, to hold those virtues sacred above all else, and to call out the sins of those who fell short of his standard.

Now, Bill Sherman was getting to meet the man he had heard so much about but had not met on Tom's earlier visit to Montevideo. This was Tom Hall, the super detective, the gentle man who had brought justice to Chippewa County. He was the man who had given Montevideo a new sense of honor and pride. Tom Hall had seen through the hypocritical veil of the community; just as he himself had. Tom Hall's name, in the short time he was in Montevideo, had become synonymous with virtue. And now, Pastor William Tecumseh Sherman would reach out to help guide Tom Hall. He relished the opportunity to reach out and show him the way, not just to help solve this mystery, but to help save Tom Hall from the sins that would inevitably try to destroy his soul if he were not given proper guidance.

"I'm really happy to meet you, Tom. The judge and half the county are still talking about how you solved those murders last year." The pastor appeared almost flushed as he blurted out his greeting. Bill Vernon was neither large nor small. His was the frame and stature of an ordinary man. Tom put his age at around fifty, his height just a little shorter than his own six feet. As always, when out in public, the pastor wore the brown wool suit that he favored. Winter or summer, he thought it was this suit which made him the man he was. Although it was beginning to show wear around the cuffs and collar, its style was timeless, and to the pastor its quality was apparent to all. The pastor's hair was carefully cut and crisply parted on the left. Perhaps the only flaw to his hair was that it was cut a little too close and a little too high on the sides and gave his slightly red hair a look something akin to a well-worn paint brush. The combination of the red hair, the brown suit, and flushed cheeks, which came from just a little too much salt, and which added to his heightened blood pressure, made some think he looked as much like a travelling salesman as a Baptist minister.

As the three men sat talking in the judge's study, Tom couldn't help but think what a simple man this was that he had just met. Tom was taken by Bill Sherman's naiveté, by the uncluttered way he came to his truths, and by the way that, although this was just a casual introductory dialogue, Bill Vernon never leaned back in his large chair, but sat on its edge as if he was going to be launched into space any moment.

As the dialogue continued, the judge saw Tom's attention wavering, and recognized that after his long journey, Tom was probably more than ready for a good meal, a shower, and a good night's sleep. From past experiences the judge also knew that, left unfettered, Bill Sherman could find endless ways to lead Tom from one subject to another until the afternoon turned into night. He owed Tom more than that. "Bill, you said you had some information that might help us; help Tom that is, as he starts his inquiries. I think we should get to the meat of it and let Tom get some rest.

"Of course, of course," responded the pastor. He turned toward Tom. "But, I can wait until another time. I'm sure you can use a good night's sleep after your long journey." Without further comment Bill Sherman was off, leaving his message for Tom unspoken.

Seven

A SHOWER. DINNER. A short walk down Montevideo's main
street to settle the dinner. Then, Tom settled slowly into his room at
the Riverside Hotel. Tomorrow would be soon enough to begin
collecting the pieces of the puzzle.

As he began to wind down Tom couldn't help but think of the
information laid out so far. Murder. A well-known woman, owner—
along with her husband—of tourist cottages on the edge of town, had
been found dead and naked in one of the cottages. A delicate hole in
her left temple, where a small caliber bullet had entered before
making a large messy exit on the right. Most of the pillow and the
sheets were splattered and crusted with her blood and brains when her
body had been discovered. Several random items were found in the
room. A large monogramed towel, still wet, lay on the floor; a well-
worn Zippo lighter with the initials "BG", was found on the floor
near the bed, and was considered to be her lover's; maybe the
murderer's. There was nothing to indicate who her companion had
been. Indications were that she had sex before being shot. Was it her
lover, or someone else who had killed her? No one had seen her lover
arrive or leave. There had been no guest card filled out, so there was
nothing there to follow up.

The husband, Darrel Swan. Had he found his wife with another
man, gone berserk and killed her in a rage? If so, why hadn't he killed
the lover? The body had been discovered on Thursday morning. It
appeared she had been dead since sometime Wednesday afternoon.

Where was the husband on Wednesday? Why didn't he tell
someone she was missing when she didn't come home that night?
Did he have a provable alibi? Where is the gun? Did the husband own
a gun? The questions tumbled around in his brain like the little cubes

in the basket at a bingo parlor. Then, like turning off a light, Tom was asleep. Two days across country by train left him exhausted, and he slept. No dreams. No fitful tossing or turning. Just welcome sleep.

Eight

TOM WAS AWAKE at first light—barely after six a.m. He had decided to stretch his travel-weary muscles with a walk. From his previous visit to Montevideo, he knew he would find a trail through the park if he walked a short way north from the hotel and crossed the little dam over the spillway behind Main Street. The town seemed to be still asleep, except for the few men making their way to Swift and Company, the poultry and dairy processing plant on the west edge of town. As Tom crossed the bridge just upstream from the dam, Harold Gillis waved good morning as he headed out on his milk delivery route. Tom waved back, then was left alone in the quiet morning. He wandered along the dirt trail until he was deep in the park, where he came upon the town's wildlife zoo. What a strange sight, here in this little prairie town. Tom wondered at the collection of once-wild animals in their cages. Three black bears shuffled back and forth, mumbling to themselves, while a short distance away a large enclosure held two adult elk and several white tail deer. A captive bald eagle perched on a dead tree. Its cage, although large, was still too small for the eagle to gain flight. Tom thought the great bird looked depressed.

Tom thought how sad it was to deprive those wonderful creatures of their freedom and to cage them up, just for the entertainment of school children and an occasional tourist. As he wandered back to the hotel Tom once again felt awake, but he also felt the burden of melancholy at the plight of the trapped animals.

After breakfast in the hotel restaurant, Tom drove up First Street Hill to see Judge Chamberlin at his home. They had agreed that Tom should come to the judge's home and hear the judge's thoughts before he started asking questions around the county. Both men were enjoying the renewal of their friendship. Small talk of happenings around the county, discussion of the depression still plaguing the country, and Tom's observation of drought conditions as his train crossed the prairie. Finally the talk led to a more focused dialogue about the recent death of Bobbie Swan. As he poured coffee from a carafe, the judge paused. "There is a second unsolved and recent death that happened since you were last here. The victim's name is – or was – Arne Thorson. It happened the summer after you left.

"I first started to be intrigued by this possible family connection when Bobbie was murdered. It was with her death that I realized she and Arne Thorson were related. Arne's death was quite unusual. Although it was almost certainly murder, it's been listed as just a drowning as far as the public is concerned. It happened just north of Watson, Tom. I'll come back to him in a bit.

"Arne and Bobbie, as we called her, were cousins, two or three times removed I guess, but related, nonetheless. That may or may not be important, but, as I said, they were related. Since neither death has been resolved, I don't think there is much of a priority as to which death you and I talk about this morning. In fact, it might be beneficial to discuss them together.

"Bobbie was killed with a gun, a single shot into the side of her head. She was found in bed and naked in one of the cabins she and her husband operated as tourist a stop-over. A monogramed cigarette lighter was found in the room but does not seem to be connected to anyone in town. We've checked out local people with those initials and found no obvious connections. The gun hasn't been found but the bullet was dug from the mattress. Its safely stored in the police evidence locker. There are no apparent suspects, although the husband hasn't been completely ruled out. Since the police found no empty cartridge at the scene, we believe the gun used was probably a revolver. It's highly unlikely the killer would have taken time to retrieve an empty shell casing. He—or she—had no way of knowing when someone might show up. The cabin has been kept cordoned off while we waited for you to arrive.

"The other victim was Arne Thorson, who came from the farm area north of Watson and Big Bend. His body was found lodged among the rocks downstream of the spillway in the Watson Sag. His skull had been smashed. There are absolutely no clues as to motive, and therefore no suspects in his death. Although we have listed his death as just a drowning, there is no question in my mind that he was murdered. His death is now more than a year old.

"You may recall the area I'm speaking of, Tom, since you spent quite a bit of time around there. The Chippewa River runs through there, just as it does through Montevideo, starting out as a creek just north of Swift Falls, and connecting with the Minnesota River, just outside of Montevideo. As part of the Lac Qui Parle Diversion Project, that's the dam building project you'll recall from your last visit, there was an overflow channel put in which connects some marginal lowland pasture to the river, and as part of that diversion, a small dam – just a small spillway really – was built. I guess the idea of the design was to raise the county roadbed above the flood level. Well, in any case, I suppose I was still sensitive to unexplained occurrences because of your brother's murder, and I spent a few sleepless nights thinking whether there might be a connection between those two deaths."

As he was about to continue his story, a knock at the door interrupted the judge. Although he hadn't been expressly invited, Bill Sherman was at the door. The judge appeared chagrined at Sherman's arrival but kept his feelings to himself and showed the pastor into his study. In a few sentences, he brought the conversation with Tom up to date for the pastor, then continued.

"On a Sunday morning last August," the judge began, "Arne Thorson's car was found, parked on the road shoulder, just east of the spillway. That probably wouldn't have caused any concern, since a lot of fellows have started to fish along the shoreline there, but Arne's car was at such an angle it looked like it might roll into the ditch, and the passenger door was wide open. After looking around without seeing Arne, Bill Stai, who lives just a bit further east, thought he should call the sheriff. Sometime later, they found Arne's body in the river, lodged against some rocks, about a quarter mile downstream.

"After finding Arne's body and clothing, the sheriff and his deputy had started a search along the river bank, initially thinking perhaps that Arne might have been fishing and that they'd find his tackle. Imagine their surprise when they found a woman's red high heeled shoe half buried in the muddy bank, just upstream from Arne's body. There was no way of identifying who owned the shoe of course, and no one in Montevideo recalled seeing Arne with a woman any time on Saturday."

Pastor Vernon sat staring at the judge as the story unfolded. None of this information had been made available to the public. Naively, he asked, "Why would a woman wear high heel shoes if they were fishing?"

Perhaps just out of kindness, Tom quietly said, "Bill, I think we have to assume that, if in fact the shoe is connected to Arnie's death, they probably weren't along the river bank to go fishing." Tom tried not to appear condescending and just smiled as he answered the pastor's question.

"Of course," the pastor sputtered. "How foolish of me not to think of that."

"Well, Tom, I think you can see where this might be going. The right side of Arne's had been crushed. The coroner couldn't say whether it came from falling from the spillway bank or from hitting it on one of the rocks along the shoreline, which seems unlikely, or if the wound, which was quite massive, came from his being intentionally struck by a rock. We haven't located the owner of the red shoe, and in fact the sheriff has kept knowledge of the shoe and some other relative information from the public all this time. And that Tom, the apparent randomness of the deaths, and the fact that the two victims were relatives, makes me wonder if there might be a connection between Arne's death and the death of Bobbie Swan here in Montevideo. So far, there no one has been identified who may have had a motive for killing either one of them."

They talked for another hour, Tom asking questions, the judge answering when he could, the pastor looking surprised, mystified, or shocked, and totally captivated.

Nine

IN THE FOLLOWING days Tom began laying out a plan. At first, he was just asking shopkeepers, merchants, and farmers close to town a broad range of questions, and randomly seeking clues which did not seem to exist. Arnie Thorson's death intrigued him. Probably, he thought, because of the red shoe and the remote location where the body had been found. After making a cursory stop by the tourist cabins, which were still cordoned off to keep curious residents from wandering through and messing up the crime scene, he decided to divide his time and at least for the immediate future, search for information about Arnie.

Tom found himself driving the country roads, working in an expanding circle from where Arnie's car had been found. He thought of solving the mystery of the two deaths as a puzzle. With a collection of small pieces, laid out on the table of Chippewa County, he hoped he would just get the fragments turned right-side up, then see which pieces might fit together. The puzzle might be made up of just a few large pieces, not yet identified, but easily slid together, then, *Wala! T*he answer would be right there on the table. On the other hand, he thought it more likely there would be a large jumble of pieces—most likely a complex puzzle, one more difficult to assemble.

He was highly doubtful of that simple scenario. He knew it was far more likely there were a hundred pieces—perhaps twice that number —in the puzzle before him. His plan would be the same in either case. He would look at the pieces and see which of them fit together, fitting two here, three or four in another place, then as if by magic, there would be no questions left unanswered. He would report to the judge, then take the next train our of town.

Tom was contemplating the strange collection of information he had gathered. His goal was to learn about Arne Thorson; in the process, he gathered a wealth of information about Chippewa County's settlers. Since his was a name and face remembered from just the last year, he was usually given a cordial, if not always a warm welcome. He visited with Paulsons, Olsons, Larsons, Clausons, Siversens, and others. These were the farmers who populated the county before towns and railroads were established. On many of the farms he found three generations of the same family, and in most cases, it was only the youngest who spoke reasonably coherent English. And yes, he was beginning to think that first Iverson couple was in fact the foundation of the county's entire population.

In a very casual manner Tom had been asking for information about Arne Thorson. Arne was a bachelor. Who might he have had an interest in, who had he been dating; where did he work, who were his family, who were his friends? The answers to these questions were like the background pieces of a puzzle; some answers were vague, the families not yet trusting this stranger. Some answers were obviously gossip, stretching a little information into vast and detailed tales which Tom knew had no basis in direct knowledge.

"You have to understand," said one Montevideo merchant, "these young people have no sense of real values. They can be seen wasting their time, drinking, going to dances, driving their cars like maniacs without regard for anyone's safety. I think since the Great War our country has just been going to hell—forgive my language. I know some people blame the stock market fiasco and the drought, but in my time we would never have acted the way young people do today."

"Yes," Tom replied, trying not to be confrontational. "I think it's the same all over the country, however. But tell me, do you really think the older generation is that much more responsible in the way they conduct their lives?"

"Of course. Young people's morals today are just laxer than when I was a boy. We would never have thought to conduct ourselves the way the young people today do."

Tom could see he would make no headway with this man. The truth was only as he saw it, and according to him, the world was going to hell in a handbasket. He was reminded of the prejudice he had encountered on his previous trip. He knew prejudice was not geographic. It could be encountered any place, triggered by age or religion, even racial differences which sparked animosities, with no regard to age or logic. Tom decided this man would be of little help solving the puzzle.

What Tom did find fascinating, and totally confusing, was how complex the structure of the expanding generations of immigrants was. Large portions of the region were occupied by Norwegian farmers, other areas were predominately German or Swedish. The oldest generation seldom spoke English, the youngest seldom spoke their grandparents native language, and in between was a generation that struggled with both languages.

Tom and Judge Chamberlin quickly got in the habit of meeting for breakfast or over a brandy in the judge's study on most evenings. "Judge," Tom laughed aloud as he tried to explain what he had so far learned. "I've just scratched the surface on the Iversons, and how they got here, but it is quite a tale. Halvor and Thea Iverson really were the foundation of the Iversons in Chippewa County and they're connected to farmers, merchants, lawyers, and almost every working or professional class existing here today. But, of course, they were not the only couple contributing to the foundation of this complex clan. I've reached out and gathered a bit of their family history. Their background and travel from Norway may not be unique in the sense that many families made similar journeys, but I think where they came from and how they came to Chippewa County may eventually help us solve your mystery deaths."

Tom started, "You were correct when you said Arne Thorson and Roberta Swan were cousins, although a couple of marriages removed.

It didn't take long to find their common ancestor, however. He was a man named Hans Iverson. Hans Hanson Iverson, actually. He came to America with his parents Hans II and Anne Iverson, when he was three-years-old, aboard a sailing ship named '*Argo*'. Following their path to Chippewa County was complicated by the fact that Hans Iverson was just Hans Hanson when he left Norway, and before that the Iversons name was Rui, taken from the farm on which they lived. In the nineteenth century the Norwegians had an un usual way of passing along their family names. Unusual to me, at least.

"Some documents call this family Iverson, some Iversson, or Rui. It seems that some two-dozen people on the Argo, shared the Iverson name and came from the same farm in Norway. They left Norway with one name and had a new identity by the time they got to Minnesota. The Norwegian method of choosing surnames is a little complicated, so let's not get too hung up on the name-changes.

"As children, and very likely as cousins, the younger Hans Iverson, and Guro Osland had crossed the Atlantic Ocean at the same time. They would have passed through the Great Lakes on a barge, or possibly on separate barges, before landing in a still mostly unsettled Wisconsin. Their families lived there for several years before moving on to southeastern Minnesota. Hans II and his wife Anne brought their three sons, Ole Hansen Iverson, Halvor Hansen Iverson and Hans II Hansen Iverson, along with daughter Helge, who was born just a year after the Argo brought the Iversons to the USA. How in the world can anyone not within the family keep track of who is who when they all have the same name?

"Then, somewhere around 1851 or 1852, the Iverson family found their way first to Whitewater, Wisconsin. Then they moved into southeastern Minnesota before part of the family came to Chippewa County and began to establish homesteads. Halvor, whose family I'm trying to concentrate on until I can make sense of this, was born in Fillmore County, Minnesota, and was the fourth child of Hans and Guro .

Halvor married many years later in Minnesota. As a young man he returned to Fillmore County and married Thea Osland. Then, Halvor and Thea returned to Chippewa County. That winter they lived in a dugout shelter near the Chippewa River with Halvor's uncle Ole, who in fact was named Olav, and was the brother of Hans II. I have to say Judge, that I have never seen so many people in one family named Ole, Hans, and Halvor!" Thank heaven, Halvor and Thea stuck with the Iverson name for their children.

In spite of being confused by all the same names, it wasn't difficult for Tom to gather a vision of the Iverson emigration from their native Norway to the prairies of Minnesota. The origins, the history, the emigration of the Iversons from their farm home in Norway, was not unlike the history of thousands who left their European homes in the nineteenth century. And, yes; Tom was almost certain they were all related. Tom's understanding of the Iverson migration to Minnesota from their native Norway was accurate, if somewhat over-simplified. It would be seven decades before their adventure was fully known.

Ten

TOM'S FIRST FEW days back in Chippewa County had been spent getting reacquainted with the community and sorting out what had recently happened there. His meetings with the judge were unhurried and comfortable. Both men seemed to just enjoy each other's company, in spite of the unusual circumstance which brought them back together.

"The Montevideo police and the Chippewa County sheriff had covered every square inch of the cabin and the parking area after Bobbie's murder," the judge told Tom. "I don't know exactly what I expected them to find, but, of course, they needed to collect anything that might have been connected to her death. The parking area is really nothing more than poorly maintained grass. There are foot paths to the cabins and an occasional path leading down to the bank of the Minnesota River. They didn't find anything of importance, I'm afraid. Some cigarette butts, and the kind of detritus that collects where people pass."

"Judge, I'd like to walk around out there. I've already spent so much time driving around the county, I just need a mental break. Tell me though, what's the story on the husband? Who are his family? Do you think he killed his wife? History shows that in deaths such as Bobbie's, it is often the spouse who did the killing. Do you really think there might be a connection between Arne Thorson's death and that of Roberta Swan? What else about these two people haven't you shared with me?"

"Tom, if I could find what connects those two deaths, I probably wouldn't have called you here! I know I have piled a lot of information on your shoulders already, but I want to share another mystery with you. Then, I'll help try connecting the dots, as it were. I had hoped, by some miracle, that even in this short time you might have found a clue to the death of Arne or Bobbie, or at least something that connected them."

On the desk of his otherwise tidy office were stacks of manila file folders. Some were thick with documents, others contained only one or two sheets of paper. "There are a lot of documents here that I can't, or at least shouldn't share with you, Tom. For many years I was the only legal resource in the county. People shared with me things even their wives or children didn't know about. Although nearly everything contained in these files has been resolved in one way or another, I feel there must be a connection here someplace. It's just an old man's hunch of course, but it just keeps gnawing at me; somewhere we need to connect these deaths.

"I'm not sure this new information I'm about to share with you will even be remotely connected to our current deaths, but it's been nagging at me a little during the last couple of days. Who knows; there might be a thread connecting these events. Or it might just be more unrelated and useless information.

"I indicated that I think the Iverson family history might be connected to the two recent deaths I've asked you to investigate." Sometimes the judge rambled, seemed to wander off subject, but Tom knew to let him wander, and actually enjoyed the distractions. "I'd like to share some other information with you. I hope it won't distract you too much.

"We're still recovering from the drought years, Tom. You'd think with the almost annual flooding of the Chippewa and Minnesota Rivers that water shortage shouldn't be a problem, but once the snow melted each spring, we found most of our county dry as a bone. A lot of our top soil is sandy, especially to the north of town, and many summers we have seen high windrows of that sand-filled dirt piled high along the fence lines and drifted across our roadways. It's only recently that we've started to improve our roads, and as you might recall, the WPA dam project Ernie worked on was part of the flood control we needed. From here to Willmar, Benson, and most of the towns around us, we had only wagon tracks and game trails until just the past few years. Don't forget it's only about twenty years since the first automobiles showed up in Chippewa County.

"Can you imagine how difficult it must have been to bring a family here and provide for them in the first years? Now, we have the railroad, but when the first homesteads were filed in the 1860's this was nothing but barren prairie. There was hardly a tree to be found here, except along the rivers. Most of our farmers north of here are Norwegians. Just to the west, in Lac Qui Parle County, the Swedes gathered to establish their farms. It seems a small difference to us today, but at that time I guess just having a common language helped make life more comfortable. Of course, by now, you're well aware of that. Both the Swedes and the Norwegians came to the

United States starting in the 1840's and Norwegians began settling claims here in Chippewa County in the 1860's, soon after the great Sioux Uprising."

"Yes," Tom replied. "I've met several families who all seem to have come from the same part of Norway. We've talked about the Iversons, Larsons, Oslands, and Larsons, of course, and there might be some truth to your belief that they've been responsible for thousands of Minnesota Norwegians in Chippewa County." With a hearty laugh Tom added, "And I really believe half of them are named Ole, Hans and Halvor!"

As their laughter calmed, Judge Chamberlin drew a folded newspaper from his desk and handed it to Tom. "Speaking of that family, Tom, I want to share this with you. I thought you might find it interesting. I've had this old newspaper clipping in my file over twenty years. I guess I'm just a pack rat of useless information, but, it might tie in with my theory of the relatives and murders being connected. Perhaps, you can spend a little time looking into this mystery, and let your mind sort out some of the Swan and Thorson information. At the worst, it is interesting reading."

Tom unfolded a faded copy of the Milan Standard. Although the newsprint was turning brown after more than two decades in the judge's files, Tom had no trouble reading the headline. In bold print it read, *"TEENAGED BIG BEND COUPLE SAVAGELY ATTACKED."* The Article went on to say the young unmarried couple had parked their buggy in the grove which surrounded the girl's farm home, as they sometimes did. While there, they were attacked by an unidentified stranger. According to Art Iverson and Inga Clauson, the couple who had been attacked, they had been courting for some months, and occasionally stopped here for some *"spooning"* before he brought her home at a respectable hour. Although caught by surprise, Art had fended off their assailant, who disappeared across the Chippewa River before Art could subdue him.

The details of the account were intended to leave no doubt of the high morals of the couple, and although the young man was bruised and bloodied, both of those young lovers were expected to recover without further complications.

"It has always seemed to me," continued the judge, "that there was more to the story than we were told." As an afterthought he added, "You'll notice that the young man named in the article is Iverson, aa cousin of both Arne and Bobbie. I can't help but wonder if that incident was intended to end in murder. Since it didn't, perhaps before long, interest in finding the attacker just faded away."

"Of course, you could be right, Judge," Tom interjected, "but isn't that something of a stretch? After all, the attack could have been for any number of reasons. Maybe he was planning to steal a horse, or even a cow, but got interrupted. Maybe he was planning to rob from the house, he stumbled on the couple unexpectedly, and just panicked, beat them up to be sure he wasn't followed. Maybe he had a crush on Inga. Or maybe he just didn't like Art Iverson. In any case, that attack took place more than twenty years ago. I find any connection to be very unlikely."

"Let me suggest this, Tom. On one of your trips out that way, just stop and visit with them. They got married about a year or so after the incident. Art and Inga live on the very farm where the attack took place. Inga's father moved the family to Watson after Inga's wedding, leaving the operation of the family farm to Art and Inga. The other Clauson children are also grown now. They all farm nearby or are in business in town. Maybe you could learn something there. Or, maybe you will just learn some more about Chippewa County."

Eleven

IT MAY HAVE been out of frustration at making absolutely no progress in solving the murders of Bobbie or Arnie. It may have just been curiosity raised by the old newspaper Article, but Tom decided to spend what he hoped would be a relaxing afternoon with Art and Inga Iverson. There was always a chance that he would not find them at home, or that they would summarily send him on his way, but Tom felt he had little to lose. Besides, he might have his first success in murder solving, Chippewa County style. Perhaps he would discover a piece of the puzzle.

The drive to the Iverson farm was pleasant and uneventful even. From the hotel he crossed over the spillway beneath Main Street and guided the coupe past Smith park, thinking for a moment about the lonely eagle in its cage. After crossing the railroad tracks next to Swift and Company, he went up the long grade to the ridge paralleling the west side of the Chippewa River. As he travelled north, Tom noticed the sandy soil the judge had mentioned. Fifteen minutes later he turned through the small hamlet with the unique name of Watson and wondered if the name might be connected to a Sherlock Holmes mystery. *"That would be fitting," he mused.*

As he left Watson, the road drifted down into another valley. A few minutes later he was following the road—now just a dirt trail—up a sharp grade. Then with a left turn, he sighted the Iverson farm ahead of him. As he entered the grove surrounding the farm site, he couldn't help noticing the look of prosperity and pride of ownership the Iversons must have felt. In spite of the recent drought Tom could see this farm had prospered.

He was greeted in the driveway by two large unpedigreed dogs, which barked with excitement at the rare arrival of a strange automobile. As he parked under the huge boxelder tree alongside the house, Inga came to greet him. Tom ruffled the mane on one of the dogs as he walked toward the house. Tom had arrived late in the afternoon, hoping that Art would be done in the field for the day. He quickly identified himself and his mission. "I'm hoping you and your husband can help me by answering some questions about the episode that took place after the church social several years ago. Judge Chamberlin, from Montevideo, showed me the old newspaper article, and we think your attack might be connected to some other mysteries in the county."

"Oh, ya! I remember that night, even after all this time." Inga replied without hesitation. Inga had a baby boy in her arms and a shy blue-eyed girl at her side as she responded to Tom. There were several other children at play, who had been cautioned to not interrupt while she visited with this stranger.

When Inga learned who her visitor was she had sent one of the children to fetch "Pa", as he was called by everyone in the household. The oldest boy and girl ran like the devil was after them to get their father, who in fact, was done in the field and was spending time repairing a section of fence just beyond the grove that surrounded the house and buildings. The cows threatened to tear it down completely if he didn't take care of it.

When Art came into the house a few minutes later there were a several moments of pandemonium. All the children yelled or screamed for his affections. Pa acknowledged his boisterous family, giving each of his children an affectionate hug or a rub on the head, then turned to his wife and Tom. As he did, Tom saw a peaceful-looking man whose strength was barely hidden in the bib overalls he wore. The plaid flannel shirt he wore was sweat-stained and stretched tight over arms Tom thought were the size of his own legs. He could only imagine the fight Art had put up that long-ago night.

Inga spoke a few words in Norwegian to her husband before she introduced Tom. "Pa, be sure you don't lose your temper when this man asks about us. Remember, we were only children and he is here to try find out who attacked us."

The moment she started to speak Tom could tell she was an educated woman. She was well-mannered and soft spoken, even as she corrected one of the excited children, who obviously loved their cheerful mother. In short order Tom learned that she, as did her siblings, had attended the University of Minnesota School of Business. As a matter of fact, she proudly stated with a slightly embarrassed blush, she was the very first woman accepted at the college. Peter Clauson had seen that each of his children, girls as well as boys, were educated.

Even after giving birth to ten children, one of whom had not survived the first year, Inga was a handsome woman. She was tall and slender, with ice-blue eyes and naturally curly hair. He noticed her hands were a little raw, red perhaps from countless hours in the kitchen, or doing laundry for her husband and a house full of children. Tom could imagine what a beauty she must have been as a teenage girl.

Her husband, on the other hand, was not so well educated. He spoke in concise sentences heavily laced with a Norwegian accent. Direct and to the point; he left flowery words to his beautiful wife. He would have stated he was going to *fix the fence,* not *repair the fence.* Art wrote and read some; enough to be sure he was not taken advantage of when he traded at the hardware or the grain elevator. The large Iverson family all became hard working farmers at an early age. Just as they had been in Norway, in America the Iversons were the working class. Their education was meant to get them through the day but had left no room for humanities and art.

While Inga was petite, well-mannered and light on her feet, Art was nearly forty years old, built for the hard labors a farmer expected. At about six feet tall, he weighed a full two hundred pounds, maybe more. Although wide in the shoulders and showing signs of thickening around the waist, he was by no means fat. Tom thought he carried himself like some of the wrestlers he had encountered while in college. He also mused that it would take a very desperate person to attack this bull of a man Tom saw before him today. With a chin which jutted out like the prow of a ship, Art Iverson would be considered handsome in any crowd of his peers. His full head of hair was straight with just a slight wave, curling to his shirt collar. It was coal black, and Tom guessed it would be that way his entire life.

Hanging on the wall of the living room were a pair of oval sepia-tinted photographs of the couple. Tom thought they were probably wedding portraits; most likely paid for by the bride's father. His reaction to the faces staring back at him was simple. He would leave home for a woman with that look, and Art was so masculine and handsome it's a wonder Inga's parents let him within a mile of their daughter. He had the look of a man other men would follow to war, if only he were to ask.

Tom waited patiently as the couple sent their children to play. Inga finally made the introductions. As the three spoke, Art and Inga occasionally reverted to Norwegian, which Tom knew was their first, and preferred, language. In fact, this generation of farmers mostly learned to speak English only when they began going to school. Parents and grandparents seldom spoke English, some were not able to use that strange new American language at all, and frequently required translators when they went to town to shop.

The conversation became easier as the farm couple became accustomed to Tom. Unlike so many town folks, he was not condescending as he asked questions or explained a point of view. "How old were you when this incident took place?" Tom kept his voice soft, matching the demeanor of his host and hostess. "Do you recall where you had been earlier that day? Do you have any idea, after all this time, who might have attacked you?" There were no recriminations in Tom's voice as he encouraged them to share the details of the attack and of that night.

While Art and Tom discussed their *incident*, Inga heated a pot of coffee on the kitchen's wood burning stove. Plain white cups, and plain white saucers were set out, along with a large plate of sugar cookies. "They're still warm," she beamed with a smile, as she poured the coffee. "I usually bake cookies or cake on Thursdays. Wednesdays, I bake bread. You might guess, we go through a lot of that. Mondays are for doing the wash." It would have been too *citified,* Tom realized, for Inga to call it laundry.

Conversation stopped for a moment as the men sipped their coffee. Tom noticed that Art, like many other farmers he had talked with, poured small amounts of coffee into his saucer and sipped it noisily. It had been explained to Tom that this habit allowed the coffee to cool rapidly. No one seemed to notice the slurping.

Inga did most of the talking for the couple, looking to Art occasionally, to verify her memory was correct. Tom thought her words rolled off her tongue like honey from a honeycomb, and there was a musicality that came from the combination of English words spoken with a Norwegian origin.

Inga explained that twenty-three years ago Art and she had spent Saturday afternoon and evening in Big Bend, at the church social. An all-day event held each year at the end of summer, and just ahead of harvest, families came to Zion Lutheran Church to celebrate their good fortune and give thanks to the Lord. Food was plentiful, and pies and cakes were auctioned off to raise money for church projects. The summer fellowship was meaningful because of the wide spread family connections. When a grandparent spoke of their home, left behind in Norway, everyone within earshot paused to listen.

Over the afternoon hours, some of the men slipped away, where they gathered around buggies or wagons to talk of crops, new-born colts and fillies, and in some cases, to share drinks from a jug of home-made liquor. Only a few members of the congregation frowned at this seemingly un-Christian-like activity. The smaller children ran and screamed, played tag and pump-pump-pull away, or cuddled dolls they brought proudly from home. Older boys, and even some of the girls, played softball. It was a great chance to show off for a prospective future date. Since the church was a central community gathering for everything, from baptisms to burials, there was something for everyone. A horseshoe pit, with room for two simultaneous games, was located just alongside the church.

Occasionally, a young couple would disappear for a few minutes. Those who noticed at all, understood. As in all pursuits of farm life, romance was intense. Art and Inga were no exception. For months they sought each other whenever possible.

Inga had been off to college in 1914. She was gone for weeks at a time, which seemed an eternity both to her and to Art. As the afternoon turned to evening, they danced and enjoyed their closeness. Each of them feeling the mounting electricity between them, as a hand touched a cheek, or as Inga felt Art's strong muscles as they danced. Occasionally, Art's hand would slide from Inga's waist, to linger for just a moment on her hip. With a smile, she would scold Art for being so bold and brazen, but they both knew she enjoyed the momentary touch as much as Art did.

As with many such celebrations, this one ended too soon; there was still a long drive home. Parents, with their children in tow, drifted off to buggies and buckboards, then disappeared as twilight covered the prairie. Younger couples found their way to part with friends and waved and yelled last minute messages to each other. Art adjusted the harness on his mare one more time, then he and Inga began the slow drive to the Clauson farm. Inga's parents and brothers had already departed. The boys would do the evening chores, so she and Art were free to wander home at a slower pace. There was a happy glow on Inga's face as she snuggled in close to Art. The mare knew its way home, and Inga and Art folded themselves in each other's arms, each knowing but secretly hoping to ignore the limits of accepted ardor.

They made their journey slower than the rest of the family, and as their buggy entered the grove surrounding the Clauson farm, Art guided the buggy to a hidden spot along the drive and called the horse to a halt. This was their favorite spot,. It was hidden among the trees but still offered a view of the moon and stars, should they care to look up from each other's gaze.

They had stopped here on many other times. It was here they discovered and explored the mysterious curves of each other's bodies. It was here in the sheltering trees they strengthened the bond that would grow into a lifetime of love. But, tonight they were lost in a tender lust that young couples had always dealt with.

"I don't know what love is supposed to be, Inga, but I can't imagine being with anyone else." Art's big hands pulled her closer as he covered her neck and cheeks with kisses. His hand moved to softly enclose her breast as he leaned his head to kiss the space between them.

"Art, don't you get carried away. I know you love me, and I love you too, but I don't want to get into trouble." All the time she held him back Inga fought the desire to reach down and discover his manhood, but she knew the risk of giving in to their desires. More than one of her school acquaintances had given in and found themselves pregnant, leading to shame or to a rapidly planned wedding.

The ardent couple would never know if this was the night their desires would win over their consciences. Out of the darkness, Art was struck a tremendous blow across his shoulders. Inches higher and his neck might have been broken, but his muscular back and shoulders took the blow. The force of the blow sent the couple flying, tumbling from the buggy.

There had been no warning. One moment they were in a passionate embrace and in the next, Art was fighting for his life as he tried to understand what was happening. The assailant charged again and by the time the Art and his attacker landed on the ground, Art began to recover his senses. His ears rang, and his thoughts were scrambled, but in a moment he turned, and saw the man in the dark shadows who had attacked him. He launched himself across the buggy's drawbar at the hulking form.

Catching her own breath, Inga screamed. She could not see who had attacked them, only that he was swinging at Art with the huge piece of a dead tree limb. "Look out!" she yelled as the branch made a trajectory toward Art's head.

By now, Art's mind was clearing and although he couldn't identify his attacker, he knew his only defense was to attack. Instead of recoiling or falling back as might be expected, he lunged forward, the powerful legs which only minutes earlier were pressing him against Inga, now drove him through the air toward his attacker. At the same time, his huge arms, made strong from days and years of labor on the farm, flailed out, spiraling toward the opponent, who was now falling back from Art.

Once. Twice. Three times, Art hammered at the man, wreaking havoc on the stranger's chest and head. With his own head lowered like a bull charging his opponent, Art drove the stranger back, into one of the buggy's wheels. Then, with another barrage, the attacker fell beneath the mare, which was shifting nervously, but still unaware of the extent of the battle taking place around her. Then, just as Art landed another flurry of blows, the mare jumped in fear, sending both men rolling across the ground.

In another instant, the stranger disappeared, charging away into the grove. The force of the horse's surge had sent Art flying and as he landed, his head struck the base of a nearby boxelder tree. When he regained his senses a few moments later, Inga had his head cradled in her lap. Huge tears cascaded down her cheeks, which were already showing the bruises from being thrown so violently from the buggy.

"Do you have any idea who your attacker was?" Tom felt as though he had been a spectator of their attack.

"None at all," replied Art. "The man just disappeared into the woods, and of course it was dark by then. I had no hope of catching him."

"When we had pulled ourselves together," Inga said in a near-whisper, " we helped each other into the buggy and drove right up to the house. I ran in and yelled for my parents, who were just preparing for bed. Between my sobbing, I told them what had happened." added Inga. "Art stayed in the spare bedroom that night. In the morning my mother and father went with Art and me to the grove. Although nothing was said about our parking there, I saw my parents look knowingly at each other. He couldn't possibly still be here someplace, could he, we wondered?"

As Tom and the Iversons talked, Tom could find no hints regarding who the violent attacker they had endured might have been. It was possible their attacker had been planning to rob the Clauson farm. It was also possible the attack had been provoked by the romance of Art and Inga, that someone present at the church social had followed them and, in jealousy, had sought to kill Art. Even if one of those scenarios was true, Tom could see no connection between that attack and the deaths of Arnie and Bobbie.

Tom was about to end his visit, admitting to himself that although the tale was interesting, there didn't seem to be any reason for him to pry further into the couple's life. Then, Art, who had become more relaxed in Tom's presence, volunteered, "When we were attacked I could hear the man yelling something. He wasn't yelling in Norwegian. Mostly, I couldn't understand him at all, but I think it might have been German he was speaking.

"When I was a boy we never trusted those Germans. Even before the Great War my father said I should not trust those German farmers, or the German shopkeepers. Of course, I didn't really know any Germans. We didn't speak the same language, and I guess everyone I knew within riding distance of our farm was from Norway. Then, one Sunday, as Pa was sitting with his brothers, they started to talk of their own father and about being boys in Fillmore County. Since my brothers and I were seldom allowed to sit in on adult conversations, we couldn't help but be interested in what they were talking about.

"It seems that when my grandpa, Halvor's pa, was about fourteen years old, his grandfather—my great- grandfather—was attacked in Rushford by a drunken German man. His grandpa was about fifty years old at that time Although he was pretty strong, this German had surprised him, and for no apparent reason had attacked him. The

German had come out of a bar, bumped into Grandpa's pa, knocking him to the ground. Then, he knocked him out by hitting him with a beer mug from the bar." "Grandpa was up in the buckboard. By the time he understood what was happening, his Pa was on the ground. Grandpa said he jumped at the man, who just back-handed him, sending him to the ground, before he stumbled away and disappeared."

"It seems to me," Art admitted, "that although the story might prove we shouldn't trust Germans because they get drunk and angry, there is hardly any proof that the incidents are connected. Maybe I shouldn't even guess my attacker was German. It was about 1856 when that old attack took place. That would mean the German from Rushford would have been almost seventy years old when Inga and I were attacked. That was no seventy-year old man I fought in the grove."

Although this new information was interesting, Tom wasn't sure it was valuable. For one thing, there were too many Pas, Grandpas and Great-grandpas, for him to keep track of. Just the attack in Fillmore County in 1856 and another attack in Chippewa County in 1914 did not prove a conspiracy. The nineteenth century had been a violent time in the American west. Undisciplined men hunted and trapped across the land, following the Mississippi, Minnesota, and Missouri Rivers, into lands that sometimes had never been seen by white men. It took men prone violence to brave primitive America as they sought their fortunes.

No, thought Tom, the attacks on two Iverson relatives in 1936, and again in 1937, were most likely just coincidental. Just having German attackers did not connect the incidents, either. *"How can I hope to connect all these incidents, happening over nearly one hundred years, based on such information?"*

Twelve

BOYD BAUER HAD spent his entire life on the move, passing unnoticed through small towns. Stealing a chicken when he was hungry, an unattended shirt or a jacket when the opportunity presented itself, then blending into the background and staying as invisible as he could. He had been comfortable with a life that was unencumbered by social norms. He had started his independent life as a ten-year-old boy who had been thrown alone into the wilderness. He had grown into a strapping teenager by the time Alice Bevins had seduced him. There was no question whether he knew how to survive. The sheep farmer Stanton learned that lesson the hard way.

In the summer of 1914, however, his luck seemed to be disappearing. After an uneventful ride atop a railroad boxcar, he had dropped into the shadows as the train stopped to add water in the small village of Milan. The bad luck started there, when he twisted an ankle as he dropped from the train. He could not remember ever making such a mistake. He had never been sick or injured so far in his life.

It was that seemingly small mishap that led to his encounter with Art and Inga. For the moment, however, he hobbled across the adjoining field, swearing at his own stupidity for the painful ankle and hoping to find an easy meal and a shelter for the coming night. A half mile to the east of the railroad tracks he spotted a farm site that promised to satisfy his needs. The Burns farm loomed large before him. The farm's crops of wheat and oats dominated nearly two hundred acres of undulating hills, which sloped gently to a huge valley with a clear stream running through it. A large white house, a substantial barn and several well-kept small buildings, were all surrounded by a well-kept grove of trees which promised Boyd protection for the night. And, it promised fresh eggs and maybe even a chicken for his next day's meal.

In the pasture west of the grove, a hundred head of brown swiss cattle lounged quietly, with no thoughts of danger. The afternoon shadows were long. Sunset was just an hour or two away, meaning the evening chores were probably completed and the farm's inhabitants would be settling in for a comfortable evening before bedtime. No one was likely to notice if he slipped into the henhouse, or if he made himself comfortable in a shed, or in the grove, for the night.

Boyd crept carefully into the yard. He stayed in the shadows and crept around the silo. He moved quietly but confidently between the granary and the hen house, watching all the while to be sure the farm's occupants could not see him. As he turned a corner his luck failed him for the second time.

The large shaggy dog, which helped herd the cattle when needed, had spotted a gopher creeping out from the granary's stone foundation and was intent of making a snack of it. Boyd turned the corner just as the dog leapt forward. Intent on survival, the gopher dived back under the granary. The dog changed course and charged Boyd, who, with his painful ankle, fell back against the building.

As he fell backward, Boyd landed a lucky blow to the dog's head, momentarily sending it to the ground. Without waiting to see the dog's reaction, he headed out of the farm yard. Although it did not follow Boyd, the dog set off a loud harangue, bouncing left and right, to be sure Boyd did not continue trespassing into his territory.

Boyd, swearing at his bad luck, swearing at the dog, swearing at the farmer for owning the miserable animal, made his retreat as fast as he could; painful ankle notwithstanding. Although Burns came to the door to see what the disturbance was, he did not leave the house, believing the dog, who was now walking demurely toward the house, had just had a bad encounter with one of the geese who also thought they commanded the yard.

Instead of a comfortable night in a barn or a granary, Boyd slept fitfully in the tall grass offered in a stand of trees growing along the Chippewa River. There were no eggs and certainly no chicken for today's meal. He salved his hunger with wild plums growing at the river's edge, then limped stealthily around and stayed clear of the next occupied farm as he continued to blame the world for his recent bad luck.

By late the next afternoon, Boyd's anger was raging, as was the pain in his ankle. As the day progressed, he found himself following a high ridgeline, moving from one pasture or wooded grove to the next. From time to time, in the early part of the day, he had seen buggies and wagons carrying couples or families, as they headed north along the prairie, following paths that could not really be called roads.

It seemed to Boyd there would be no better time than now to find a free meal at some unoccupied farm. Late in the day he came to the grove surrounding the Peter Clauson farm. A long driveway wound through a grove made up of Boxelders, Chinese elm, and Hackberry, and opened onto a huge yard decorated with young Norway pine, more elms, and several Linden trees. A huge house, with a wrap-around porch, looked out over the yard. Granary, hog house, corn crib, a well house with an electric generator, and a chicken house as large as many homes, flanked the big red barn, itself looking over the river valley that was a mile wide. A half-dozen huge draft horses lounged in the shadow of the barn, as well as two dozen lazy dairy cows which were contentedly chewing their cud. The presence of the cows told Boyd that, although there was no one home at that moment, there would be activity to feed and milk the cows before sunset, or at least soon thereafter.

Past experiences told Boyd that the most likely and the safest place to find food would be in the well house. That simple white structure, sheltered by huge trees on three sides, would be the logical place to store smoked meats, or milk, or even freshly butchered chickens, for the Sunday meal. His guess was right. Boyd slipped inside, closing the door behind him. The room was dark and cool. A large tank containing cold clear water held several sealed glass jugs, each one offering thick and creamy milk. He quickly sliced a large section of ham from a hanging pork haunch, stuffing it into his mouth as he sliced several more pieces that were put into his pack. He took a mason jar filled with buttermilk from the water tank and it was consumed in one large gulp as Boyd's eyes scanned the room.

He sliced more ham for his pack then grabbed two coils of smoked sausage as well. Although he was tempted to see what treasures were available in the house, Boyd thought discretion should prevail; take the treasure of food and disappear before the family returned, he decided. The wisdom of that decision soon proved true. With the warm feeling of a full stomach, he retreated into the grove, skirting the farm buildings. As he did, he heard the creaking and thumping that signaled the return of the Clauson buckboard, followed by a second wagon containing several additional family members.

Boyd realized he had stayed at the Clauson farm just a little too long, realizing also, that he might not have been paying quite enough attention to his surroundings. He had been too comfortable in the solitude of the well house. Now, he had to decide if he should try to sneak unseen across the nearby open field or stay in the grove until nightfall.

Since the weather was mild, it seemed just as smart to find a comfortable place in the woods and wait for darkness before venturing out. Besides, he thought, where do I have to go, why should I rush away? No one is waiting for me, so why don't I just make myself comfortable for a few hours. Enjoy a nap. Forget about that damn dog. Forget how much my ankle hurts.

The next thing Boyd knew, it was night-time. It was dark, but not still. He had fallen comfortably asleep in the grove of the Clauson farm, and he might have slept through the night, except for the sound of voices nearby. At first, he thought the Clausons were searching for him, that they had discovered his intrusion and were searching the woods for him. As he listened, staying immobile behind a tree, he realized he was eavesdropping on a conversation between a man and a woman which nothing to do with him. It was just two people, in a quiet, intimate conversation that was interrupted occasionally by a chuckle, a giggle, a crooning, or a sigh.

Carefully, as quietly as possible, he moved to where he could hear them better. They were just visible in the wooded darkness. He could now tell it was a young man and a young woman; maybe just a girl. They were wrapped in each other's arms, leaning now one way, then the other, as they embraced and fondled. They were in a buggy, with its top laid down, the horse was standing patiently in the night.

When she turned just right, Boyd could see the young woman was beautiful, gorgeous even. He could tell she was slender and was wearing a form fitting dress. He could see the swell of her breasts as she moved next to her companion. The sight of her brought back memories of Alice Bevins, memories of her passion, her aroma as they made love, and of all the mysteries of sex which she had solved for him.

This woman was everything Boyd could imagine possessing. Even in the moonlight, he could see her high cheekbones, see her teeth sparkle as she smiled at the man next to her, hear her joyous laugh as he whispered in her ear. At one moment, he thought they were going to lie down on the buggy seat, that he would be tortured by the sight of them make love right in front of him.

Boyd was captivated by her. Now, she took the man's hands in hers, as she whispered, "No, Art. We must not. We have to wait until we are married. I do not want to get into trouble, pregnant, like some of the girls I know. Just think how wonderful it will be though, when we are husband and wife, when I am no longer just Inga Clauson, but Mrs. Art Iverson. Think how much it will mean then, when we can make love without worrying about it. Think of how we will live in our own home and raise children of our own."

In that instant, the spell was broken. Inga was no longer an innocent girl to Boyd. She was no longer the symbol of beauty and chastity. She was just a possession of Art Iverson. She was another prize, held by another Iverson, another reminder of all he had lost, of all his own father had lost because of people named Iverson. Iverson. Iverson. Iverson.

How he hated that name; Iverson. They were the cause of all the losses in his life. Iversons were the reason he was forced to live alone, to wander from woodland to town to village. It was because of an Iverson he was alone on nights like this; cold and alone in the winter, always kept from living the good life he deserved. As he listened to the couple, cooing and murmuring, laughing at some secret known only to them, Boyd's mind conjured the image of the shack where he had taken the lives of his mother and grandmother. That would never have happened if some Iverson had not ruined his father's life so many years before. And now, he was being subjected to this.

Lying next to him in the grass was a large branch. It was five feet long and four inches thick. It was just what he needed to exact revenge for all the privations caused by people named Iverson. He grabbed the smaller end in both hands and leapt from his hiding place. He screamed loudly as he ran the few steps toward the buggy. He swung the limb at the man with all his energy.

At the last moment, as if by some divine intervention, Art turned. He moved just enough to keep the weapon from crushing his skull. The blow landed on Art's shoulder. The blow was not enough to kill him, as Boyd wanted. Then, Art recovered and retaliated. In an instant the two men were on the ground pummeling each other. They fell under the horse, flailing at each other, neither gaining the advantage. In an unexpected moment, Art was thrown against the root of a nearby tree. Realizing he was himself in danger, Boyd fled. If Iverson had chased him, Boyd knew he would be caught. His damaged ankle screamed with pain, but Boyd had no option but to run as fast as he could.

He was a mile away before the pain in his ankle forced him to stop. All the while, Boyd had been screaming silently, cursing all the Iversons who had ever lived. Finally, as his pulse quieted and as the pain grew unbearable, he dropped into the grass and passed out.

Thirteen

BOYD BAUER'S LIFE had been lived in cycles. Highs and lows, mostly lows. There had been times when he almost joined normal society and was almost ready to no longer be a person of the night. After his encounter with the couple in the farm grove, he wandered without focus or purpose. From rural Chippewa County he had drifted to the small town of Morris, then across the state line into South Dakota, where he had toiled as a laborer for a summer, helping build a new road across the dry prairie.

The pattern continued. Desperation drove him to legitimate labor. When that happened, he was excited that he might have found new meaning in his life. Sometimes within a day, sometimes a month, Boyd saw the disparity of his wages to the massive profits being made by his employer and the great new job became just a good job before becoming another despised job, to be put behind him as soon as possible.

His last day on one job came when he heard the foreman praise a man named Iverson, that despised family name. He had pushed the man from a scaffold, breaking the man's arm and several ribs. He angrily drew his final wages. It was time to leave so-called normal society behind again.

In Huron, South Dakota, Boyd set fire to a church where he had labored, deeming it proper that the disrespectful pastor should lose his symbol of superiority. When he left his ranch job, just west of North Platte, Nebraska, he cut the fence enclosing two hundred head of fattening cattle and spooked them onto the prairie, after first killing three of the steers.

In the spring of 1917, Boyd found work in the Oklahoma oil fields, sweating and busting his back for a consortium that never saw how hard he was working and how he was making them richer by the day. After drawing a meager final paycheck, he sneaked back at midnight, beating the foreman into unconsciousness, before hightailing it across the state line into Texas.

As the months p[assed, Boyd found himself back on the northern prairie. He was looking for a safe zone, some place where he would be accepted. He passed through town after town; he was not successful. It seemed the entire world had turned against him.

Boyd Bauer's life had fallen apart. He had survived, some days cursing God and all the mystery surrounding Him. Some days Boyd thought perhaps God did exist and there were days he thought he was just being tested. But, mostly, Boyd just felt his life spiraling down; no good luck, no good fortune, no success. No longer was the prairie his friend, no longer was he comfortable sleeping in a sheltering grove of trees. He was no longer confident that he could survive alone through another winter, and no longer confident that he had successful control of his life.

As autumn was turning to an early winter, Boyd wandered into the village of Benson, Minnesota. He had never been this far north, never so far from the hills of southern Minnesota. His long journey of uncounted failures across North and South Dakota, Nebraska, Oklahoma and Texas, had brought him in an irregular circle and back to the Minnesota River valley. He was just miles from the place his downward spiral had begun.

Benson was not much of a town, he thought, but it was the county seat of Swift County, and it had a railroad running through it. Boyd thought maybe he would just catch a ride in an empty box car or flatten himself atop one if none offered an open door. He would do anything to get away from this unfriendly countryside. He must get away and regain some sense of success. There must be something he could do.

For a while he sat at the edge of a small grove of trees, with his back against a huge elm, which had already lost its leaves. The barren tree was a precursor of the coming winter. Along the eastern edge of town there were numerous small businesses; a men's clothing store, a hardware store, another that provided general goods for farmers and homemakers. Boyd could see nothing in this hamlet that encouraged him to stay. There were no easy pickings in sight. The train depot looked like all the others Boyd had seen as he had wandered across the country. There was a bleak, one-story depot building and a long platform, with a row of flatbed carts lined up along the platform, ready to haul baggage, or mail, to and from the train. There was an uncomfortable looking wooden bench on each side of the ticket window. And standing alongside the depot there was a middle-aged, dumpy, policeman in a wrinkled uniform, who had not yet spotted him but who looked like he was primed for trouble.

If he was going to sneak aboard a train, it would have to be out of sight of the train depot. Boyd gave the depot and the policeman a wide berth, circling behind the building, then making a fast exit behind the nearby row of businesses. As he rounded a building corner, he caught the eye of a tall man who had been watching for someone just like Boyd. The man wore a uniform of olive green, pressed, fitted, impressive. On the sleeves of his uniform were the chevrons of a sergeant, U.S. Army. Unlike the policeman, this man smiled at Boyd and motioned, in a friendly way, for Boyd to join him.

Fourteen

THE TALL YOUNG soldier seemed not to notice Boyd's tattered clothing or his unkempt appearance. "You look like a man who could use a good meal and a shower," he volunteered. There was no sign of condescension in his manner. Boyd felt welcomed by him. They walked together into the nearby office, where he was offered a hot shower, followed by the promised meal.

While Boyd ate, the soldier explained why he was hanging out by the railway station in Benson. "We've got a war coming on," he began. "I discovered there are dozens of brave men such as yourself, maybe hundreds of men, who need just a little opportunity to change their lives for something better. I don't beckon every man I see into my office. You have a look about you. Something that tells me you have far more potential than most of people see."

The man had Boyd's attention. It was obvious to Boyd that this man was successful; just one look at him, all clean and pressed and happy to be alive was enough to gain Boyd's respect. It had been months, possibly years, since Boyd had felt so welcome anywhere. After Boyd had taken the hot shower, the sergeant had gone to a large locker where he continued to talk over his shoulder as he rummaged through a collection of clothing. Boyd was given a new shirt, a pair of khaki trousers and socks. He felt like a new man. A second full helping of hot food took the final edge off his suspicions regarding the soldier's motives.

The two men spent over an hour at the table. All the while, the sergeant extolled the life of a soldier. "You can do something good for your country while you make a new life for yourself, Boyd. We both know you deserve better than being forced to live in the shadows. Let me help you; the army will feed and clothe you while you get your life back together. Oh, yes, I know there's going to be a war. We think the United States might be in it for a short while. The president doesn't want to put our citizens at risk just to help the French and English out of a pickle they should never have gotten into in the first place. But, we need to protect our country. Believe me, enlisting in the army is a choice you won't regret."

Boyd knew nothing of an impending war. Newspapers were not delivered to men who ate stolen food and slept in farm groves. That news seemed of little value compared with the life being offered by the smiling sergeant.

"Boyd, this is a once in a lifetime chance to put your life back together. I'll even give my personal recommendation on you application papers. Trust me, you'll love army life."

For the first time in years Boyd felt like he was a man welcomed to the table. The sergeant was convincing, although from time to time Boyd questioned the man's motives. After all, he had not been born yesterday. His years on the road, working menial jobs, just surviving, had taught Boyd that everything that sounded true might not be quite that true.

The army put Boyd up in the local hotel for the night before he and three other new recruits boarded the morning train to Minneapolis and to the new life promised them. For the most part, Boyd did love army life. Basic training was a piece of cake compared with living under a bush beside the river, and far better than mindless work for men who only cared for their own prosperity. He learned in short order not to talk smart or strike back at drill instructors who put their faces inches from his own and yelled at him. He gloried in the hand-to-hand combat training, even if it was with make-believe weapons. He was a survivor. More than that, he was being recognized on a daily basis for showing a ruthless spirit.

After five weeks of training at Fort Snelling, private Boyd Bauer was put aboard a train with three hundred other recruits. It was a wild and exciting trip, non-stop to New York City, where they joined another three hundred-forty men. For the first time, Boyd travelled in a coach instead of a boxcar. He was served meals by an orderly. In Kansas City and again in Chicago he lined up with his companions and was served in a huge open kitchen, then given a half-hour break, before being put back on the train. In another three days, they all disembarked and were shuttled to a mysterious military establishment. Two weeks later, private first-class Bauer and his platoon were on their way to glory in the French countryside. He was ready for his great adventure. He had not only a grand-looking uniform; he had a duffel bag filled with everything the Army told him he would need. His aggressive spirit had earned him early promotion and although the feelings were not actually universal or unanimous, Boyd had a squad of friends at his side.

Boyd was now thirty-six years old, thought by most of his companions to be too old to be fighting in any war. The *old man,* they called him. *Gramps*! The glory in France was short-lived, however; instead, it was fleeting, non-existent and out of reach. Instead of glory, they found foxholes which they shared with dead and mangled bodies. They found trenches, meant to protect them from bombardment, but which turned out to be long, twisting mass graves. And they found miles of concertina wire, with barbs that tore at their flesh and their clothing, trapping unfortunate doughboys, while German machine guns tore their bodies to shreds, leaving their unidentified bodies for the crows. He was there with all the young men who were dying in the trenches, or in the muddy fields that had recently been covered with wheat or oats. Now the fields were just covered with the dead bodies of men and boys.

Now, he was corporal Boyd Bauer, U.S. Army Infantry. As men died all around him, promotions came quickly. Corporal Bauer was just more cannon fodder as the German Artillery pounded the fields with their big guns. It looked like he was going to be just another sacrifice to the greater glory of freedom, the living and dying barrier that was meant to slow the tide of German aggression. He was just more meat being sacrificed to stop the tide that was trying to engulf Europe. This world war would bring a final peace to the world, they said. For Boyd, it had offered the most expedient way to escape being put in jail, or to spend another cold winter looking for shelter, but Boyd wondered where the glory had disappeared. There were no crisp, pressed uniforms here, no clean-shaven young men, laughing and enjoying life. It was like that construction site in Huron, South Dakota, or like the Oklahoma oil fields; except that instead of opportunistic employers, there were German soldiers intent on killing him.

Then, almost without warning, the Great War, the war to end all wars, was over . The Armistice was signed. Corporal Boyd Bauer was discharged and sent back into the unfriendly world—just as America was beginning to experience its great depression.

Fifteen

THERE WERE DAYS Tom felt as though his time was running out. He sometimes felt all the trips back and forth across Chippewa County, all the hours spent seeking an unknown, unidentified murderer, were being wasted. Summer had become fall; frost now sometimes covered the ground in the early morning. Tom knew that winter would soon settle again over the Minnesota River Valley. Before long, the prairie that was so fertile and lush through the summer and fall, would settle into a cold white sleep.

And then—what? Tom had no idea how he could expect to solve the mystery deaths of Bobbie and Arne with absolutely no clues to guide him. The only positive result of his time here, other than his deepening relationship with Judge Chamberlin, was the pleasant time spent with Mary Collins. Yes, he would miss her when he left. He and Mary now spent most evenings together, going to a movie, eating a burger at the Bungalow Café, sometimes a walk along the river.

September was nearly over. Thinking of it as a going away celebration, Tom had suggested he and Mary spend Saturday afternoon just touring the valley in the little coupe the judge had made available. They drove for hours, up the east side of Chippewa County as far as Big Bend, then west to Milan, where they shared a burger at the Norse Café. As the sun settled lower, they crossed the newly formed Lac Qui Parle Lake on the new steel bridge just west of Milan, then followed the shoreline south on the dirt road which led up a hill to Anthony's Resort. They spent an hour at the grand roller-skating rink the Anthony's had built right along the lakeshore. After watching the light reflect on the lake while they shared a Coca Cola, they slowly made their way south again.

At the last moment, Tom turned left. Instead of continuing up the hill to the village of Lac Qui Parle, Tom drove across the bridge and dam Ernie helped build; the project where Ernie had been murdered. It looked very different today. The road was now a smooth macadam instead of snow-covered dirt. The shoreline of the river, which had still been under construction at Ernie's death, was now lined with large granite slabs, stacked edge to edge in the hope of minimizing erosion. The shore on both sides of the river had been planted with elm and ash saplings, which were soon going to lose their leaves. All the huge construction equipment which had lurked along the river had been moved to new sites. In their places, random automobiles were parked haphazardly by a dozen or so fishermen who seemed to have stopped with no specific plan but had a need to get to the river's edge as fast as possible.

It was as if he was being drawn by some unseen force. Tom slowed the car almost to a stop as they passed over the bridge. Then, without commenting to Mary, he turned in front of Buster's Roadhouse and parked in the huge gravel-covered lot. As they sat in the car, Tom told Mary the tale of Ernie's death and the subsequent series of events that now was nearly two years in the past. It was the first time Tom had returned to Buster's, and the first time he had talked about his dramatic trip to bring Ernie home. Images of that deadly winter flashed before him. As Tom recounted his emotional tale, Mary sat quietly, holding Tom's hand, without saying a word.

Finally, his emotions spent, Tom leaned back and laughed. "Wow! I had no idea that was going to happen. It's like I had built a wall around that whole episode. Now… let's make a clean breast of it and go inside for a beer before I take you home!"

As they entered the bar, Tom's emotions were like electricity on a silk scarf. The place seemed strange and unreal. At the same time it looked familiar, as if he had been in there just days before. The wide-plank pine floors were swept clean, except for some newly dropped peanut shells under the bar stools. A girl Tom guessed to be sixteen or seventeen years old was sprinkling salt across the floor of the dance area. He knew that before long the local band would set up; the afternoon beer drinkers would be replaced by the singles and couples coming here to celebrate the end of another work week.

Tom knew it was going to be just a one-beer stop at Buster's. It was almost surreal; memories flooded his thoughts. The images of Ernie, probably sitting in this same booth with his work companions, mixed with images of today's farmers and fishermen leaving, as their replacements wandered in.

As Tom and Mary were finishing their drink and getting ready to continue their journey, a middle-aged man in bib overalls approached the booth. Without asking, he signaled the bartender for three drinks, then asked if he could join them.

Tom started to turn down the drinks and was about to say they were just leaving, but stopped short when the stranger said, "I know who you are, Mr. Hall. I think I have some information you might be looking for."

Although he did not seem to be hiding his conversation from the others in the room, the stranger spoke in a barely audible whisper. Those living in the area would not have thought he had an accent, but to Tom the Norwegian-laced voice was very lyrical, and in some ways it was hard to understand.

"I farm just over here in Kragero Township, Mr. Hall. My pa and his brothers were some of the first to homestead here in the 1870s. I got to know your brother before he died, and I'm awfully sorry he was murdered. I guess you know, there were some pretty violent men working here then.

"Well, I know you've been asking about Arne Thorson. I suppose everybody around here has already forgotten that he was killed over in the Sag last summer. Most people don't realize he was murdered. That business was all kept pretty quiet, and of course, life just goes on after a while.

"I knew Arne pretty well. We grew up together; more or less. The Thorson farm isn't too far from ours; just two sections north, toward Appleton. I'm a bit older than Arne, but we both went to the country school just a couple of miles from here. I stayed with my family on the farm, but Arne took a job at the grain elevator up in Holloway. The drought has kept everybody pretty poor, but Arne was a good worker and hauled a lot of grain for us and other farmers while we were growing up. He didn't hang around here too much, though. His family farmed nearer to Appleton, which is twelve or fourteen miles north of Watson, and he just found friends up that way after he started at the elevator. With his work at the elevator, Arne got around pretty good; spent his free time in Bellingham and Morris more than he did around here.

"What I was wondering was, whether you had a chance to talk to the girl Arne brought in here the day he was killed?"

An electric jolt jumped through Tom. He was so shocked at the news that he was momentarily speechless. Of course, he knew, or at least had cause to believe, that Arne was with a woman because of the red shoe found by the river. But, there had been no sign of that woman. Except for that shoe, she did not exist. Not one person he had spoken with had even hinted at a woman in Arne's life.

"I'm sorry," Tom stammered. "Tell me your name again. Sometimes my brain jumps out of gear, and I apparently just wasn't paying attention when you told me."

"Oh, no. It wasn't you. I just began telling you about Arne and neglected to introduce myself. I'm Carl Blom. We get so used to everyone here knowing everyone, I just forgot my manners."

"Please, Carl, join us for a few minutes. I'm interested in hearing everything you can tell us about Arne and this mysterious woman. Do you know her name, where she lived? What did she look like, what was she wearing? Wow!" Questions raced through Tom's mind. "After all the hours I've spent and all the people I've talked with, I had no idea who Arne was with. And, for some reason, it never crossed my mind to come here to Buster's and just ask around. I guess I thought eventually I'd visit enough farmers to have talked with everyone in the county."

The minutes became an hour. Tom ordered hamburgers and beer for the three of them as Carl talked about Arne, about their growing up, about school, everything that came to his mind.

"Arne was a confirmed bachelor. With his job, he travelled daily, and not just to the farms around Big Bend, Holloway and Milan. Over the months he made friends as far away as Benson, Willmar, and Ortonville. Mostly he made day-trips though, hauling corn here, oats and wheat in other places.

"What I remember most of that day is that Arne and this real beauty showed up about nine o'clock. They had obviously been drinking somewhere before getting to Buster's, but I think they spent most of the night here dancing, not drinking. Then—around midnight—they were gone."

"I assumed that when they left Arne was going to take her home, wherever that might have been. We don't have any hotels anywhere near here and Arne lived about twelve miles away. I guess that means, since Arne died sometime that night, that she lived, or was staying, somewhere near here. The spillway over in the sag is not on the way to Arne's place, so I have no idea why they'd go in that direction."

"Tellme what you can about the girl. Had you ever seen her before?"

"No, never. I'd say she was twenty-five years old, or so. Of course, it's hard to tell. And they were so wrapped up in each other, I don't think they stopped dancing long enough to talk to anyone all night. I do remember, she had this great head of hair, short, almost like a boy's haircut, and dark red, like a red roan horse. She wasn't put together like a boy, if you know what I mean. I'm sorry, miss, if I'm being vulgar. It's just that her figure was, I guess you'd call it voluptuous. She wasn't fat or anything, but she had… Carl shrugged his shoulders and blushed as he described Arne's date. She had great hips, and when it got hot in here, her blouse clung to her. I mean… a man almost couldn't take his eyes off her.

"I remember now, she was wearing a rather short skirt, much shorter than we are used to seeing around here. It was bright red. Her blouse looked like it was silk, kind of gauzy; it was black, with big red flowers. I guess I said before, it stuck to her body, you couldn't help but stare at her. And then—I remember—she was wearing red shoes with high heels. Man, oh man, she was something else to look at."

Tom and Mary were mesmerized. What an impression this girl – or woman – had made on Carl. Tom wondered who else might have noticed her. How could any man there have missed seeing such an attractive woman?

Although Carl was embarrassed as he shared his memory of the voluptuous young woman, Mary could only smile. She knew that in this remote country setting the sight of a beautiful stranger would certainly inspire wild thoughts in a man. "Carl, did you ever hear her name? Did Arne say anything you can recall?"

"You know, "Carl responded, "I've been trying hard to think of that. With the music playing loudly, and everybody talking at a high pitch, it was really almost impossible to hear anybody more than a foot or two away. But, as I think about it, I seem to recall Arne saying Lori, or Laura, or Lorna. Something like that; but I could be wrong. I'm sorry I can't be more help than that."

Eventually, the conversation with Carl diminished. Tom and Mary could think of no new questions. Carl Blom had exhausted his memory of that Saturday night, of Arne Thorson's memory, and of the woman wearing the red shoes and red dress. Tom thanked him for all he had shared, then paid for the food and drinks as he and Mary left the tavern.

As they left Buster's, Tom turned the car east, almost unconsciously heading toward the Watson Sag and the spillway where Arne's body had been found. He and Mary were bubbling with excitement over the new information. By now, the sun was long set, but the moon cast bright light on the road and the fields sweeping by. Then, Tom pulled the car onto the road shoulder as they came to the small dam where the Chippewa River crossed under the road. They sat for a moment, looking at the spillway, the meandering river, and the pathway beside it as it disappeared into the night. Tom mused, "This might be the very spot Arne parked the night he was killed." Tom was almost whispering, as if speaking the words aloud would erase the image he now had in his mind of Arne's last hours alive.

By now, both Tom and Mary had similar thoughts of that night. "I suppose it's improper of me to say this Tom, but do you think Arne and that girl stopped here for some romance?" Mary was slightly embarrassed to say such a thing, but she thought Tom could handle the intimacy of her comments. Although there had been no romance between her and Tom, she felt a growing closeness, and was certain Tom had similar feelings.

"I can't believe we have all this new information. It makes sense, of course; the red shoe, the open car door when the car was found in the morning. I have so many new questions to ask the judge. And the sheriff. I can't imagine where this information will lead, but I know now, that I need to widen my search. Tom and Mary were walking slowly on the well-worn path along the river. Past the spillway, they looked back at the car, then Tom continued. "Arne's body was found way down there" Tom said as he pointed to a rock cropping further downstream. "I think the shoe was found about here."

"It seems to me," Mary whispered, "if I were looking for a romantic spot along the river, this is as far as I might go." They both laughed as they recognized they were each imagining Arne and a beautiful stranger, wrapped in romantic ardor, stopping at this exact spot, shedding their clothes, falling to the grass.

Then, as if the power of their thoughts was too strong to resist, Tom and Mary found themselves in each other's arms. No word was spoken as they settled onto the grass, it was as if they were re-enacting the tableau they had been imagining only moments before. They shed their clothes, piece by piece, helping each other out of blouse, slacks, shirt. Then, naked, Mary drew Tom to her, circling her arms around his neck.

They didn't say a word for a long while as they lay close in the grass. Both were now overwhelmed by their spontaneous passion and the feeling that this was right, inevitable. The only question was—now what? Where do we go from here?

"It just dawned on me for the first time, Mary, that no one ever said if Arne was dressed or naked. I just took for granted he was dressed. No one ever suggested anything different. I suppose it would be inopportune," he chuckled, "to tell the judge what prompted that question."

Sixteen

MONDAY MORNING TOM was at Judge Chamberlin's office. He arrived at seven thirty, as did the judge, who told Tom, "Arne's clothes were found among the rocks and brush in the river. Yes, he was naked. His clothes were found among the rocks. Somehow, that distinction was never discussed. That information was never made public. I'm not sure why it never came up as you and I talked about Arne's death. Do you think it's important? Is it possible the woman you described could have killed him? Maybe, Arne was pressing her too hard; she might have been fighting him off and struck him with a rock. That might explain why we haven't heard from her. Of course, if that's the case, this probably disproves the Iverson conspiracy."

"No," Tom replied. "I think it's unlikely she would have waited until Arne was naked to respond by striking him with a rock. I think it's more likely she and Arne were both naked, or nearly so, and were attacked by someone else. The question, of course, is who that person was, and why he killed Arne and not her. There's still a lot we don't know about Arne's death, but I doubt the woman was the killer."

Tom was back in a business mode now. Discussing Arne's death was his primary interest this morning. The drive into Montevideo on Saturday night had given Mary and Tom time to discuss their own feelings and how they should conduct themselves. He and Mary had agreed they should have a day or two apart. After their first embarrassment they agreed that for the time being they should just enjoy the closeness they were feeling.

Saturday's revelation about Arne and the mystery woman brought new enthusiasm to Tom. "I think I should spend a little time trying to locate this woman. Probably talking to law enforcement and maybe even pastors in some of the towns not in Chippewa County.

All indications are that Arne knew her from his work, perhaps he met her while delivering grain to some neighboring town. I can identify those towns by talking with Arne's employer. "What do you think, Judge? This might be the first real lead in Arne's death. Even if there is no family conspiracy, we might be able to solve Arne's death."

The answer to the mystery of Arne's death was a lot closer than Tom knew. He just didn't know where to look. Arne's last night on earth was so normal that no one seemed to notice as his final hours clicked away.

Seventeen

SATURDAY NIGHTS AT Buster's. It was the place to be, the place where it all happened. Arne's job driving a grain truck for the local elevator brought him to most of the small towns in the area, and Arne was single, almost always available to a pretty girl. Laura was pretty, and Laura was available. That Saturday night found Arne at Buster's. Yes, Carl Blom had been correct when he guessed the couple had been drinking before arriving at Buster's.

Arne and Laura had first met at the Farmers Co-op Elevator in Danvers. Laura's family farmed a sandy patch of ground north of town, and Laura had taken the job of secretary at the elevator shortly after finishing high school. It was a job that didn't have a future, and didn't pay well, but it was a job. With the drought and depression, any job was a good job. Six days a week, Laura took her Pa's 1929 Ford pickup to Danvers. The job was dusty and boring. The workday was long during the harvest season. She knew all the area farmers by name, of course. She thought the ones who needed a bath the most and smelled the worst were the bachelor Andersen brothers. The two men usually came to Danvers as a pair, and it seemed each of them teased and encouraged the other until some lewd and stupid comment was made to Laura.

"Betcha can't guess what Darrel's got ahold of in his pocket." She fell for that one just one time. As she stood and leaned over the counter to see what Darrel was hiding, her dress sagged at the neck, giving the two men a free look at her breasts. They roared with laughter as they took turns suggesting what wondrous pleasures they might bestow on the poor country girl if she and they could sneak out back of the elevator for a few minutes.

After two years of being treated like a mindless bimbo, Laura got fed up and took a waitress job in Benson. Her Pa's pickup ran just well enough to make the daily drive. There were still 1 lewd or suggestive comments from time to time, and the school boys tripped over each other when they came into the café for an ice cream after school, but the job was an improvement in every way. She no longer had to wear a plain old house dress, covered by a sweater or a jacket in colder weather. At the café she could wear a nice skirt and blouse and she traded her high-top lace shoes for penny loafers. Now, she started each day with a bath and shampooed her hair, which she cut into a page-boy rather than wearing it in a long-twisted bun. Laura thought the biggest blessing that came with the new job was that the Andersen brothers never came to Benson.

The first time Laura and Arne met was a Tuesday. Laura had taken advantage of a quiet time in the cafe and, put a nickel in the huge juke box against the wall. She was swaying to *Red Sails in The Sunset.* It was a new recording by Whoopee John Wilfert, the popular bandleader from New Ulm, and she thought it was just dreamy. As she whirled slowly between the tables and the booths, she was unaware Arne had entered, until he swooped in and swung her in a circle, then laughed loudly as he sat in the nearest booth.

Laura couldn't decide if she should laugh or be mad at his rude intrusion, then decided laughter was the best remedy. Within minutes both she and Arne knew they had found soul-mates. For the next several months Arne stopped for coffee, or lunch, whenever he passed through Benson. She learned he was single—expected to stay that way. She learned that first day he had a great sense of humor, was well-spoken, especially for a farmer, and that he liked to dance. They had never been on a real *date* before going to Buster's.

Although she was a stranger in the crowded tavern, thanks to Arne she felt right at home. They had spent a wonderful afternoon together, driving from town to town, stopping for a sandwich, stopping for a cold beer, laughing and teasing each other, engulfed in the foreplay of young adults who knew how the day would progress.

They had arrived at Buster's just before sunset and walked across the road to watch the water cascading through the spillway of the new dam. They walked slowly across the bridge deck, and they threw small stones into the swirling river, then embraced each other tightly and kissed with nervous passion, before returning to the rural majesty of the roadhouse.

As the sun set and the afternoon became evening, they drank and ate in a dream-like state, enthralled and engrossed in each other. Laura felt she actually glowed. Arne, more than any other man in her life before, made her feel like a completed woman.

About eight o'clock the small band began to gather in the corner. Art, Harlan, Sig, and Roland pulled chairs in a semi-circle and uncased their fiddles, a guitar, and an accordion. The members of the band were in fact local farmers, just a group of friends who came together on weekends. After a week of farm work and livestock chores it was a relief to spend a few hours together, entertaining the crowd that was usually made up of friends and neighbors. Waltzes, schottisches, and polkas ran together for hours. Occasionally, one of the band members told a joke, made fun of someone in the crowd, or just related some recent news. As the night wore on the heat and humidity grew, as did the exuberance of the crowd.

Arne and Laura were swept along with the excitement. Finally, with flushed faces and sweaty bodies, they headed for the door. Laura had no doubt that before long Arne would find a quiet place to park. His passion on the dancefloor would turn to passion for each other. After hours of dancing, feeling the sweaty touch of fiery skin through shirt and blouse, she would free herself of skirt, blouse and undergarments, to be enveloped in Arne's equally sweaty body. She had no doubt that the passion she felt building would be satisfied as he held her and entered her steamy body. She knew that after their fiery sex they would lie together and fondle and kiss until Arne's passion rose again and then, possibly, even once more.

By the time they left Buster's the moon was up and full. Trees were brightly lit by the moon, as were the fields of wheat and corn as

Arne guided the car along the dirt road. Only once did he see another automobile, far behind him. He wasn't sure just where he and Laura were heading. He just knew this would be a night to remember. Mile after slow mile, they drove east, up long hills and around curves, where he was driving almost too fast. They continued, teasing and fondling each other, keeping their passions alive.

When their mutually exciting teasing finally became too much, Arne pulled his car to the side of the road. On this remote and deserted country path, Arne had little concern that another car might come by. In moments they had leapt from the car and were wrapped in each other's arms as they sought some perfect private spot to stop. They followed the faint path which was lit by the moon, and then they sank to the ground. The deep summer grass made them a bed as they groped and began to shed their clothes. Only a few yards away, the Chippewa River gurgled over the spillway, as it moved otherwise quietly to join the great Minnesota River, just a few miles downstream.

As Arne began to settle onto her, Laura caught a movement over his shoulder. Before she could scream there was a flash of movement that ended with a sickening crunch, as a large rock connected with Arne's head. Arne slumped forward, the weight of his body pinning Laura to the earth. Then, a red-haired man swung the rock again as he yelled obscenities to Arne. He grabbed Arne's now lifeless body and pulled it away from Laura. As he was about to swing again, Laura lurched to her feet. Without thinking of covering her naked body, she smashed a shoulder into the red-haired man. Just one violent rush was enough to send him backward through the tall grass and, off balance, he caught his foot on a rock lining the river and tumbled backward down the bank.

Laura did not have to think to realize that Arne was dead, and she began to run in panic. For a moment, she could not think, then realizing her nakedness, she turned and grabbed the clothing she had so willingly shed only minutes before. Then, not knowing where she was, or where she was going, she ran as if her life depended on it, because she knew it did. She stumbled through the grass and along the brush lined river for what seemed like forever, before she found a cow path leading up the bank from the river.

Sobbing frantically, she followed the path a long way, before stopping to put on her clothes. Panties, bra, skirt, blouse, shoes. Shoes! Only one red shoe in her hand. Somewhere back there was her other shoe, but Laura knew there was no going back. Just run.

When the sun came up Sunday morning, Laura was miles away, walking in a daze beside the country road. She had begun to calm herself, torn as to what she should do. No cars had come along the road as she walked. She knew if one would come into view she would hide, rather than be caught by the man with the red hair.

Just ahead, she saw a livestock truck idling alongside the road and knew what she must do. There were no livestock in the back of the truck. The driver had stopped to relieve himself before continuing his journey. As he went around the truck, Laura ran on the other side and threw herself into the truck box. She lay there, shaking and crying, as the driver renewed his journey. Three hours late, the truck slowed and turned into the livestock yards in Morris. Now, dressed again except for her shoes, Laura cautiously lowered herself from the truck and disappeared.

Eighteen

TOM DECIDED HE deserved a weekend free of intrigue. Friday night, he and Mary went to the college football game and watched as the University of Minnesota at Morris shellacked the Windom College team from Montevideo.

Tom was beginning to feel as though he was not soon going to be leaving Montevideo. Too many clues, not just a few promising bits of information, left him feeling that something was going to break in his favor— and soon. It looked like Tom Hall was going to be around for Thanksgiving. And maybe for Christmas, although until now, that possibility had never crossed his mind. Remembering his last visit to Minnesota sent shivers down his spine, but his discomfort at the thought of Minnesota in the winter was offset by the pleasure he was finding in Mary's company.

Saturday morning Tom met Mary at her home, then they started a leisurely drive south of Montevideo. It was difficult to put the investigation aside, even for a few hours, but both knew they needed a day away from mystery and the hustle of shopping day Saturday in Montevideo. With no conscious plan, they left town, travelling south on the dirt road that would eventually take them through the small village of Wegdahl. From there, they could follow the Minnesota River for another dozen miles. They thought they might go to Granite Falls, and from there they could choose to follow the river south, through the Upper Sioux Indian Agency, or head west across the open prairie to any of the other small towns that would be filled with farmers doing their weekly shopping and relaxing.

Unlike the prairie north of Montevideo, the river valley to the south had large outcroppings of granite rock. Along the eastern wall of the valley surprising clusters of cacti showed up from time to time.

Here, large cottonwood trees lined the river and stands of river willow crowded the banks in places. In some ways, it reminded Tom of his home in Ohio and as they drove, he realized he hadn't been home in more than a year. When his mother had died, he found he had no important connections there. Now, with both mother and Ernie gone, he had little reason to return to Ohio.

In Wegdahl, they stopped for a soft drink and walked the short distance to the river, where they leaned on the bridge rail and watched the brown water slowly glide beneath them. Fall was in the air. Mary dressed for a possible autumn walk, or perhaps lunch somewhere along the way. She wore a Scottish tartan pleated skirt, topped with a crew neck blouse and blazer, an outfit suitable for whatever the day might bring. Tom, feeling the need to not be in "work attire", also dressed for a day of pleasure, wearing tan gabardine slacks, a turtle necked sweater and a short leather jacket. On the days he was searching around Chippewa County, he just wore blue jeans and a chambray shirt. With the weather getting cooler, he now threw his leather jacket on the car seat, in case the air turned chilly.

The romance between the couple was blossoming, and as they stood on the bridge Tom held Mary's hand. As the water swirled beneath them, Tom realized that although he was not a celibate, he had never really had a girlfriend. How strange, he thought; girlfriend. Neither of them were teenagers, yet this romance had a captivating innocence to it. They each seemed uncertain what their relationship really was, and neither of them—so far—was brave enough to ask what future the other saw for them.

"Your skirt is lovely," Tom offered, "I haven't seen you wear it before. It certainly doesn't look like you bought it in Montevideo."

Mary laughed and twirled lightly in front of Tom. "We do occasionally have the ability to buy nice clothes in Monte, Tom. But, you're right. It's really a hand-me-down, I guess. In its previous life it was a kilt. It is one of the few things that survived when my family came here from Scotland. My grandfather and his brother walked to

Montevideo from some place in New York state after they arrived from Scotland. Somehow, the kilt, as well as a couple of other MacGregor heirlooms, survived the trip. You wouldn't know, of course, but I'm related to the Heinrich's, and of course, all of the MacGregor's around the county. My grandpa knew I always admired the kilt, and before he died he gave it to me. I thought it was too beautiful to leave in a drawer or in the closet, so… here it is. I just wear it on special days. Like today.

Nineteen

TOM AND MARY were leaving the Riverside Hotel Restaurant where they had lunch after first attending church, and something was scratching away at his brain. It was as if a light had flashed on in midnight blackness. "I don't know what it was, Mary." The words stumbled out of his mouth. "I left the church feeling as if I was getting some kind of message, or I should have understood something which had been said, but whatever it was has just slipped out of my brain."

Although Tom professed to not being very religious, he had been attending various churches around the county. Zion in Big Bend, the Methodist and Lutheran churches in Montevideo, and the Lutheran church in Watson as well. Some Sundays Mary joined him, and today they had sat together on a hard pew at the back of the First Baptist Church in Montevideo as Reverend William Tecumseh Sherman droned on. With a dour expression, he was promising each parish member, and every guest, a limited choice of ethereal salvation and reunion with loved ones; or eternal damnation, fire, brimstone, and agony beyond comprehension. It depended on a person's ability to lead a good life and make the right choices.

Unfortunately, the light which came on for Tom, came on without focus. Tom knew something did not fit but couldn't put a finger on it. Today's sermon, more pointedly the tenor of Pastor Sherman's voice, something in his body language, had awakened a memory, but Tom couldn't tell if it was a word, a phrase, or a telling body language. Something… something was hiding in the recesses of Tom's mind. He was sure it would come to him if he could just gather his thoughts, but for the moment, it would just remain an unanswered question, to be solved in its own good time.

Mary was little help in solving Tom's problem. "I think you're just trying too hard to find a clue in each conversation you have or hear, Tom. I've gone to this church my entire life, and honestly, I didn't hear or see anything different today. I just saw Pastor Sherman being that strange Pastor Sherman."

"I know Mary, but haven't you ever woke up one morning, or left a room somewhere, thinking you have missed something important?"

Mary jabbed Tom in the ribs and laughed, "I think you are suffering from a case of good old Protestant work ethic. You have been running all over the county, talking with people, or asking questions, nearly every day since you stepped off the train. I think your brain is just overloaded. Besides, maybe no one will ever solve Bobbie's and Arne's deaths. Sometimes, it's like that you know." By the end of the day however, Tom had developed a plan. It was time to try something different before he got demoralized and walked away.

Monday morning Tom stopped to see Judge Chamberlin. "I'm going to be gone for a few days, maybe all week. I have some nagging questions, and I think this trip might bring some answers." Tom had told the judge about the new information he acquired at Busters, and without going into detail, he expressed the unsettling feeling that came over him on Sunday. "I don't think it's going to ever be possible to connect all the unanswered deaths that have taken place in this county over nearly a hundred years, your honor. I'm not sure there is any connection at all, but the only way I can think of to clarify some of those questions is to check the courthouse and church records I've told you about. If the death of Arne and Bobbie are tied to the assault on Art an Inga, and if all that goes back to the Rushford area, I really need to do some on-site research. On the other hand, if there is no real connection, this trip should put that theory to rest."

Tom's last stop before heaving town was at the train depot. He had not warned Mary of his plans, and although he and Mary had talked about his revelation that something seemed wrong, out of place, he still could not identify the real source of his new concern.

For the time being, he had to just stop thinking about it and let the questions ferment while he made this trip.

"I think I am misjudging or misunderstanding too many things, Mary. I really need to check some records, flesh out some of the details and corroborate some thoughts I'm concerned about. It's time to eliminate some of the possibilities we think are probabilities. I just have too many unanswered questions."

By mid-morning Tom was guiding the little Ford coupe, loaned by the judge, eastward along the newly established and paved highway 212. By week's end, he would have visited newspapers, courthouses, libraries and churches in Mankato, Rushford and Highland Prairie, before arriving in St. Paul, where his first two stops were to be the Ramsey County Courthouse and the office of the Veterans Administration.

Twenty

IT HAD BEEN a long and busy, but fruitful week for Tom. Now, as he and the judge sat together, Tom began bringing the judge up to date on his trip.

"I think I was looking for answers to too many questions." Tom and judge Chamberlin sat in the judge's library on Saturday morning. After his long week's journey Tom was still trying to piece all his newly gathered information together. He was trying to find something that would tie current day Chippewa County activities to the wealth of information gathered on his trip to southeastern Minnesota, and to the State capital.

"There may be some connection yet," Tom continued. "When I left here Monday, I couldn't see how a vendetta could continue from 1843 to 1937. If a young German had attacked Hans and his wife aboard ship, and almost by accident, attacked Hans again in 1856, I can see some possible connection might exist there. But not again in 1893, and then again in 1914. By 1914 our earlier attacker would have been more than sixty years old, and now might even be in his seventies or older.

"This mystery just seemed to go around and around. I couldn't find any logical connection between the shipboard attack in 1843, the 1856 attack in Rushford, the recent attack on Art and Inga Iverson in 1914, and then the murders of Arne Thorson and Roberta Swan. The great time span, to say nothing of the geographical distance just kept the incidents from logically being connected. But now, I just may have some new information that could make sense of the conspiracy idea, although conspiracy might be too formal a word for the connection.

"Although I still need to tie some information together before I can be certain of my convictions, I can at least bring this puzzle into a little better focus. Judge, I think Arne Thorson and Roberta Swan just might be tied back to the first conflict aboard the Argo. I'm just not sure how. Our Chippewa County killer could be the grandson, or even the great grandson of the red-haired man who attacked Hans Iverson in Rushford. If that is the case, we won't be able to prove the connection unless we get a confession from the killer of Arne and Roberta. We're nowhere near having that happen. I'm stuck somewhere between thinking there is a slight possibility of a connection and the very strong likelihood that there is no possible way the events can be connected."

Tom had spread his notes on the judge's dining table. He had over a dozen pages; photos of newspaper articles, names and dates from various sheriff's offices, church records and notes of questions and answers to thoughts while he was driving. Rushford, in 1854, 1857 and 1858. Highland Prairie Lutheran Church in 1861. There were several pages of notes taken at locations in St. Paul.

Ramsey County and St. Paul governments proved to be the most difficult to deal with, and in the end perhaps could be the most valuable, but he still had a lot of questions awaiting answers. The state capitol was home to city, county and state records, and Tom spent two days searching just the county files.

"What, exactly was it that you were looking for, Tom? I don't yet understand what you were trying to connect."

"When I started, I was just looking for a name that might have shown up frequently in news accounts or law enforcement records. Back in the 1850s and '60s, what few local newspapers in existence across the area made big headlines of violence, hold-ups and robberies. Remember, Minnesota was only made a Territory in 1849, and when it became a state in 1858, the entire population of the state was less than five thousand people. Those few newspapers were also a good source for information about weddings and births and were vital in the settling of the prairie. I started cross-referencing newspaper reports, sheriff's records, and church records. Although it was strictly arbitrary, I was looking for German names, since the Iverson's were first accosted by a German man.

"In Rushford Township, which was settled by mostly Norwegian immigrants, I came on what I thought was the first possible connection. I was talking with Willis Knockleby, who is the publisher of the Tri-County Recorder. When I asked for any specific reference to violence in the early community, he broke into a smile and took me into his office. There, he had a collection of old newspapers going back to the county's beginning. As we started through the stack of newspapers, he told me that when Minnesota became a state in 1858, Rushford was expected to become the Fillmore County seat. Because of that possibility there was a lot of news coverage in the county.

"Farmers, merchants, trappers; they all came through there," Knockleby said. "The Root River connected Rushford to the Mississippi River, and the Mississippi was the main connection to the Minnesota River. Decorah and Waucon, Iowa, were stopping off points near the last civilization before heading into the remote prairies that were to become Minnesota. In fact, most people today are unaware that the settling of Minnesota and the Dakotas initially came from the north as trappers and fur traders followed the Red River down from Canada. That, of course, is another story altogether.

"My great grandfather, Cyrus Knockleby," he continued, "brought a printing press from Joy, Indiana, and began a weekly newspaper called the County Recorder. My grandfathers, then my father continued publishing the Recorder. I took up the task when I finished my schooling. We changed the newspaper's name several years ago. *'Here.'* He pointed to his collection of nearly five thousand newspapers. "This is the entire nineteenth century history of our little part of Minnesota." In his office he had a copy of every week's news for the past ninety-seven years! Each week's newspaper had been carefully saved and filed in Knockleby' s office.

"Of course, the oldest newspapers, which I was interested in, were, by this time, nearly brown and fragile with age. We carefully separated out 1855, 1856, and 1857. One by one, he helped me—very carefully mind you— search each one. These early journals were mostly just one large sheet. The news of the week was frequently limited to sighting and shooting of a bear, or an unfriendly encounter between a settler and the Indians, who were being displaced at a rapidly increasing pace.

"Then, there it was. The news I had been looking, for but truthfully, never expected to find. In 1856, spread over several editions of the Recorder, was the account which I think connects to our current Iverson name. Because of the lengthy time-span I think it ties not just to a single perpetrator, but a dysfunctional family that might—I repeat— might be connected to Chippewa County's unsolved deaths of Bobbie and Arne. Initially, however, I did not recognize the connection; that came later."

Twenty-One

"IN EARLY JUNE of that year, 1856, a series of violent encounters took place in and around Rushford," Tom was saying. "At first, they were attributed to travelers passing through. About that time, a lot of men with no family connections were moving west,. They were getting away from what they saw as over-populated big cities such as Chicago, St. Louis, and Kansas City. There was talk of gold in the Black Hills, and in addition, the government was encouraging men to kill all the buffalo they could find. No doubt about it—it was a bad and lawless time, even in the soon to be new state of Minnesota.

"Most of those men were malcontents who did not fit into normal society. They wanted no restrictions, no rules, no one setting limits on their activities. Keep in mind that there were no railroads here yet, not even any real roads connecting the small towns that were being formed. A military road had been cleared along the Mississippi River towards Wisconsin, but what few small villages there were had only wagon trails which followed small rivers and wandered through the hills, from town to town.

"As I read through the series of newspapers from that summer, one name stood out and was repeated in several of Knockleby' s editorials. A little at a time, the newspaper's coverage began to better identify one of the violent hooligans rampaging through the territory. He was finally named by those he had beaten up or robbed. By August he had been identified, with certainty, as having been the primary perpetrator in several violent incidents, and was arrested, soon to be tried by a circuit judge who was expected any day.

"This man was named Max, short for Maximillian. Bauer. Maximilian Bauer. Apparently, he was as viscous a man who had ever come to this territory. He was described many ways, but every description included sociopath, drunkard, immoral, mean-tempered, violent without cause; he was just a bad actor. At the age of twenty-five or twenty-six—no one seemed sure of his age—he towered over most men at something like six feet tall. Perhaps, at one time he had just been physically strong; now, he had begun to deteriorate from too much food and alcohol. He weighed by some guesses around two hundred forty pounds and was still extremely strong.

"At the time, no one knew where Bauer lived. Certainly, he was not farming a homestead in the area. And apparently without a family, he would just show up in Rushford, drink and cause trouble for a week, then disappear. When he as finally arrested, it was by accident, and only possible when, on leaving Rushford after a particularly violent encounter, Bauer spurred his horse as he was going across the river at the edge of town. The horse reacted to the painful spurring, began to buck and threw Bauer into the river where he struck his head on some rocks and was rendered unconscious.

"Several men, encouraged by local merchants, hog-tied him and carted him to the town's one-cell jail. Well, once they had Bauer locked up, they threw every charge they could think of at him, hoping something would stick and they would be rid of him once and for all. People claimed everything from wanton destruction to armed robbery, attempted murder and rape. The nearest law was out of Caledonia, some twenty miles away, and Bauer was just going to be held in jail until the judge could reach Rushford.

"As they waited for a judge to show up, the summer drew on, it was found that although nearly everyone knew someone who knew someone who might be able to identify Bauer, not a soul could be found who had actually been accosted, threatened, or attacked by him. The circuit judge arrived in August and was about to release Bauer, since no one had come forth as a victim, when, at the last minute, Edwin Wilner, who owned the general store, brought up the farmer and his son, who had been attacked as they loaded their wagon in front of his store earlier in the year.

"And that," smiled Tom Hall, "is where this history got interesting! That farmer, who was finally traced to his homestead several miles from town, was none other than Hans Iverson. Yes. Hans Iverson, whose son Hans and his descendants came to Chippewa County. Hans Iverson and his son were brought to Rushford and testified against Bauer. Iverson ended up having his name in the newspaper. He needed an interpreter at the trial, since he spoke no English, but was a more than willing witness. He told the judge about Bauer's attack on his wife aboard ship, about Bauer wielding a knife in their fight, and how, without provocation, Bauer had attacked both Hans and his son in Rushford.

"Bauer apparently became a wild man in the court room. He screamed and yelled at Iverson, threatened to beat him within an inch of his life before killings his son in front of him. The town was in a frenzy. It seemed that by now, everyone knew what a bad actor Bauer was, and they all wished him the worst punishment possible. There was such chaos that the judge recessed the trial until the next morning, hoping the crowd would disperse and everyone would just go home, so he could do his job without interruption.

"During the night, Bauer's friends broke him out of the tiny jail. There was no guard of course, so all they had to do was break the lock on the door, take the key ring from the desk, unlock the cell door and they could disappear in the night. And, that is just what they did."

"My gosh, Tom," the judge blurted, "That's as fantastic a story as I've ever heard. I know the men and women who settled our country and our state, came from all backgrounds, but that is just unbelievable. And to think we know of this now just because you had a hunch. And, that you followed it, of course. But, as remarkable as that information is, how does that lead to a connection with our current events here in Chippewa County? That business in Rushford happened over eighty years ago."

"You're absolutely right, Judge. We're a long way from solving the mystery and we're still far from connecting 1855, or 1856, to 1937. What I now have, however, is a name, a date and a record, to begin with. If—and I repeat—if, there is a connection, I think we'll find that Maximillian Bauer passed his hatred on to someone else, who is still seeking revenge against Hans Iverson by attacking Iverson's relatives, no matter how remote the relationship is. Old hatreds can grow, just like a festering sore. The longer it's there, unattended, the more malignant it becomes."

Tom had asked some contacts, in St. Paul and other places, to see what information they could find on Max Bauer. Several days passed before he had news regarding Maximillian Bauer or anyone who might be connected to him. Then, as he was having breakfast at the Riverside Hotel Restaurant, one of the Chippewa County Sheriff's deputies came to his table and handed him a neatly folded note. As he handed it to Tom, the deputy quietly said, "The man on the telephone said it might be quite important."

Tom unfolded the piece of paper, read, then re-read the note, hoping to find something important. The message, however, was short and did not hint at why it might be important. All it said was: *"Got your name from Harry Parker, who said I should give you a call;"* signed William Wilhelmson, New Ulm, and gave his phone number.

After a short phone conversation with Wilhelmson, Tom dialed Judge Chamberlin's office, telling him of his impromptu decision, then called Mary to ask if she could have dinner with him when he returned. Then, with no more distractions, Tom headed for New Ulm.

Two hours later, Tom was face to face with Bill Wilhelmson. He wasn't sure why he felt an urgent need to get to New Ulm, but he had pressed the little Ford as fast as he thought he dared. All that time, he couldn't help but feel he was on the verge of uncovering momentous information. *Maybe, I can add just one more piece to this crazy puzzle*, he thought.

Bill Wilhelmson was a man Tom thought could easily be described as a son of German immigrants. He appeared to be in his mid-forties and, although Tom would profess to having no prejudices, he fit the stereotype Tom carried. Wilhelmson, had he actually stood as Tom entered his office, would have been about five feet ten inches tall, filling his uniform comfortably at about two hundred twenty pounds and showing a mid-morning glow to his cheeks and nose that Tom was certain to have been caused by one night among many of hoisting steins of beer until the bar closed. He fit Tom's stereotype.

Wilhelmson's small office held the clutter one expected to find when a man took every task seriously. Everything he did took first priority for that moment—except the paperwork. Tom categorized the man as a creative thinker, a vertical filer, whose most important project was the on the top of the pile.

Wilhelmson went immediately to the reason he had contacted Tom. "Mr. Hall, I'm not one to rush to judgement, to shout fire at a slight provocation, but I think, between us we have a lead to solving both your puzzle and mine." He pushed a stack of papers, police reports, and news Articles across the desk. "I was on the telephone two days ago with Harold Conrad, a detective with the Minnesota Criminal Investigation, out of St, Paul. Somewhat backhandedly he mentioned you and your interest in Maximillian Bauer, or anyone who might be connected to Bauer. As it happens, we have an open case file dating all the way back to 1899, nearly forty years ago. While reviewing it recently, I spotted the name Bauer. Of course, it meant nothing at the time, but it sure caused a flash in my brain when Harold mentioned it. Well, I dug out the file. That's it in front of you."

Wilhelmson gave Tom a few minutes to look through the file, then, methodically, began to fill Tom in on the full story.

Twenty-Two

"SOMETIME AFTER HIS scrape with the law in Rushford in 1856, Max Bauer ended up in Mower County, and a more miserable son of a bitch may never have been born." Wilhelmson referred only briefly to the file Tom had just reviewed.

"It's amazing that Maximillian Bauer survived nearly forty years. He was a thief, bully and just an all- around bad actor, moving through southern Minnesota and the Minnesota River Valley, without being jailed—or killed, for that matter. We've learned that after escaping from the Rushford jail in 1856, Bauer lived on the edge of civilization, occasionally re-emerging here and there, only to create havoc. There is no telling what the total of devastation he created might be as he wandered through southern Minnesota.

"Common law marriages were common on the prairie in those days, mostly because access to churches, justices of the peace, and so forth, were limited. In most cases, couples formalized their marriages when the opportunity arose, but some couples just continued to live together as husband and wife, without ever being formally married. Somewhere, in the 1860s, Max Bauer took a wife, who followed him from one camp to the next as he marauded across the territory.

"There is no written record of his marriage, but by piecing together snippets of news from the region, it seems his wife was a young German girl, left parentless from what may have been an Indian attack. From the late 1850s, until 1862, there was a lot of violence between the whites and Indians, which culminated in what we call the Great Sioux Uprising, in 1862. Settlers, who had already begun farming and establishing small communities in the southwestern part of what was now the State of Minnesota, fled to the relative safety of places like St. Paul, Mankato, and New Ulm. After the conflict with the Indians was over they began resettling the region in 1864 and 1865. That marks the major settling of western Minnesota, and of course the establishing of the Iverson families in Chippewa County.

Wilhelmson continued, "...let's get back to Max Bauer and his common law wife. She was only fourteen or fifteen years old, a good dozen years younger than Bauer. It may be too kind to call theirs a marriage, but that label will have to suffice. During the following year, Bauer became a father when his child bride gave birth to a daughter of her own in 1863 or 1864.

"Reverend Nils Nygaard, who was pastor of the Highland Prairie Methodist Church for several decades, wrote in his daily ledger that, on one occasion he had found the girl and her baby, huddled in a shack near the Willow River. They appeared nearly starved and were filthy from living in such miserable conditions. When he tried to convince her to come with him to his parsonage, she fled into the woods, screaming in German, as though she thought he was going to harm her.

"Imagine the parson's despair—and fear—when two day later, Max Bauer rode up to the parsonage and leveled a gun at him. Just as with the young mother, the horse Bauer rode was thin and dirty, in such poor condition, the pastor stated in his notes, that he was surprised it could carry the massive bulk of its rider. In a broken combination of German and English, Bauer screamed at the frightened man, wheeling his horse wildly in circles until it appeared the horse would collapse. In a final frenzy of fury, Bauer charged the minister, knocking him to the ground before, galloping into the woods.

"Over the ensuing days, Pastor Nygaard told his parish of the incident, believing that Bauer was gone and that somewhere in the hills nearby there was a frightened starving girl and her baby. Over a period of several weeks, a cursory search was made of the area, without ever finding Bauer or the girl and her baby.

"It wasn't until a couple of years later that Bauer surfaced again, and then just another passing encounter. Near the Iowa border, an immigrant couple reported being accosted by a gigantic, dirty, red-bearded man, who was accompanied by a young woman with a child. They had no way of following them, as Bauer took their only horse, leaving the family with only a cow and a wagon without a horse to pull it.

"In 1878, or '79, Bauer became a grandfather, when his daughter gave birth. More accurately, he became father to his daughter's son. Not only had he kept his child bride a slave, he had also begun abusing his daughter, both physically and sexually. Mother, daughter and son were occasionally seen hiding in the shadows as Max Bauer rampaged across the territory. They were seldom seen in the same town or village twice, which meant they left no real trace of recognition. They just lived in the shadows. It's just a coincidence, that over the following years, members of various communities tied their sightings together. Even that may not have happened, except that Bauer's gigantic stature and bad demeanor left lasting impressions, wherever he went.

"It was meaningless to those he encountered, of course, but in his drunken rages he frequently ranted about the Norwegian farmer who was responsible for all his troubles. 'He attacked me aboard ship, as I tried to make a new life in America,' he lied. 'For no reason at all, he had me thrown in jail. He told one lie after another. He would yell out his hate to anyone who was unfortunate enough to be captured by the screaming drunken man."

"Over the years Bauer continued to move west. Following the Minnesota River, he bullied and drank his way across the prairie. At every encounter, he laid tirades of verbal abuse at the Norwegian farmer, whom we now know, was Hans Iverson. And with all that abuse, his incest-born family was treated in unimaginable ways. Apparently his first grandson died somewhere in the wilderness. Max Bauer finally came to a bloody but well-deserved end in1883, and had it not been for the extreme abuse he rendered on his incest-born family, that might have been the end of the Bauer story.

"So," Wilhelmson continued, "in early spring of 1883, Max Bauer's daughter gave birth to another of his children; this time, another son. This birth would signal the end of Maximillian Bauer. At that time, Max and his miserable family were squatting in a shack just south of New Ulm, in Brown County. Their home was some combination of sod hut and log lean-to some other family had abandoned, I guess. I'm sure they never occupied any place a normal family would deem fit.

"It had been an extremely bitter winter. Cold, wet, seeming as if it would continue forever. Max stumbled into the shack the family called home for the time being, roaring drunk, with vomit on his shirt and jacket, and urine soaking his trousers. He literally fell to the floor as he entered. There, in the dank, reeking hovel, his latest son-grandson had just been born within the hour. 'I get no thanks from you, you worthless lot,' he roared, as he stumbled across the single room. 'I've done my best for you all, and this is the thanks I get.' Ignoring the fact that he was the father of the new son, and that he repeatedly raped all the women of the family, he raved on. 'You tell me, who is the father of that red-faced bastard. I know you have men here all the time. I can tell you're all just whores, expecting me to give you the good life.'

"In his drunken rage he charged across the room, looking as though he was about to beat the new mother and baby. He stumbled and fell to his knees. He grabbed for the rickety chair near the bed, halting his progress for a moment. Wide eyed, his wife, now moved toward her daughter, screaming for Max to stop, to come to his senses and leave the new child and his mother alone.

"But, Max was not to be deterred. As he raised himself up, screaming and frothing at the mouth, she could see Max would not be stopped this time. Without another thought, she grabbed the short-handled axe kept next to the stove and swung at Max with all her strength. The first blow broke Max's collar bone, the next nearly severed his arm at the elbow. The final blow took the rear of Max's head completely off, sending blood and brains in a maelstrom, across the room. As she sunk to her knees, she could only think that if it hadn't been for Hans Iverson and his rotten family, she would not have had to kill Max, that she and her children could have been happy. But, now, what could she do?

"What happened next was mostly a matter of bad timing and bad luck. Because Max's body was so huge, even with the both women working together there was no way to carry it outside. They tied a rope around Max's feet and tied the other end around the neck of Max's emaciated horse, planning to drag the body to the nearby river and send it on its way downstream.

"Unfortunately for the family, the horse panicked at the smell of Max's blood and the sloshing and gurgling sounds it made as they wound their way toward the river. With no way to control the horse once it panicked, they could only run after it, yelling at the top of their lungs, which scared the horse even more.

"After crossing over the second tree-covered hill, Max's body became lodged between two rocks, and with a jolt, the horse slammed to the hard ground, breaking its neck.

"By now the very distraught family was in a panic. They might just have left Max and the horse where they were. There were no roads or farms within sight, so Max's death could have just gone un-noticed. But, two fur trappers, checking their spring beaver traps along the river's edge, had heard the commotion and then saw the flight of the family as it tried to catch Max and the runaway horse.

"Max's family was just deciding to leave him and his dead horse to rot where they were, when Harley and Rodney Willard topped the hill with their traps and pelts in tow. There was no turning back now, of course, so the family just sat down on the wet earth and cried. The Willard brothers calmed the Bauer family, who tearfully told them the cause of Max's unfortunate demise, and the brothers, sympathetically agreed to help them get into New Ulm, and to verify that there had been no option but to kill Max. It was their report to the local sheriff which put this whole episode on record.

"By this time, in 1883, New Ulm had a population of over twenty-five-hundred people, making it a major trade center, with all the trappings of a growing community. The Great Sioux Uprising was history, with the only remaining chore that of bringing to trial and hanging the Indians that had caused havoc in the entire region. Doctors, bankers, attorneys, shop keepers of all manner, had rushed to the region after the uprising had been quelled. It was here that Max Bauer's family was finally brought. It had taken two weeks to notify the Brown County Sheriff of the strange incident. By then, Max Bauer had been buried. The horse was left for the wolves and other carrion eaters. The Bauer family was a horrible sight. Two women— mother, mother-daughter, and a grandson barely three weeks old— not a piece of warm clothing between them.

"The local Lutheran minister found an empty two-room cabin at the east end of town for them and called on the members of his congregation to bring clothes, food, and firewood, or anything which might help them survive.

"When the minister tried to learn their names, it came as a shock that they really did not have names. *Ma*, the mother was called by the younger woman. *You*, the only name for the other adult woman. They were given the names Emma and Eunice, sounding near enough to the guttural names they used. The tiny baby boy was nothing more than a tiny skeleton, ruddy complexion and wild red hair and was just called *Boy*.

"The bedraggled group stayed in the small cabin just over a year before disappearing. The sheriff and minister determined that Maximillian Bauer's death was self-defense and left the miserable women to themselves, which itself posed problems within the community. Neither of the women, one just a child, even though she bore a son, could read or write, and they seemed to understand only German. This, by itself, was not much of a problem, since New Ulm was heavily settled by German immigrants. Their lack of social skills, however, led both Emma and Eunice to fall into bad company. It might have been that they were just predisposed to being treated poorly, because of their years with Max Bauer.

"Over the next several years they were occasionally seen in small town bars around the county or picking through the refuse behind eating establishments. When drunk, both mother and daughter ranted about what a good father Max had been; what a good father and great provider, and how much he was missed. They ranted that if not for Hans Iverson and his son, the good-hearted Max would not have been driven from Rushford and forced into such a low life. Instead, his family would have been respected members of the community.

"All that time, the boy who was now known as Boyd, was growing into a surly, mean spirited, incarnation of his father. At the age of five, he nailed a cat to a tree, head down, and watched it die as he pelted rocks at it. At the age of ten, Boyd nailed the cabin door shut and set fire to it, with his mother and grandmother inside, screaming for their lives while they burned to death. Then, Boyd Bauer disappeared, cloaked in the physical scars from his frequent beatings and the deep emotional scars from the mental abuse inflicted by his mother and grandmother. In 1893, at the age of ten, Boyd Bauer disappeared. The fire, the deaths and the disappearance of Boyd Bauer have been an unsolved mystery ever since.

Twenty-Three

I HAD JOINED Tom for a cup of coffee at the Bungalow Cafe. In one of his free moments, he was filling me in on his mystery search and I was gathering bits of my family history from him. I always thought of my family's history as an Iverson history. But, of course, it turned out to be much more complex than that.

In addition to the emigration of the Iversons and Oslands from Norway, I had my mother's family, the Logan's ancestors, to consider, as well as the Heinrichs'. The Logans crossed over from Canada, following the Canadian routes of trappers, traders, and hopefuls of all sorts. The Logans had come from Nova Scotia, and prior to that from Ireland, but ultimately, it was a French family which traced its roots to Normandy, France. It follows, naturally I suppose, that with a name like Heinrich, the Heinrich family would have come from Germany.

I also knew, if minimally, that my grandfather Howard Logan had married into another family of immigrants. His mother-in-law, Maggie Heinrichs, my great grandmother on that side, was a MacGregor. Her father Charles B. and his brother had walked across the USA in the 1860s, during which time C. B. MacGregor had taken a wife by the name of Lucinda Lyndsley as they passed through Ohio.

In the true American way, Lucinda and her sister Sylvinia had been adopted by the Michigan Lyndlseys when the girls were orphaned at ages ten and seventeen. Henry Robison, the minister of a black congregation in Michigan, had spirited the girls across a hostile countryside and freed them from their servitude, when they were adopted by the Lyndsleys. They passed easily into the Lyndsley family. They were somewhat darker of complexion than the other children, and although no one knows for sure, we are told that

Lucinda owed her tawny complexion to a Negro mother and a father who was a minor chief of the Ojibway nation. Lucinda was just fifteen when she married Charles MacGregor, who found her beauty captivating. Without a backward glance, they made their way to Minnesota, bringing Sylvinia with them.

The MacGregors were among the earliest settlers in Chippewa County, and their daughter Maggie my great grandmother, was born while the family lived in a sod home near town. Maggie MacGregor would grow up to marry John W. Heinrich, who was known as Jack, and sometimes as Bing. Jack's father, Werner Heinrich had come to America in 1857, at the age of thirty. One year later, in Clayton, Iowa, he married Dorothea Stein, who also born in Germany. While it had taken the Iversons nearly ten years to cross to the Minnesota Territory, Jack Heinrich's father had made the trip in only a year.

Dorothea Heinrich was a prodigious diary keeper, making it relatively easy to track the Heinrichs family to Chippewa County. She gave birth to six children, including Jack in 1871 while the family was still in Iowa, then two more children were born as the family moved west.

I had borrowed the diary from a cousin, who had inherited it. From the diary I learned that Werner Heinrich had brought his skills as a shepherd with him from Germany. The diary was fascinating reading; the woman chronicled every day and detail of their journey. In Minnesota, Heinrich tended his flock of sheep as the family grew, staying where the grazing was good, then moving on. This was a family of survivors, with high energy and the resilience needed to survive in that primitive land. When the Heinrichs reached Chippewa County, they were well suited to become prominent farmers. And in no time, they were a respected part of the community.

Although the search for my family was moving along, Tom's mystery was far from being solved. I recognized that when Tom and I visited about my search, he was also using that time to give voice to his own questions. "It's so unlikely that the Heinrichs and the Bauers would have crossed paths, don't you think, Tom? With hundreds of square miles of mostly unsettled land and no roads to speak of, it seems like a one in a million chance they would have met."

"Keep in mind," Tom responded, "at that time there were no roads across the state, but what trails existed primarily followed the Minnesota River and its tributaries. Anyone heading toward Chippewa County would have stayed in—or near—the Minnesota River valley. If the Heinrichs were tending sheep, they could easily have spent six months or more in making that trip, and that means there is something of a greater likelihood they may have met the Bauers than if they were travelling further north, as some settlers did. The diary doesn't make any note of meeting the Bauer family, so perhaps they never did meet. We do know the Bauers were in the same region as the Heinrichs passed through.

"We lost track of Boyd Bauer in 1893, somewhere near New Ulm, which means that there was a ten-year old boy, unattended and completely on his own. No parents or other relations; how do you suppose he survived? And, where did he go?"

"What happened to Boyd Bauer? In our modern and civilized world of 1938, it's inconceivable that a ten-year old boy who spoke little or no English could survive. Perhaps, he could steal food and clothing to survive the summer, or even longer, but in the strange and undeveloped country that was Minnesota in the 1890s, how did he survive the winters where temperatures could frequently fall below minus twenty—or even minus thirty degrees— and where a blizzard might last a week, leaving two or three feet of new snow on the ground?

"But remember," Tom continued, " Boyd Bauer was a survivor in the true sense of the word. He had never had the luxury of a warm home or a loving family. On a good day, his mother might remember to feed him twice. Even one meal a day was probably a luxury. With the death of his mother and grandmother, Boyd Bauer may have felt as if a burden had been lifted from him. With the enthusiasm of youth, Boyd may have just followed the river. At the age of ten he knew how to fish and even how to shoot a gun. He had no qualms regarding stealing, or whatever he needed for survival, and within days Boyd was probably well provisioned for life on the prairie. I suspect young Boyd Bauer had no qualms about his odds of surviving."

Although Tom humored me as I searched for my family, he seldom lost his focus for long. Our conversation soon shifted from Max Bauer, somewhere in the wilderness, to Tom's more immediate mystery. Although he had gotten temporarily side tracked from the mystery of Roberta Swan while searching for an early connection to the Iverson name, he was still looking for answers to her murder.

Twenty-Four

TOM COULDN'T HELP but wonder: what happened to Boyd Bauer? In the modern and civilized world of 1938, it seemed inconceivable, that a ten-year- old boy who spoke little or possibly no English, could survive on his own. Perhaps, he could steal food and clothing to survive a summer, or even longer, but in the strange and undeveloped land that was Minnesota in the 1890s, how did he survive even the first winter?

With the death of his mother and grandmother, Boyd felt as if a burden had been lifted from him. No one nagging him, no screaming shrews who could only find fault in his every action; and finally, no tirades about how the Iversons had ruined their lives. Even if it was true, that Hans Iverson was responsible for all this family misery, and Boyd believed what he had been told all his life. He was just plain tired of hearing about it. With the enthusiasm of youth, Boyd just followed the river.

Although early settlers followed the rivers upstream as they searched for unclaimed land, ten-year-old Boyd trekked down-river, following the muddy Minnesota River as it wandered past New Ulm and then on toward Mankato. It was from downriver the immigrants came. It was from down the river the barges and mule trains of goods arrived. Downriver must be where a better life could be found, and it was downriver Boyd knew he should go.

Boyd had found his way to the village of North Mankato which was located on a huge bend in the Minnesota River, the wide muddy waterway that would connect with the mighty Mississippi River, a hundred miles further downstream. The few hundred people calling North Mankato their home relied on traffic from river-trade for their livelihood. Southbound barges carried wheat, oats, corn and farm goods, as well as occasional passengers, heading for St. Paul, which was known as Pig's Eye Landing until just a few years earlier. On the upstream voyage, barges brought the wide variety of goods new settlers had not brought with from their previous homes. Although there were some hand-poled barges seen along the river, a weekly paddle wheeler loaded to the gunnels carefully plied the river's treacherous channel as far upstream as Granite Falls, where the rugged rocks forming an obstruction—called Minnesota Falls by the locals—stopped their upstream movement.

The rough and tumble collection of residents along the river had to put up with floods in the spring, muddy quagmires of trails and roadways all summer, and bitter winters, made nearly intolerable as north winds blasted their way through the river valley. The few businesses, located facing the water along North Mankato's River Street, could best be described as shabby. Most had never seen a coat of paint, many had roofs with missing shingles and broken windows. The boardwalks, intended to keep mud and dirt from being tracked into the businesses, were warped and in some places were missing boards altogether.

Residents and patrons of North Mankato appeared to have been cut from the same cloth. There were no fancy suits and top hats and no ladies in brightly flowing satin gowns. On even the best autumn and winter days, heavy boots with mud clinging to them, were more the order of the day. Men and women alike pulled their heavy wool mackinaws close as they struggled along the streets; the men, wearing coarse woolen caps with earflaps pulled tight, while the women insisted on a feminine hat, held in place in cold winter by a durable scarf, which they knotted in place before wrapping the tails around their exposed necks.

It was here, in North Mankato, that Boyd came to find shelter and food. It was a blustery October day and Boyd was having a difficult time. He had grown out of the last coat he had stolen just a month ago, and he wondered where and when his luck would bring him another one. On days such as this, he wondered if he had made a mistake burning down the cabin with his mother and grandmother inside. Not that he was sorry for their deaths; but the cabin might have been alright without them around. He told himself he would just have to make-due with what he had. His knife, his rifle, and a partial box of ammunition for shooting a rabbit or a squirrel, an extra shirt that still barely fit. Before long though, he knew he needed to find shelter for the coming winter. Maybe he could get on a barge and make it to St. Paul. Surely, there he would be okay. At ten, he knew how to fish and even to shoot a gun. He had no qualms regarding stealing whatever he needed, and within days of setting the cabin afire, Boyd Bauer thought he had been well-provisioned for life on the prairie. As the weather had turned colder however, he now sometimes worried about his future.

As he was scrounging through trash behind a ramshackle tavern on the edge of town, he was accosted by its owner. A large woman grabbed him by the scruff of the neck. Plopping him down on an empty crate, she shook him and yelled "Get out of my mull, you little ferret." The only word he recognized was Mull, which in German meant garbage. The rest of the tirade was beyond his comprehension. He spoke no English and her tirade went from English to German and back again, with no apparent consideration that her mixture of languages was unintelligible.

The woman stopped shaking the boy and yelling at him when he responded in German, the only language he knew. "I'm just hungry, you old hag., You've thrown away enough food to feed me for a week. How can you care that I feed myself?" He had hoped to gather a pack-full of scraps and just disappear—until this old hag showed up.

Before long Boyd and the old woman stopped screaming at each other. "Tell me your name boy, before I cuff you behind the ear again. "

"I'm just Boyd," he snarled at her. "Boyd Bauer," he added, relishing the rich sound of his father's title; "and turn me loose before I cut your eyes out."

She swatted him again, then once more, just to be sure he knew who was in command. "Here, come inside," she continued in German, as she dragged him through the door and into her kitchen. Once indoors, her voice softened. "Just sit here. Let's start over, you and me." Her manner softened a bit as she took in the boy's condition. "Tell me, what's a handsome boy like you doing in my mull? You should be home this time of the day, not scavenging about like this."

She yelled over her shoulder to someone in the tavern. "Johann come help me here. We have a young man who needs a grown man's touch."

As she waited for Johan, she turned to Boyd. "I am named Anna Brockhaus. This place is mine. My skinny husband likes to make people believe he is the owner but make no mistake about it; I own this place and I am the boss." The woman who still held him by his shirtfront was much older than his own grandmother had been before Boyd had set the cabin afire. If Boyd had known anything about weights, he would have known she weighed nearly three hundred pounds. She seemed to Boyd to be as wide as she was tall. Her gray hair was tied in a huge bun; that was not unlike the way his mother had worn hers. She wore a smock that dragged nearly to the floor, a coarse material with grease stains up and down the front—in spite of the apron hanging about her neck and cinched around the waist. Boyd had never seen such large feet, even on a man. She wore scuffed brogans that reached up to the bottom of her dress. On one of them, there was residue of meat and gravy, probably two days old.

She cleared her throat of phlegm, spitting it into a rag she kept in an apron pocket, then in a quieter voice, she continued to learn about Boyd. "Just sit calm, little man. I want you to tell me who you are and why you were digging around back there. " As she leaned over him, Boyd thought the woman's arms wobbled, like the fat on an old hog. Her breath was heavy with the aroma of garlic and she seemed to have the smell of a kitchen long past the time for cleaning. I am not going to hurt you, and if I like your story I might even feed you a good meal. Of course, if I do not like it, I'll just kick you in the rear and throw you back out the door." She laughed loudly at her own joke, then turned to her husband.

If Anna could be described as a large old hag, Johan could only be called a stack of bones tied into a pair of dirty overalls. He closed the rickety door which separated the kitchen and living area from the rest of the tavern and took a chair across from Boyd. As he had foraged across the country, Boyd had seen his type before. He was sure this old man was just a small version of the description he had of his father. Boyd was certain when the words came, that they would be vulgar and violent. He half expected to be cuffed beside the head again at any moment. Although he had never heard his father's voice, his mother and grandmother never spoke kindly of Max. Never, that is, unless they were recalling their woes and how their misfortune was the fault of the hated Iversons, and what a wonderful man their Max was.

Imagine his surprise when the voice coming from the old man was soft, almost like syrup flowing across bread. Even speaking in the sometimes harsh and guttural German language, the old man's voice was soothing. The words could not possibly be coming from the bony old man. "You are much too handsome a young man to be out in that dirty alleyway. We must find you some hot porridge, some strudel as well. Come, let's all sit over here and eat some of Anna's good food," he continued, as he turned his chair toward the table. Still uncertain of his future, Boyd could only follow suit.

Although the tavern became more boisterous as the evening progressed, Anna and Johan made sure Boyd was comfortable. Their voices soothed him. Is this what a family is supposed to be like, he questioned himself? For the next several hours they plied him with questions, and with surprisingly little hesitation, Boyd told them of his life. He left out the parts about the cat, the fire, and a few other details he thought were his business, not theirs. But he gave them to know he was a man, even though he was only ten years old, that he could take care of himself and needed no help from anyone.

The kitchen contained a huge wood-fired stove, with six grates and two large water reservoirs, one at each end. On the stove were kettles and pans, filled with dumplings and sausages. The smells that filled the room made Boyd question what other wonders would be lifted from them. Anna had put a huge copper boiler over two burners and filled it with water, which soon began to steam.

"You need a good bathing, young man. We have a huge tub over in the corner and you're just going to have to scrub away all that dirt. We have some clothes in a trunk that will fit you. We had a son a long time ago, but he is no longer with us. You will stay with us for a while— until spring, maybe."

That idea did not seem too bad to Boyd. He had not thought of exactly how he would get through the winter, even though the past several nights had been cold and uncomfortable as he slept in a shed across town. He had never seen a calendar and could not read the words on it, but the one hanging near the wash basin indicated it was October. November and colder weather were only days away.

A light blanket, hung from a wire stretched across the end of the room, was pulled so Boyd could have some privacy as he bathed. Interesting, he thought, as he slid down so only his head was above water; I have never done this before. I thought everyone bathed in the river, or a lake, if there was one nearby. By the time the water cooled, it was the color of an old gray buggy wheel. He had never held a bar of soap, and the coarse, lye-impregnated tallow made his skin sting. When he stood to get out of the tub, his skin was wrinkled like an old rag. It glowed bright pink as he dried with the huge, if somewhat threadbare towel, Anna had left for him.

The next morning, Anna and Johan were up with the sun. There actually wasn't any sun. Instead, the day was framed by a cold rain, driven by a north wind. Winter would soon be here. Boyd was instructed to sweep the boardwalk in front of the tavern. The hand-painted sign read Anna's Kitchen. Smaller print pointed out German cooking and beer on tap. After sweeping the boardwalk, he swept the tavern front to back, straightened the chairs and tables, then with a bucket and a rag, he washed all the tables.

It seemed like easy work, but Boyd couldn't help think he could have slept in a shed and stolen food from out back just as easily. Anna fed him three times that day and fed him liberally every day. Soon, the routine felt okay. It was warm, and that counted for something. He even had another bath just a week later. There was a small attic, reached by a ladder just inside the rear door. Up there, Boyd now had his own bedroom; actually just a cot, a pillow, and two blankets, but it was his alone. Anna and Johan slept in the big saggy bed next to the kitchen. He wondered how Johan kept from sliding downhill into the cavern Anna created when she fell, exhausted, into bed each night.

The three of them drifted into a comfortable routine as winter closed around them. There was never a loud word. Anna and Johan were apparently loved by everyone. Each noon, the same men came for a beer and lunch of potatoes and sausage, or a huge bowl of thick soup Anna labored over three times a week. In the afternoon, men started to come in about sunset. Never women, seldom a child looking for his father; always a quiet evening with the men commiserating over steins of dark German beer. Anna served good humor along with the beer. Johan was cordial, right up to the time he might slip into a stupor if it was a slow night and he emptied too many steins of beer.

Christmas came, and Anna explained to Boyd the mystery of Jesus, men on camels following a star, and the animals in the stable where Jesus was born. It was confusing to Boyd but being able to tell him the story made Anna happy, so what was the harm.

Some afternoons, Anna retrieved a bible from her cupboard and read to Boyd. She taught him print his name, and eventually, to write in cursive. It made little sense to the ten-year-old boy; just accept the task and make Anna happy.

Twenty-Five

ANNA AND JOHANN treated the boy like he was their own son. Anna hugged Boyd, scolded him, joked with him when they sat together for a meal. It was a revelation to Boyd, who had never had a comforting conversation with anyone in his entire ten years.

Johan took Boyd with him on nearly daily journeys to the market along the river. Fresh produce came upriver from St. Paul and Anna needed it for her customers. Although the couple had a cold storage room, cut into the hillside behind the tavern, they enjoyed the occasional exotic fruit and other produce the barge made available to them.

As the two wound their way to the market, Johan pointed out the attributes of their small community. "The river flows right past us; it brings people upriver from St. Paul. Every week, there is another whole clan of travelers from Norway or Germany—Ireland, even. We get the benefit of people from all over the country, who want to eat Anna's great cooking. Our tavern is located where everyone coming upriver sees us before they see any of the other businesses. We will be rich before long. You can stay with us and you can also enjoy our success."

It made little sense to the boy. How could these old people call themselves rich? They were dressed in dirty rags, just like all their customers. Oh sure, they were warm and well-fed. But rich? Nah. It would take more than their smiles, laughter, and occasional hugging, to make Boyd believe they were rich, or even going to be rich someday. And, it was the same routine every day. Sweep the boardwalk, sweep and mop the tavern floor, clean tables after strangers left their mess. Who would consider this being rich?

What Boyd wanted was not just to be warm, but to feel rich and respected. Even at the age of ten, now getting close to eleven, he could tell the difference between poor and rich, like the banker across the street, or the captain of the paddle wheeler that brought finely-dressed women to little Mankato now that the ice was off the river once again. The women with their superior smiles, their condescending comments to Anna and Johan, as they sat smugly over the meals the couple – and Boyd – worked so hard to provide. Then, there was the Presbyterian minister and his prissy wife, who looked at Boyd like he was a scabbed-over sore on a horse's leg; something to be ignored with the hope it would disappear if ignored.

As spring advanced and the muddy Minnesota River swelled nearly over its banks, Boyd found he had more free time for himself. Longer days meant he could wander about the village after the evening meal was finished. He had made no friends of the children in North Mankato. It seemed they sensed he was just a temporary resident here. He had not joined them in school during the winter. The one-room school building on the hill behind River Street seemed to be a gathering place for children of the rich. Working-class families did not have the funds to waste on an old-maid teacher, who just blathered on about the three-Rs. What use would that be to someone like Boyd, even if Anna and Johan could afford it?

Boyd knew it would be more important to know how to stalk a deer or a rabbit, to fashion a wire snare to catch one of the northern pike or sturgeon idling in the back-water of the river. He listened to the wizened men, who gathered in the evenings, telling their great tales of hunting and fishing successes. He heard and remembered their pride, when they spoke of how easy it was to outwit the sheriff, to lift a stoneware crock of liquor from a passing wagon, or, beat some poor Injun into submission over just about anything of value. Boyd knew there would come a day when he would leave Anna, Johan, and North Mankato behind. He collected pennies and an occasional nickel left on the bar or found on the floor next to the brass spittoon, and put them into a spare sock, left behind when its partner was finally worn beyond repair. When an un-wise passenger from the paddle wheeler left a suitcase unattended Boyd became the owner of an entire male wardrobe. The shirts and trousers were too large but eventually Boyd knew they would be just right; when it was time for him to resume his travels. He knew the day would come when he would venture out on his own once again.

At the end of August, Boyd was enjoying a quiet hour along the river. There was a pool of quiet water, just under a huge willow tree, where he had sometimes snared a fish. When that happened, he brought his prize to Anna, who would crush him into her ample bosom. Today, he was patiently waiting, hoping, but not concerned, whether he caught a fish or not. The secluded pool was just downstream and far enough around the bend in the river to be out of sight of the town's activities. Boyd seldom saw a single person when he lay in the grass and watched for an unwary fish.

He was spread full-length in the knee-high grass. Peering over the bank, holding the long wire snare motionless as he waited, when Willard Wiggins approached him. He came quietly, so quietly that Boyd, who heard even a mouse as it scampered through summer grass, was not aware of his presence until the man stood directly over him. Boyd had seen Wiggins before, but never away from River Street. Wiggins was a clerk in the bank, always nattily dressed, seemingly sweet and self-effacing with all the bank's customers.

Boyd had never really given any thought to who Wiggins was. To Boyd, he was just a middle-aged, wimpy guy, who worked at the bank. In fact, Wiggins was thirty-five years old, single, and not well thought of in North Mankato. He fawned over men and women alike, smiled and made inane comments, which he thought were worldly and humorous and sometimes risqué.

He asked Boyd if he could join him, and without waiting for an answer, he removed his suitcoat, and sat by the boy. "I don't think we've been properly introduced, but I know who you are. I'm Willard Wiggins." Boyd was caught by surprise, but continued to lay, looking over the bank. What did he care if old Wiggins wanted to sit there also?

Wiggins would not have thought of himself as prissy, nor middle-age. At thirty-five, he still had a spring in his step. He was certain his banking career would continue to flourish. Bank owner, Stanley Masters, had personally told him he was an asset to the bank. "Continue to do well and you can go far," he had commented to Wiggins on more than one occasion.

Wiggins had shown up in North Mankato three years earlier. He brought with him a certificate, indicating he had graduated in good standing from a college in Indiana, had worked, temporarily, for a large corporation there before feeling the need to move west and prove himself. Masters had been impressed with the well-dressed young man and never made an inquiry about either the education or previous employment.

In truth, Wiggins had barely scraped though an ordinary-school education in Indianapolis, Indiana and had been involved in several scandals before fleeing to the infant state of Minnesota. For six months, he had struggled to gain enough banking knowledge in St. Paul to save a low-level job. Then, he disappeared on a Thursday, with two thousand dollars belonging to a customer who would be surprised and devastated a week later, when she learned the funds never reached her account. Willard Wiggins had secrets.

As Boyd lay looking over the river bank, Wiggins casually spoke of the weather, the spring flood, the muddy summer. He droned on about a variety of subjects, unknown and uninteresting to Boyd. "I have watched you fishing here several times. You seem to have a real knack for that snare. How did you ever learn that?"

"I just learned it," Boyd responded. What he thought was, "What a dodo this guy is."

Wiggins folded his suit jacket, lay it neatly next to Boyd and lay down next to him as he peered over the bank. He reached forward, pointing. "Is that a fish?"

"It's just a shadow."

For fifteen minutes Wiggins disturbed Boyd's silent quest for a fish, occasionally reaching out to touch Boyd's shoulder, sometimes letting his hand rest on an arm for just a moment.

Boyd had not seen a fish in the pool below him since he arrived and was getting bored. Occasionally, his eyelids drooped for a moment. It would not be long before he gave it all up for the day and headed for Anna's Kitchen. Supper was beginning to be on his mind.

Before he realized it, Boyd found Wiggins had draped his arm across his back and turned half-way towards the boy. Before Boyd could complain, he found Wiggins kissing his neck. When he tried to move away, shocked at the advance, he found Wiggins had tightened his grip, holding Boyd firmly to the ground.

"You should just let me show you how much I like you, Boyd."

Boyd tried to rise, but his eleven-year-old frame was trapped. As he stared wide-eyed at Wiggins, the man now seemed maniacal. His eyes sparkled, and he had a smile Boyd had never seen on any man's face.

"Turn me loose, you son-of-a-bitch!" He writhed and kicked, but Wiggins had a firm hold on him and continued to press kisses on his neck, trying in vain to kiss him on the lips.

"Come, come, Boyd. I'm going to show you something wonderful. Your life will never be the same."

What he was thinking was altogether different. Wiggins's mind raced. *"There's something wonderful, exciting fulfilling even; sodomy has so many benefits. No one ever complains, and little boys are just so smooth, so innocent."* His mind raced as he thought of this easy conquest. This little fool never had a clue, never expected to be overwhelmed as he lay here, waiting for some stupid fish. Wiggins smiled, then laughed loudly as he started to force Boyd over, even as the boy kicked and screamed. No one could hear the commotion as he wailed to be set free.

Before he could move out of the way, Boyd made a move that completely changed the dynamic of the moment. A jagged rock was just within his reach, and Boyd slammed it into the side of Wiggins' head. As he flinched, not quite sure what had happened, Boyd struck him again, then, as Wiggins slumped to the ground, Boyd forced himself free. "You think I am just some stupid kid?" He slammed the rock into Wiggins head, again, and again, all the time shouting at his now unconscious attacker.

Although Boyd did not actually understand what Wiggins attack was about, he did understand that his well-being was at risk. When Wiggins feebly began to move again, Boyd reached into the grass and grabbed the steel wire with the loop he had hoped to slip over the head of a fish. Now, instead of yanking a fish over the bank, Boyd put the loop over Wiggins head. Then, standing with one foot on either side of the stricken man, he pulled the snare tight. He pulled it tighter, screaming all the while.

Finally, he was exhausted and fell to the ground, letting out great sobs. His tears blurred his vision. Beside him, Wiggins life flowed onto the ground. The wire snare had cut deeply into his neck, severing a jugular vein, ripping his larynx and nearly decapitating the now dead bank clerk.

For fully fifteen minutes Boyd at motionless, looking at the man he had just killed. He felt frightened and yet exhilarated at the same time. The little boy had just become a man, had bested his attacker, who was now dead at his side. But, now what should he do? Boyd was relatively unscathed, a few splatters of blood from Wiggins final throes, and his exertions in pulling the snare had cut into his hand. Mostly, he was terrified. Should he run to Anna's Kitchen? Should he confess that he had been attacked and had then killed the usually well-dressed banker? Why should he expect anyone to believe he had killed in self-defense, how could anyone believe he was a victim and had not waited in the shadow of the willow tree, attacking Wiggins as he, not Boyd, lay on the ground?

Boyd had lived his almost idyllic life for nearly a year. The boy who relished nailing a cat to a tree and stoning it to death, who had spent his first ten years unknowingly becoming an incarnation of his father, and who had killed his own mother and grandmother by burning them alive, had almost left it all behind. Boyd came close to leading a normal life and might have become an accepted member of North Mankato society, if not for Willard Wiggins. Now, that was all behind him.

At the moment, however, Boyd needed to make a decision which would be hard for an adult, let alone for an eleven-year-old boy. As he sat with his back against the willow tree, Boyd made an amazingly adult decision. The man lying dead at his feet just needed to go away. The river was right there, so where was the problem? Boyd, the survivor, all eighty-pounds of him, shaking and sobbing, rolled the one-hundred-forty-pound dead man onto his back, then stripped his trousers, shirt and shoes from the body before rolling it over the bank.

The sun was nearly setting. By morning, Willard Wiggins would be locked in a submerged brush snag, a dozen miles down the Minnesota River. When he did not show up at the bank, Stanley Masters would first send his messenger to Wiggin's small apartment, then quickly do an audit to be certain the bank was not going to suffer from Wiggins disappearance. When he went home for his evening brandy before dinner, he would comment to his doting wife, "I suppose the worthless little shit is sleeping it off in some whore's room in St. Paul by now. Good riddance."

With adult acumen, Boyd folded Wiggin's clothes neatly and left them hidden among the roots of the willow tree, along with the shoes, which he would later find to be just slightly too large. Slightly over two hundred dollars from Wiggins' wallet fit nicely into Boyd's pocket. As he walked slowly back to Anna's Kitchen, he formed a plan, and the following morning, after a hearty breakfast with Anna and Johann, Boyd excused himself, took his rifle, his pack with his few possessions, some food wrapped in an oil cloth, and left by the rear door of the tavern. He did not look at the garbage, which a year ago had provided a banquet. Instead, he walked confidently to the willow tree to retrieve his new treasure. Unlike Willard Wiggins, who went downstream, Boyd turned and followed the river upstream, back

to the west. The Willard Wiggins episode would wake him screaming for a long time to come.

Twenty-Six

DURING THE NEXT five years Bauer crept into small towns or villages, or into remote farm buildings, to steal whatever he needed to survive. A chicken, taken quietly from its nest in the middle of the night, was food for two or three days; more if need be. Maybe, he would be lucky enough to grab an egg or two, which could be eaten raw, as he retreated into the night.

By the time he was twelve, he had developed all the skills needed to make his way alone. He felt content most of the time with the life he led. Occasionally, he felt angry with the unfair circumstances that had cost him his family, and frequently struggled with memories of Willard Wiggins. When anger rose, he sought redemption, finding relief from the anger by killing a sheep or a calf, just because he could, as he passed through a remote farm. Sometimes a dog would venture from its safe haven in a ramshackle shed to seek Bauer's kind stroking, and then as the dog leaned into him, not wanting this moment to pass, Bauer would hug the needy dog. As he felt it relax, Bauer would quickly grab its neck and jaw, twisting it violently, breaking its neck before smiling and walking casually away. When that happened he felt better as he thought it might have been Willard Wiggins, sometimes it was someone named Iverson.

By the age of fourteen, he began to feel the urges of manhood. He knew about sex, of course, even though he struggled with the memories of that day in North Mankato. Before the untimely death of his mother and grandmother, Boyd had lain on the straw pallet that served as his bed, captive audience to the carnal moans and giggles of both women, as they shared their bodies with men they would probably never see for a second time.

In the beginning, Boyd was confused by the physical change that arousal brought to his body. He was left unsettled, when he would wake in the middle of the night, his trousers wet from the involuntary ejaculation of a carnal dream.

His first actual carnal experience with a woman came quite unexpectedly. In addition to the transition to manhood, Boyd made one more, huge, step which had nothing to do with sex. He had quietly entered a small town on the Iowa border, planning to spend his small reserve of money for a seldom occurring hot meal, before retreating once more into the shadowy world in which he was most comfortable. It was late in the day. It was cold and stormy, with little chance that the weather would soon improve.

As he sat quietly at a small table in the corner of the restaurant, he tried his best not to attract attention, but his dirty condition and shabby clothing were hard to miss. If a person looked past the grime and the filthy clothes they might have noticed that Boyd was almost handsome, in a primitive sort of way. Although undernourished, he had a certain look of self-reliance. A light beard, slightly more than a fuzz, coved his features. A shaggy mane of dirty red hair was kept in check by a well-worn and shapeless hat. Strangers of any kind were rare here, and one so needy in appearance caused sidelong glances from everyone who entered.

As he finished his meal, sopping up the last of the gravy around his plate with a last small bit of bread, a woman approached, and without being asked, sat across from him.

To Boyd she seemed old, but in fact was only in her early thirties; to Boyd, thirty was old. Her name was Alice Bevins. Life had already been hard for Alice. She wore a shapeless dress, which showed the tattered signs of long wear. Her face was haggard, tired from long days of thankless chores; her hands were red and her fingernails dirty from the day's labor. On final analysis, in spite of the shabby clothing and the fatigue which was difficult to hide, Alice was still a handsome woman.

Alice had been married at sixteen to the man she was sure would be her Prince Charming, but who had been far less than charming. They had eloped, because, he said, there was little reason to put her parents through an expensive ceremony. She had ridden behind him on a horse of poor quality for a full day before they came to his rundown cabin on the Crook River. He was a trapper, he had told her, working up and down the river, fishing right there in the river at times and catching suckers or carp, which he smoked for eating during the winter, or just frying the fish over the open fire in good weather. Hanging from a tree next to the house was a freshly killed deer, its guts still spread beneath it, the blood and bile oozing into the dirt.

There had been no courtship. The honeymoon consisted of Axel Bevins tearing her dress and mauling her as he threw her onto the hard bed, where he continued to violate her from sunset until sunrise, pounding her delicate body over and over, while she whimpered in pain and embarrassment. In the morning she woke alone, with no sign of her new husband. Her face was red and swollen from the frequent slaps he had rendered on her when she asked him to stop his punishment. Her arms and thighs were covered with bruises, the space between her legs was torn and swollen, and she felt pain as never before in her life.

Alice had left her table and slowly approached Boyd, who shrank back in his chair. He was about to bolt from the room, saying that he was causing no harm to anyone and would soon be on his way, when she spoke quietly to him. "I couldn't help but notice you here. You didn't see me across the room, but like you, I eat alone." She smiled tentatively, a soft look in her eyes. "My name is Alice. Alice Bevins, actually. I hope you don't mind if I sit with you for a bit." There was a softness in Alice's eyes that caused Boyd to relax just a bit. Boyd's eyes were more like a cat, more yellow than brown.

She looked at him with eyes that were dark and clear. And, although they had a tenderness, there was also a hardness that came from living alone and being wary of everyone who came close to her home. "The weather will soon be quite unpleasant. Those heavy clouds to the southeast will probably bring snow in a day or so, I think. Tell me your name, won't you?"

"It's Boyd," he replied with a shaky voice. "Why would you care who I am?"

"It is good to meet you, Boyd. People like you and me don't seem to gather friends easily. I just thought it would be nice to talk for a while. I live alone just a way from town," she added, and then wondered if she should have been quite so forthcoming with the information.

Little by little, Alice drew Boyd from his shell. Before long, they both found occasion to laugh once in a while. Darkness covered the town by now, and the wind was chasing hard rain drops against the building. "I think you should come to my home for the night, Boyd. It's not so far, and you can be away first thing in the morning, if you like. Or, maybe you can stay on for a few days if you would like to help with some repairs I need before winter comes to stay."

Boyd was not sure exactly what this strange woman really had in mind for him, but he knew at least he could find a dry place for the night. He couldn't read any clear meaning in her look or in her eyes, and hoped she could not read his mind, but there were hopeful thoughts that he might find more than a dry place for the night.

Alice's team of bay horses was just outside, tethered to a rickety rail. Boyd collected his pack, including his well-worn rifle, from the shelter of the building, and threw them in the back of the wagon, which contained a meager collection of supplies. The supplies had been the reason Alice had come to town. Steam rose from the horse's back as Alice turned them into the wind and toward her cabin.

There was little to say as the couple hunkered into their coats, trying to make themselves small as possible to keep out the cold rain. The team seemed to know its way and followed the faint track along the bank of a small stream. The otherwise quiet of the night was broken by the squish and squash of the horse hooves, the jangle of their harnesses and the slapping of the rain on the wagon and on the two quiet travelers. Nearly an hour later, Alice guided the wagon into a clearing next to the stream they had been following. The team was turned into the lean-to and the harnesses hung on pegs under the lodge pole roof, then Alice led Boyd into her home. As she lit a kerosene lamp on the table, she directed Boyd to lay wood in the stone fireplace and build a fire so they could dry their clothes and warm their chilled bodies.

The small house showed a woman's touch, tidy and organized. It was beyond any luxury Boyd could imagine occupying for more than a night. The large main room was kitchen, dining and living room. The simple furnishings, all showing wear, but also showed loving attention.

Both Boyd and Alice were timid, not meeting each other's eyes while moving slowly around the room "You should get out of those wet clothes," Alice said in a whisper. "Get over by the fire." As she said this, she left the room, going into her small bedroom. A minute later, she came back, wearing a flowered robe and carrying another robe, which she held out for Boyd.

Boyd had shed his shirt, and self-consciously unbuckled his trousers, letting them slide to the floor, turning away from Alice as he did so. As he stepped out of the wet pants Alice held up the robe, but rather than slide it over his shoulders whispered, "Turn this way, you dear man." As Boyd turned, his eyes were drawn to the open front of the flowered robe Alice was now wearing and to Alice's naked body, now exposed to him. In an unhurried motion she reached out and draped the second robe around Boyd, drawing herself in close to him as she did so.

Boyd was aroused in an instant, and moved to turn away, but Alice giggled, "this may be something new for you, Boyd. Don't be embarrassed. I have been without a man in the house for a very long time, but I think you and I can comfort each other on this cold night." With that, she took one of his hands and gently placed it over one of her breasts, then moved her own hand downward. As her hand circled his manhood, she kissed his neck and gently but firmly squeezed Boyd's engorged penis. "Be slow, Boyd; relax and enjoy our closeness. There will be time for more passion, but now let us just enjoy this wonderful feeling."

The next hours brought Boyd to places he had never imagined. In the beginning, Boyd's body shook with anticipation. He had never been with a woman. His childhood memories of his mother and grandmother sharing their beds with strange men did not compare with this. Now, he was a man. This woman's place in his mind held no connection to his memories of the past. For hours, they petted and stroked, they laughed, they moaned with ecstasy. And they slept in the warmth of each other's arms. Boyd's thoughts were only of Alice; the memory of North Mankato was, for the moment, erased.

For the next seven days and nights Boyd and Alice were seldom out of each other's site, or out of each other's arms. There were no major chores to be done, the repairs and reparations Alice had mentioned were not spoken of.

The cold rain eventually stopped, and, as their passions cooled, the unlikely couple began to talk and get to know each other. Although Alice was quite open and needed to share intimate parts of her lonely life, Boyd was less forthcoming. How could he tell her he had murdered his mother and grandmother, that his grandmother had killed his father on the day he was born. How could he confess that he lived by stealing food, clothing, or whatever items he needed or wanted, in order to survive. How could he explain he sometimes would kill an animal for the pleasure of being powerful enough to take its life. What would be gained if he told Alice about his experience with Willard Wiggins? Those were experiences he thought best kept to himself.

Twenty-Seven

THE IVERSON CONNECTION to Max Bauer surfaced again in 1898. This time the connection was with Max's son. The actual connection would not become apparent for several years, and if not for Dorothea Heinrich's diary we might never have become aware of that connection.

Charles and Lucinda MacGregor had arrived in Chippewa County, poor but industrious. Through the early 1880s, as Montevideo prospered, so did the MacGregors. The first railroad was established through southwestern Minnesota and Montevideo became a hub, providing a gathering and shipping point for the region. The MacGregors, with true Scottish zeal, built a roadhouse directly across from the Chicago, Milwaukee and St. Paul depot, and proudly named it MacGregor House. Charles kept the stables, providing service for all those who needed horses and wagons tended. Lucinda kept the roadhouse and attended to the personal needs of travelers. As the MacGregor family grew, the five daughters each had individual responsibilities to attend to. The two MacGregor sons, not quite as driven to succeed as was their father, preferred to spend their time hunting, fishing and squandering their lives.

By the time the Heinrich family arrived in Chippewa County, Jack was a strapping teenager, and Maggie MacGregor, with her mother's good looks and wild spirit, was, in spite of the strong Baptist restraints on social conduct, immediately drawn to him. How could these two pioneer children who were raised in the prairie wilderness not immediately fall in love?

The Heinrich-MacGregor wedding was an extravaganza the community had never envisioned. Both families were devout Baptists. The parents were far more conservative than their children, of course. MacGregor House was overflowing with guests the entire week before the wedding. The wedding celebration found some of the guests sleeping in the stable, some finally just collapsing on the lawn when the celebration became too much to endure. Dorthea's diary captured the beauty of the wedding, but being a good mother, she left out much of the ribaldry.

In the days following the wedding, Jack and Maggie set out to celebrate their wedding with a honeymoon journey. A whole month was set aside for their buggy journey through the hills of southern Minnesota. Both Jack and Maggie were well-aware of the difficult journeys their families had made to establish new homes in Chippewa County, and now they wanted to trace at least a part of their parents' journeys.

Their first day's travel brought them to Granite Falls, just seventeen miles downriver. They spent carefree hours there, watching as barges, which had come upriver from Minneapolis, were unloaded. They watched with fascination as passengers boarded for their journey downstream to New Ulm and Mankato, and for a few minutes wondered if they should have planned a river cruise instead of taking their buggy on the journey across the state. In the end they agreed they would rather share their honeymoon trip with just each other.

From Granite Falls, they followed the military road to Morton, where Jack guided the buggy aboard the ferry, which transported them across the Minnesota River. A half-hour later he and Maggie wove their way up the long, wooded hill toward Redwood Fall, which had been the site of a major Indian battle in August of 1862. It was there the Sioux had ambushed army troops from Fort Ridgley. After visiting the battle site, the honeymooners spent the night with Harold Conners, the local Baptist minister, and his wife. They attended church services with the Connors the next morning, before continuing their journey.

It was going to be two more days of travel before they expected to arrive in New Ulm. The young newlyweds travelled at a leisurely pace, following the edge of wooded hills as they went. The trail from Morton to Sleepy Eye was sometimes vague, but Jack assured Maggie that as long as they continued south or southeast, they would eventually reach New Ulm. In Sleepy Eye, they found lodging at the county home of Ester and Frank Farnsworth. After washing the day's dust away they were treated to a sumptuous dinner and an hour-long history lesson, as Frank told an elaborate tale of his summer-long skirmishes with Indians during the uprising. The next morning the honeymooners were on the trail once again, promising to stay in touch with their hosts and newly found friends.

Jack's father had specifically asked for them to call on Adolf and Marion Slayton, fellow farmers and pioneers, whose friendship they enjoyed as they crossed the state on the way to Chippewa County. The Slayton farm, Wilhelm had told his son, stretched over two hundred acres of rich hilly land above the Minnesota River and was located just a few miles south of New Ulm. Jack had been just a boy when the Heinrich family passed through the area on their way to Chippewa County. He was sure he would recall the Slaytons and thought visiting them would be one of the highlights of their honeymoon.

As Jack guided the buggy onto the long driveway winding its way up to the Slayton farm site, he and Maggie could see that a major gathering was taking place. Although his first reaction was to turn around, return to New Ulm and come back the following day, Jack thought it better to at least give his greetings to the Slaytons. As they neared the farm yard Jack could see the reason for the gathering. A dozen buggies, some buckboards and saddled horses, were located beyond the house, at the base of an elevated section of land. In their midst, gathered solemnly together and dressed in somber attire, the visitors were listening as final prayers were being said for Adolf Slayton.

Jack was embarrassed to be arriving unannounced and in travel-soiled attire. Maggie was mortified, thinking to meet the Slaytons privately, hoping they would forgive her frazzled hair and soiled clothing. As they left their buggy at the end of the driveway, they were met by a stranger they were sure was not Adolf Slayton.

When Jack introduced himself and Maggie, the young man told them of Adolf's death, leaving out the gory details of how his body was discovered. He also assured them they were not going to be judged for their travel attire.

Jack and Maggie joined the crowd surrounding the grave. When the mourners moved off, Maggie joined the other women in serving a hearty lunch to the attendees. As the crowd dwindled, Adolf's widow took Jack aside and assured him that he and Maggie should certainly stay the night. Later, Jack helped with the evening chores, while Maggie and Mrs. Slayton did the things that needed doing after serving a large crowd.

By next morning, the newly-weds had discussed their honeymoon plans and decided to put off the rest of their trip. After learning of the death of Adolf Slayton, it seemed almost sacrilegious to continue; by noon they had begun the return to Montevideo.

Twenty-Eight

IN THE EARLY days of their relationship Boyd and Alice seemed to be on a path for a long and loving relationship. For the first time in his short life, Boyd was loved, doted upon, and treated as a man. He seemed to be settling into the life of husband and farmer. They worked side by side, toiling in the field, repairing their modest home, even butchering a hog in the winter and salting the meat, which they stored in the storage dugout they also created together.

Little by little, however, the bloom went of their romance. When Alice needed the strength of a man to hoist timbers for a permanent roof on the livestock shelter, or when she wanted Boyd to help store potatoes, picking them from the field and wiping them clean one by one, he would lose his temper. "You're trying to turn me into a goddamn farmer, like that bastard Iverson and his stupid son!" he would rant.

The first time he struck her was in response to her demand that he show her more affection. After a long day of breaking sod for a new field, Boyd found himself angry with the world. He hated the repetition of walking the single furrow, created as he followed the bay mare back and forth, hour after hour. He hated the flies that attacked him, drawn by the rich aroma of his sweat, crawling on his neck, biting him behind the ear. He hated the sweat running down his back, turning his shirt and pants to heavy wet manacles. He hated the stink of the mare, as she also sweated and flashed her tail to rid herself of the flies.

By the end of the long day, Boyd hated everything, and everybody connected with his life, and he hated the final minutes of the long work-day, when he had to brush and curry the mare, who had given him a full day's work without ever questioning why she had been chosen for this job of pulling a heavy plow back and forth for hours.

And most of all, Boyd hated Alice Bevins for the seduction which had brought him to this ignominious task. He hated the smile and the soft words that had drawn him from his solitude, into her home and into her bed. He knew he deserved to share the warmth and comfort she had provided, and he knew he could have found that warmth and comfort any place he had chosen. He just hated that she had seduced him, had used him for the many household and farm chores he was coerced into doing, just for the gift of her body. There was no doubt in Boyd's mind why she had chosen him. A man, young, innocent in the ways of women, trapped by the promise of her soft body, of the false affection when she cupped his face in her hands, when she softly caressed his manhood as she guided him into her, as she moaned with the pleasure he brought to her. He hated the cooing sounds she make as she threw hers hips up, and he hated the soft giggles as he retracted, spent from giving her satisfaction.

As he lay back that night, clenching his fists, needing to expend physical energy, just needing a moment to his own thoughts, Alice had whispered how glad she was to have him to herself, to be able to rely on him when she needed just such a man. It was in that moment Boyd understood the relationship between a man and a woman, between all women and the men they seduced, controlled, and secretly ridiculed when that man was unaware of their scornful laughter.

In an instant, Boyd leapt from the bed, turned and struck Alice with his clenched fist. A single blow— it felt so good to release his anger and frustration. He hit her again, his feet spread wide as he stood naked by the side of the bed. He began to scream obscenities as he continued striking her, in the face, on the head, on her chest, and in her stomach, which had so recently been held tight against his own.

When he finally stopped, Alice lay bloody before him. Her jaw sagged, broken by the beating. There was no expression on her face, her eyes were wide but unblinking. Boyd had only lost his temper with this woman once. It would never happen again, because Alice Bevins was dead.

Deep in the darkness of his mind a haunting noise intoned, "*...this is because of Hans Iverson. He set this in motion when he ruined my father's life. He caused all our unhappiness, ruined our family. If I ever get the chance I will kill him, make him lose everything, just as I have had everything I might have had or loved stolen from me.*"

Boyd moved from the side of the bed. As he pulled on his trousers, his thoughts were confused. He was sick at the sight of Alice's tormented body lying on the bed. He nearly vomited as he realized what he had done. But, another place in his brain raced with excitement. The power he had felt as he hammered at Alice's body surged in his brain. No one could be this powerful, so much in control, he thought.

His fists were painful from the beating he had given Alice. His shoulders ached, for although he had grown stronger here at Alice's farm, this violence had been a new demand on his body. When he regained control, Boyd looked dispassionately across the room at Alice's broken and mangled body. Then, as if in a trance, he dragged her body from the bed. Without any show of emotion, he covered her naked body with her own robe, then he lay on the bed they had so recently shared, and in moments he was soundly asleep.

When he woke in the morning, Boyd had a plan. It was early May, and most nights they had put a fire in the stove to keep away the chill. Now, he stoked the fire, opened the flue, lit the flame. But, instead of closing and latching the fire-box door, he left it ajar, knowing that at some point a spark might escape. But, that was Boyd's intention.

Boyd gathered his belonging and put them outside the door. Everything he might need, he now had; his jacket, an extra shirt, trousers and sox. From the covered jar on a high shelf, he took the few dollars Alice had managed to save. His own rifle, worn, with its cracked stock, he left in the corner. Instead, he took Alice's nearly new

.30 caliber Winchester lever action from its cradle, and with it, two boxes of ammunition from the drawer of the rickety bed-side stand.

Then, once again, he was ready to disappear. He placed Alice on her bed and covered her naked body with a quilt, then gathered his pack. As his last task, he pulled a smoking ember from the stove and dropped it on the rug Alice had so proudly braided from the rag remnants of their clothes which were finally too worn out to be repaired one more time.

Boyd knew he could have taken the mare, but he also knew it could—and likely would—connect him to the fire and Alice's death. He opened the gate, so the livestock cold just wander out when they finally got hungry. The animals could fend for themselves until someone discovered them. For now, Boyd just wanted to put distance from this place before anyone happened by. He felt safe again; alone, but not lonely. It felt good to be a free man once more.

Over the summer Boyd travelled, quietly and unseen, as he moved westward. He followed game trails, and occasionally a wagon track, but he liked his solitude and stayed out of sight of civilization when at all possible.

For nearly a year Boyd wandered the wilderness of Minnesota. The vague borders between Minnesota and Iowa meant nothing to men such as him, and he occasionally showed up in Iowa villages, without giving thought to such mundane details as which state he was in. His feral life seemed to suit him. He was his own company by an evening fire, or in an abandoned cabin, when he found one. That winter he shared a hovel with a tramp heading for the Red River Valley, where the man expected to hire on as a field hand in the spring.

As he moved across the unsettled hills and valleys, Boyd's life philosophy began to take shape. In the time he spent with Alice Bevins he had grown from boy to man. Anna Brockhaus had given him a rudimentary education. Although her bible verses meant nothing to him, he could read a bit and write his name. Alice taught him to read and write with a bit more skill and he had taken her bible with when he left her behind.

Twenty-Nine

WHILE THE HEINRICH-MACGREGOR wedding was drawing near, Boyd Bauer was nervously following a trail as it meandered near the Minnesota River. As Jack joked with his brothers about becoming a husband, and as Maggie frolicked playfully on a hillside, gathering wild-flowers for her wedding bouquet, Boyd was creeping carefully toward a doe standing, unaware and un-worried, in a woodland clearing.

The day would end in laughter for Jack and Maggie. But, for Boyd it would be spoiled when the doe leapt into the brush, leaving Boyd frustrated and meatless for another day. And with a growling stomach Boyd screamed out his rage.

On Saturday, Jack Heinrich and Maggie MacGregor smiled, kissed and ran joyfully from the small Baptist church in Montevideo. Brothers, sisters, and friends from across the county, cheered them on as they began their new life together. The reception lasted the afternoon, followed by a huge party, which lasted well into the night- and which was very un-Baptist like.

On Sunday, Jack and Maggie, along with friends, and family, gathered in the church for a final lunch and gift opening party before the couple's planned departure later in the week. A hundred happy celebrants joined with the couple and wished them a happy journey, which was planned to take them back across Minnesota. They would be following the trails their families had used a generation earlier; to Redwood Falls, New Ulm and Rushford, with a final journey—time permitting—to Jack's birthplace in Iowa.

Boyd Bauer knew nothing of the Heinrichs, the MacGregors, or the wedding and honeymoon plans. His angry thoughts were focused on finding a meal. He just wanted food, red meat he could dig his teeth into.

As he had travelled alone through the wooded countryside, Boyd had begun talking to God. It was a new experience for Boyd, this God-talk. Anna had started his religious training in North Mankato. Alice Bevins had tried to further introduce Boyd to religion as she helped him improve his reading and writing. Alice used the tattered bible she had inherited from her mother, who had inherited it from Alice's grandmother. Alice had limited success in explaining the religious history laid out in the Old Testament. She hoped Boyd would just find and accept the love and the hope she found in the New Testament. "You sometimes just need to accept things on faith," she offered. Patiently explaining the wonderful messages there, she had worked to improve his reading skills.

At some moments Boyd seemed filled with the Lord, seemed to grasp the love, hope, and history. There were times he seemed to accept Alice's religion. At other times, however, Boyd rebelled, screaming obscenities that none of the gibberish made sense. Only strength, revenge, and redemption, could be counted on as the path to survival. Deep in his heart Boyd knew survival by any means was the true course of action, that stealing a chicken when he was hungry was more righteous than having his stomach complain for lack of nourishment. All the evil and mean things around him, the good life he was deprived of, the anger so deep in him, could not be overcome by those words in her bible. That was his faith.

But, he tried. Even as he beat Alice to death with his fists, Boyd had screamed bible passages aloud. Now, alone as he wandered the woodlands, he occasionally thought of bible passages, and thought perhaps somewhere, sometime, he might make sense of the bible and find peace of mind.

Today, however, Boyd's stomach was screaming for food. Today, his thoughts were consumed by the anger of his actually starving to death while farmers all around him had more food of all kinds than they could use. Then, as if Providence was answering his need, there, in a cleared pasture Boyd saw a flock of sheep. Big fat ewes, tiny lambs, more even of in-between sizes.

For a few minutes, he sat quietly by a large tree as he formed a plan. How simple, to just walk up to an ewe, or a lamb, and bash its head, then drag it quickly into the woods. In minutes, he knew he could skin it, cut it into manageable pieces, then skewer it over a fire.

As he scanned the pasture he could see no buildings, no farm house or barn, if there was one; nothing in sight for half a mile.

He ran swiftly to the nearest lamb, grabbed it by the neck as he smashed its skull with a rock, and scurried back into the woods. The flock of sheep were only momentarily spooked, running several yards before stopping and looking back. But, there was no danger in sight, so they resumed grazing. Only the ewe who had her infant taken from her side seemed confused and concerned. She wandered left and right, bleating for her lost baby.

This is working out well, thought Boyd. I guess maybe God does provide for those in need. Without another thought he set about preparing a hearty meal of freshly killed lamb.

Boyd found some wild onions growing in a low damp area and added them to the stew he was making from the remains of the lamb. He was confident that he was safe. With so many sheep, the farmer couldn't possibly miss one lamb.

Before preparing his lamb banquet, Boyd had travelled down-river a quarter-mile before setting up a substantial camp. He gathered dry wood for a fire, cleared a hollow in the roots of a huge cottonwood tree, and spread pine boughs from nearby trees for a soft and fragrant bed. He had been taken by the soft beauty of the lamb's hide and decided to scrape the fat from it, then fashion a pair of mittens. Just because he could.

Well fed, relaxed and feeling good about his life, Boyd failed to notice later as Adolf Stanton strode into Boyd's camp. As he had entered the campsite, Stanton had paused, assessing the scraggly red-haired man lounging under the trees. Stanton paused beneath a large oak tree, scanning Bauer's attempt at making a woodland home from nature's bounty. He saw Bauer, relaxed on the pine boughs, his campfire, which had turned to a bed of glowing embers. Draped over a low hanging branch, Bauer had hung his threadbare shirt to dry after rinsing it in the creek. On an adjoining branch was the skin of Stanton's lamb.

"I presume my lamb was tender, satisfied your hunger."

Bauer jumped at the sound of Stanton's voice. He was surprised that he had not heard Stanton enter his encampment. In all his years, Boyd had never been caught by surprise, and now he was immediately on his guard.

"Nothing to say?" queried Stanton. "At least I thought you'd have the decency to offer some vague apology, 'I was starving,' or 'you have so many sheep I did not think you would miss one'."

"You know," he continued, "from time to time I lose a sheep to a wolf, or a coyote. On a rare occasion some transient family in their desperation will take a lamb. In most cases, I am asked, offered some labor in return for my own endeavors. But you, for some reason unknown to me, you just took one of my lambs and disappeared into the woods."

Boyd had not moved from his pine bough bed. While Stanton continued to berate him, Boyd kept his eyes focused on the glowing coals of his campfire. In the corner of his eye however, he kept Stanton's location.

At first, Boyd accepted that he was going to be chastised, maybe even insulted, but as Stanton droned on, Boyd became weary, could not help but think this damn farmer had overstayed his welcome. It was obvious to Boyd that this lanky farmer, in his bib overalls and flannel shirt, was going to continue his harangue without end if Boyd did not do something.

"It was only one lamb," he remarked. "It's not as if you cannot afford to lose just one of the miserable creatures. You do nothing. You just turn the sheep out on the grass, where they breed and pop out lambs, with no work on your part. You should close your trap and shuffle back to your farm. I'll be gone in a day. We can both just forget we've ever met."

By now Bauer was sitting, reclining against the big tree. Although he seemed relaxed, his nerves were tensed. The time had passed for this foolish talk.

As he reached out to touch the soft lamb skin draped next to Boyd's shirt, Stanton turned his back on the intruder, and in a firm voice stated, "It's obvious that God has not entered your life. I can only feel pity for you. Yours is a life wasted. No doubt of that. Who, but a man lost to God, can skulk in the woods, hide from the world, as he sleeps on a bed of pine boughs! To say nothing of killing a lamb with no thought of its provenance. Yours is a life that is doomed—I say it is doomed."

Boyd had not actually planned to kill Adolf Stanton. It just happened. If the old fool had stopped yelling at him, Boyd would have walked away, and they both would still be alive. But, as Stanton droned on, Boyd began to seethe with anger. *"Who is this stupid farmer to call me lost and a thief? What does he know of me and what I have endured just to survive in such an unfair world? What does he know of my mother, or my father? What does he know of how this life of pain and loneliness started, when a stupid farmer, just like him, ruined my father's life? Without cause, the man attacked my father aboard ship as my father was coming to America to start a new life. Full of hope, my father was already a victim. And then, in just a few years, that same farmer lied to a judge, claiming my father had attacked him and his son."*

Stanton was oblivious to Boyd Bauer's anger. He was no longer chastising him, Boyd thought, but was now proselytizing, preaching to him, as though Boyd was some ignorant fool, who needed saving by this self-righteous fool of a farmer.

Finally, unable to bear the older man's tirade, Boyd grabbed a fist-sized rock near the fire and charged. He caught Stanton completely off guard, and with a single blow, knocked Stanton to the ground. Then, viscously, he continued to smash the rock into Stanton's head until both men were covered in blood.

Bauer dropped to his knees at Stanton's side. "You fool! You stupid old bastard!", he screamed. " What right do you think you have to criticize me, to call me Godless? You are just like all the others who have tried to ruin my life. I hope you find it worth it to lose your life over just a lamb."

As he calmed down, Boyd looked around him, as if he were not connected to the bloody scene. His complexion began to clear, and his breathing became calm once more. Without looking at Stanton, Boyd stepped past the body and scooped some lamb stew from the kettle, then sat once more with his back against the giant oak as he slurped the broth from the cup. As the sun was setting, Boyd put more wood on his glowing fire, then cut another large pine bough, which he laid over Stanton's body. When the morning chill woke him just before sunrise, Boyd gathered his belongings and disappeared one more time.

Thirty

TOM WAS STILL looking for just one clue, some tiny object or bit of information that he hoped would spring his investigation into Roberta Swan's murder forward. Only days before, he had re-visited the tourist cabins, where Bobbie had been killed.

The cabin was still cordoned off. A sign on the door warned curiosity-seekers to stay away, but Tom had been given carte blanche to come and go throughout the county. Without going into detail to all concerned, Judge Chamberlin made it clear that he expected unhesitating support from the Chippewa County Sheriff and from every police agency in the county.

So far, however, Tom had returned empty-handed from every excursion into the countryside. He had looked for clues in the cabin on two previous occasions and had wandered back and forth across the property with his head down until his neck was sore. Now, as the sun settled behind the trees lining the river bank, Tom was ready to accept that the killer had left no clues. The grassy lot around the cabins was comprised of a mixture of wild timothy and quack grass, with the quack grass threatening to take over. Tom's attention was drawn to the base of a huge cottonwood tree. Along the side and behind the tree, as seen from the cabin, the grass was matted and trampled down, as if someone had stood there for some time. He wondered that he had not noticed this before. Tom walked carefully around the tree, keeping some distance between himself and the matted grass. After finding no tracks, he stepped carefully behind the tree, turned slowly, and looked across the parking area, toward the cabin, not more than fifty feet away. What he saw took his breath away.

From behind the tree he couldn't see the bathroom or the bed, which was what he expected, but the late afternoon sun acted as a spotlight. Through the window, fully visible and brightly lit, was the bed. Its full length lighted brightly as a theatre stage, reflected in the large mirror hanging above the antique dressing table. Then, as Tom moved to the opposite side of the tree, the mirror reflected more of the room, but from his first angle there would be no secrets, no hidden passions, no wanton lust hidden from someone standing out here in the shadows.

Now, Tom's interest was piqued. He could imagine a man, or a woman for that matter, hypnotized by the mirror image, afraid to move for fear of being seen, or perhaps mesmerized, as the couple inside became lost in their passion.

As if hypnotized himself, Tom crept slowly across the grass, imagining what must have been going through the mind of the peeping Tom. He had never previously considered that the murderer might have done anything other than open the door, shoot, close the door, and escape. New possibilities now emerged. *Was this a voyeur, who finally lost control and became a murderer? How often had the bedroom been the focus of the killer? How often had Bobbie used this cabin for her illicit affairs? Why? How? Who?* The questions raced through Tom's mind, but no answers came with their questions.

Tom stood outside the cabin for a few more minutes, letting his mind absorb the surrounding area, thinking of the various emotions that might have gone through the mind of the killer. During the past weeks his thoughts had flown between Arne Thorson, the Iversons and Bobbie Swan. *Not connected? Connected? In what way? What was the motive, or motives?* He knew he should have given more attention to Bobbie Swan's death. He should not have wandered around Chippewa County, should not have taken a spontaneous trip across the entire state just looking for some unknown answer to an unknown question. His brain snapped question after question as he left the cabin and wandered toward the river. Why, he asked himself, would someone have killed Arne, then a year later killed Bobbie, and how could those two deaths possibly be connected to the attack on the Iversons more than twenty years earlier?

Although there seemed to be no logical connection to the events, Tom's gut was telling him this was all connected. Somehow, these deaths, that attack, were connected all the way back to 1843, and the Argo. As he wandered along the river now, following the game trail he knew would eventually take him to Smith Park and the wild animal captives, Tom felt certain there was a connection. If only he could find it.

At a small bend in the river Tom, bent and picked up a small flat rock from the sand. Casually, letting his mind wander, he threw the rock and watched it skip across the water. He skipped another, and then a third rock; it was relaxing. As he bent to retrieve yet another stone, he noticed a crumpled paper lying partly buried in the sand. Out of curiosity he picked it up, and as he unfolded the squashed paper, he recognized it as a chewing gum wrapper. He was about to throw it into the slowly spinning water, but then with no real reason, thought better of it and put it into his pants pocket.

By this time, Tom's walk along the river brought him nearly back to the Riverside Hotel. He considered going to his room, but since his car was still parked by the tourist cabins, he decided to retrace his steps and get the car. It was only a half-mile back to the car, and Tom, by now had become accustomed to having such easy transportation. It was an easy decision to make.

The next morning, Tom decided to have breakfast and coffee with the judge. His latest revelation regarding the cabin, the trampled grass, and the view into the room where Bobbie was killed, would be of interest to the judge. Tom thought talking with him about the discovery might spark some new insights.

"It's always inspiring, having coffee or a drink with you, Tom. I'm constantly amazed at your ability to find new clues or spot some vague connection and make sense of what everyone else just finds confusing. Tell me more about your experience at the cabin. What can I do to help your search?"

Tom had learned to let the judge ramble, to vent his excitement at small discoveries Tom brought to him. The two men had developed a true affection for each other, and both enjoyed the excitement that came with sharing these moments.

As their conversation rambled on, Tom reached in his pocket and drew out the wrinkled gum wrapper, planning to throw it in the trash. With a quizzical look, the judge commented that he did not know Tom chewed gum.

"No, I just found this on the beach as I was walking along the river yesterday evening. I thought I shouldn't just leave it to pollute the river, and I forgot to throw it out before I left my room."

The judge paused, looking at the wrinkled wrapper, then said, "I think we should go over to the evidence storage room, Tom. There's something I think you should see.

Few minutes later, Tom and Judge Chamberlin were looking at a loose collection of items on the evidence room table. "Until you dropped that gum wrapper on my desk I hadn't given this box of evidence a second thought since it was put in here. In all the time we have spent together, I never considered that it might be important for you to actually see what was collected from Bobbie Swan's murder scene.

The judge carefully spread the items from the box on the table. The mysterious cigarette lighter, Bobbie's lipstick and compact, her undergarments, a piece of note paper with a scribble on it, a collection of miscellaneous trash from the room—and three wrinkled gum wrappers.

"Where did these come from? Who found them? Where were they found; are there any more of them?" Tom's mind raced as he questioned the judge.

"I don't actually know where the wrappers came from. I assumed they were found in the room with everything else. I suppose the investigation report made at the scene should answer those questions. But let's see, Tom. Are they the same brand of gum? Can you guess how long your find was left in the sand?"

Judge Chamberlin promised Tom he would have the investigator's notes before the day ended.

Thirty-One

WHILE TOM HALL was looking for a killer, I was wandering around Chippewa County, looking for relatives and for stories I could bring home to my family. I spent hours at the Chippewa County courthouse, making notes about births and deaths, and about marriages, divorces, and property transfers. From time to time, Tom and I would meet to discuss our progresses. My Iversons had married and now were tied in history to Heinrichs and MacGregors and from a seemingly endless list of immigrants from all over Europe.

Tom, Mary and I, met for breakfast on a Saturday morning at the Stavos Cafe. We knew that by noon the main street of Montevideo would be jammed while people from all corners of the county did their weekly shopping. As we ate and drank our strong coffee, George Stavopolis joined us, George was Greek and had escaped through Italy, then across France, just before the Great War. He cut an imposing figure, and when he had arrived in Montevideo, it was only days before the eligible, and sometimes the not-so-eligible, women were at his doorstep.

George stood about six feet-two. In 1912 he weighed a respectable and powerful, two hundred fifteen pounds. His great size was capped beneath a massive spread of curly black hair. Now, twenty-six years later, the still curly hair was laced with a dignified gray, and George's smile had to fight its way past a mustache which threatened to engulf his entire face.

In his youth, George bragged that he had been the strongest man in his home village— if not in all of Greece. When I looked at his massive arms and his barrel chest, I had no reason to doubt him. It hadn't taken George long to select a beautiful Chippewa County maiden, to marry, and father four children in as many years. "I would have had a dozen," quipped George. "But, my poor wife couldn't keep up the pace. She died giving birth to my beautiful baby, Georgina."

We always enjoyed George's company. He was outlandish in his joy for life, making and taking ridicule with equal aplomb. This morning, however, George's mood seemed dark, troubled even, as he joined us. "I'm troubled by the death of Bobbie Swan," he offered. "She was a vixen, that's for sure, but I can't believe somebody shot her.

"I get to see a lot of things that happen," he continued. "Some people would be embarrassed to look in my eyes if they knew what I know about their secrets."

As George spoke, Tom drew squiggly lines on a paper napkin, doodling, with no apparent motive, as we passed the time. He looked up from his doodles, commenting, "You seem like you're trying to redeem a secret, George. You might feel better if you shared the burden. Unless, of course, you think it's a secret best kept to yourself."

"I'm a good catholic, Tom. I was Greek Orthodox before I left home, but I guess Rome's church is close enough for me, now. I thought I might feel better if I just went to confession, but as a matter of fact, I'm not sure what I know is meant to be shared in a confessional, or that what I think I know is actually true. It's just confusing to me, Tom."

Tom, Mary, and I, exchanged looks and leaned toward George. Whatever he knew was important enough that he seemed willing to share the secret with Mary and two strangers, but not with his priest or the friends he had known for years.

"I've known Mary here since she was a kid," He looked at her for a moment and continued, "until this moment, you're the only one I could possibly say this to. Now, I've gotten to know you two guys and I think you can be trusted to keep a secret. If it should be kept, that is." George seemed to shrink into himself and stared down at his coffee mug while he stirred a sugar cube into it. "I can't believe I'm about to say this, Mary… Tom. I've given it a lot of thought; if there is any validity to my hunch, I hope you can help me know how to deal with it.

"I've known for some time that Bobbie was fooling around, seeing other men while Darrel was working. I guess fooling around doesn't really cover it properly. She was having sex with a lot of men; strangers and neighbors alike. More than once, she suggested she and I should spend an afternoon in one of those cabins where her body was found. I could never bring myself to cheat on her husband, even though she made the idea appealing.

"When her murder was first reported, I reacted like nearly everyone else in town. I suspected Darrel had found out about her infidelity, gone crazy, and killed her. It was an easy conclusion to make, but of course, Darrel was cleared. It's interesting, that before long, no one even thought about her death anymore.

"Over the past couple of weeks my mind kept wandering back to Bobbie, seeking any strange or unusual pattern of activity. I'm here before five a.m. every day you know. I see lots of things not known to everyone. I also work late, sometimes I'm here all night, baking, or preparing for a busy weekend.

"I couldn't help question, in my mind, all the men who I thought might have been tempted by Bobbie. Harold at the Coast to Coast, whose wife died a couple of years ago, came to my mind. There was Ollie Hansen, who has the implement dealership; I knew he couldn't resist a girl in a tight skirt, but eventually I wrote him off, too. I found myself watching my old friends to such a point that I was afraid to even ask how their families were, for fear I'd learn that one of them was the killer. At one point, I was sure it was our postmaster, Daniel Hauk. He's up early and is never where you expect him to be. I even asked my friend, Howard Logan, if he thought Daniel was acting suspiciously. Howard just laughed and told me I had too much time on my hands.

I could see that Mary was on the edge of her chair, nearly screaming for George to just tell us what he knew, but obviously knowing such a question might stop George's resolve, she just fidgeted and waited.

Tom had stopped his doodling and held his pencil so tight I thought it might snap. "George," he asked, "do you really think you know who the killer is? This is too important to make wild accusations, and yet, if you have some sort of lead that can help me, you just have to say it."

"I think I do, Tom. It's so hard for me to accept this, that I'm beside myself. I'm afraid that I might accuse someone and be totally wrong. The man I think is responsible for Bobbie's death is so respected in town, I could never forgive myself if I'm wrong about this."

By this time, I could hardly contain myself. I wanted to know who George thought the killer was and why he thought it possible. I also knew it was not my place to pose the questions. After all, I was the ultimate outsider. Tom, or even Mary, should be the focus for George's answers.

George gave Tom a long sad look, then sat back in his chair. As he leaned forward and began to speak, there was a tremendous crash from the kitchen. It was as if all the metal shelving, the pots and pans, and the dinnerware, had come crashing to the floor.

George leaped from his chair, knocking it backwards as he rushed from the dining room to learn what catastrophe had brought our conversation to a sudden end. He bolted through the swinging double doors as we sat, spellbound. A moment later we heard George's scream; not a name, not a profanity, but a scream that sounded like a man being murdered.

That is what had just happened.

thirty-two

"IT WAS ONLY a minute!" Tom explained to the judge. "Certainly, not more than two minutes. I should have gone to the kitchen with George as soon as we heard the noise. Instead, I just sat there until I heard his blood-curdling scream. Then, we all bolted for the kitchen, and found George dead, tangled in the wire shelving. He was covered with cooking oil, flour, who knew what else. I suppose I wasted another minute or so seeing if he was alive. I should have known, just by his look, that he was dead."

There was chaos everywhere. The café doors were quickly locked and a "closed" sign hung on the shuttered door. Mary and I were speechless as we stared from one to the other, then scrambled to the kitchen's rear entrance, which opened on the alley. There was no one in sight in any direction. The alley was muddy from a night of autumn rain. There were no footprints in the mud, no tire tracks. How could that be? The chaos had taken place only minutes earlier.

I grabbed the goose-neck telephone next to the cash register and told the operator to get the police chief here, on the double. "Yes, it's an emergency," I yelled, but did not give her any details. "Just get him here!"

I ran south, to the corner nearest Ree Motors, the auto dealership that consumed nearly a half-block of Main Street. Eddie Masterson, Ree's manager, sat in his glassed-in office, but there was no one in sight in either direction. Mary had scurried north but saw no one from the corner which looked west to Howard Flynn's coal and fuel oil warehouse. Looking east and up a slight rise, Mary could see only Main Street itself. She ran to that corner, both hoping and dreading that she might see George's killer. There was no one who looked even slightly suspicious.

Across the street, people were beginning to crane their necks, wondering at the commotion down the street. Police Chief Bill Mathiason left his car running at the curb, its door wide open, and the rotating beacon on the roof flashing it's red message of emergency in progress. One by one, they arrived; Bill's deputy, then Sheriff Andrews, Doctor Burns, who had just been in the drug store, and Royce Schwitters, who had planned to spend the day cleaning the Hollywood movie theater but could not help but run to the Stavos Café to see what the commotion was all about. Pastor Oswaldson, from the Methodist Church, and Reverend Sherman, joined Doctor Burns' nurse Helen Evers, crowding in to see what help they could provide.

I let each one in, then locked the door behind them. We now had more people than we could deal with, all crowding to see George and offering their perspectives. *Who did it; how did anyone get into the kitchen; was someone hiding there, still?* There were no answers; just more questions.

Judge Chamberlin arrived, and I let him in. He huddled with Chief Mathiason and Doctor Burns. Then, he turned to the crowded room. "Let's just all leave the café. Doc Burns and Bill Mathiason will take charge. Tom, you and Mary, please stay. Everyone else, please leave your name with Mary before you go. Of course... we'll keep in touch, but we have to clear this mess up and you are not helping at the moment."

I was disappointed, but of course, I left with the crowd. One by one, the rubberneckers wandered away. "Bill Mathiason will take care of it, " said one.

"I didn't know George, but I heard a lot of people were concerned about him; he was Greek, you know." That comment seemed to infer that George himself must be guilty of something.

It's Saturday, and I have my week's shopping to do," commented another. It seemed life would continue with only slight disruption for the rest of Montevideo's residents.

Thirty-Three

IF THERE WAS such a thing, Tuesday was perfect for a funeral. It was blustery, cold and foreboding. The rain was driven by a northerly wind that threatened to bring an early winter. I stood with Tom and Mary. We were just behind the Stavopolis family. The Sunset Memorial Cemetery accepted Catholics as well as Baptists, Lutherans, and other repentant sinners. W e huddled together, hoping our umbrellas would not tear apart, or be torn from our grasps by the wind, as the priest gave final absolution to George and then wished him safe journey to heaven and his final redemption.

George's children said their final goodbyes to their father as the casket was lowered slowly into the earth. They turned tearfully to each other as they offered and sought consolation before trudging to their cars, which were lined along the dirt path meandering through the cemetery.

Tom was nearly inconsolable, feeling that if he had rushed to the kitchen with George, he may have saved him from his violent death. In the days following George's murder, Tom and I had searched the kitchen for clues, and had wandered the alley behind Main Street in the futile hope that there would be any hint that could lead to the killer.

"I don't understand it," Tom moaned. "How could the killer have disappeared so completely in such a short time? How would he have been aware that George was very likely going to identify him to us?" We had assumed we were alone in the café and had neither seen, nor heard anyone, in the time we sat with George.

Our search was in vain. We thought we had looked in every dark nook, pried at every locked door, the length of the alley, and questioned a dozen people whose rear business doors could have given access to an escaping assassin. It was all to no avail.

After three futile days, we were forced to admit our failure, admit that the killer would likely walk free, unless there was some future slip-up to betray him.

Now, as we left the cemetery, Tom, Mary, and I looked at the others who were leaving. They trudged to their cars, shook the water from their umbrellas, and stamped the mud from their feet, before finding the protection of their cars. A hundred people or more moved back toward their relatively normal lives. Doctor Smith and his wife and daughter retreated to their comfortable, but unpretentious home, overlooking Lagoon Park. The Morehouse brothers and their children left the cemetery in their big Studebaker sedans, and drove the short distance to Bruce's home, where they gathered around the table in the formal dining room, to pray for George Stavopolis and for their own safety, in a world which seemed to be plummeting into sin.

Raymond Prentice, Montevideo's only dentist, retired quietly to his home, while the Browns and Moresetters clutched their wives and children closely, as they left the cemetery. Throughout the small town, families consoled one another at the loss of George Stavopolis.

It seemed all the town leaders came to pay their respects. Ministers from the Lutheran, Methodist, and Episcopal churches and their wives stood together in a show of public unity, as did Reverend William Sherman, from the small Baptist congregation. Unmarried, he seemed to be not quite included.

I bid a somber goodbye to Tom and Mary, then watched, as they drove slowly away after we promised to meet in a day of two, hoping against hope that our luck would change and that we would be led to the killer, whom we were now certain was responsible for at least three deaths in the community.

Thirty-Four

ALTHOUGH TOM KEPT his room at the Riverside Hotel, he was spending less and less time there. He still had breakfast at the hotel most days, and occasionally lunch or dinner, but the nights were now spent in the quiet comfort of Mary's home. In spite of his concern for Mary's reputation, she insisted having him near was far more important than any gossip generated when his car was parked near her house overnight, or as he was seen driving away in the early hours of the day.

Now, their sadness at George's death drove them close, as they slumped on the mohair couch in front of the fireplace and shared the sadness of George's funeral. "I'm angry beyond belief, Mary," Tom uttered. "I feel like I have somehow gone blind and can't see. What am I not seeing? Where am I supposed to look? What is it that must be absolutely and completely apparent. George was with us one moment, and in the next he's dead, and the killer's gone, as if it never happened. What am I not seeing or hearing?"

As they sat in front of the fire, Mary held Tom's hand in hers, patting, soothing, speaking only to assure Tom that he had been doing all that could be expected. The only light in the room came from a single floor lamp in the corner, and from the glowing fireplace. When they had arrived at her home, Mary had changed from her wet clothing, and was curled next to Tom in her large, soft, warm, terrycloth robe.

"It's time to change the subject, Mr. Hall," she whispered. "Lean back and close your eyes while I fix you a drink." He could hear Mary's movements as she put ice in a glass, then poured a generous portion of scotch over it. With his head back and his eyes closed, he began to relax and to put aside the pain and anger that had held him.

When Mary returned with Tom's drink, instead of handing it to him she placed it quietly on the end-table, then leaned across Tom's lap and kissed him gently before he could open his eyes.

As they kissed, Mary unknotted her robe, letting it slip from her shoulders, then sank gently, straddling Tom's lap. With a start Tom opened his eyes to see Mary, naked under her robe, reaching her arms around his neck. "I suppose the ice will melt of course, but right now you need to make love to me."

Mary unbuttoned Tom's shirt as they continued to kiss, then stood while she undid his belt and allowed his trousers to slide to the floor. Then, once again her arms circled Tom as she turned slowly to lie back on the couch.

For the next hour they cuddled, fondled and made love; at first with near violent passion and later with a slow, melodic gyration that seemed to last forever.

Thirty-Five

SUNDAY MORNING FOUND Tom and Mary, like most couples and families in Montevideo, going to church. They had chosen once again to visit the little Baptist church overlooking Montevideo's main street and the panorama of the river valley.

The Sunday greeter shook Tom's hand, somewhat hesitantly Tom thought. Then wished him and Mary God's blessing, inserting "nice to see you both seeking God this morning." Mary blushed, and Tom thought perhaps his temperature rose just a bit at the perceived implication.

It was communion Sunday, and both Tom and Mary partook of the thimble of grape juice and dry cracker offered in place of Body and Blood. They were sure Mrs. Coyle, seated behind them, mumbled some retort at their participation, knowing she was sin-free, while Tom and Mary were neck-deep in irredeemable sin. They ignored the implication. Tom and Mary joined the congregation as it shuffled slowly from the church. Rambunctious children, now freed from their hour-long confinement, rushed noisily into the church yard, disregarding their parents' admonitions to be civil.

As on most Sundays, neighbors and friends who may not have seen each other during the week, paused to visit before going home for a comforting dinner. Coles and Bensons, Cushmans and Iversons, huddled for a moment before moving on. MacGregors and Heinrichs, the bee-keeping Morehouse brothers, along with their wives and children, wished each other well before turning toward home.

As Tom and Mary moved quietly toward Tom's car, Jack and Maggie Heinrich greeted them. "Tom, we're happy to have you here. And Mary, we don't see much of you these days." Maggie hugged

Mary lightly as she spoke. As they continued their conversation, Tom and Jack moved to one side, allowing others to pass.

"I can't help comment to you Tom, about George's death. I can't believe he's no longer with us, and I just cannot believe all the violence in our small town in recent months."

"I somehow feel almost responsible for George's death," muttered Tom. "One minute we're all having a serious conversation and in the next moment, George is dead. And so violently."

"His death…" Jack spoke slowly, then paused as if looking for just the right words. Tom thought the man's voice resembled the sound of gravel being rolled around the bottom of a bucket as he responded, "His death made me think of the funeral Maggie and I attended; or should I say that we happened upon. We were on our honeymoon and planning to visit Adolf and Clara Stanton. The Stantons farmed near New Ulm. As we neared their farm we saw a crowd gathered, and found it was Adolf's funeral. He had been murdered, apparently without reason, and we just happened to arrive during the service.

Maggie and I were on our way down to Steele County. My father had tended his sheep there on the way to Montevideo. I was still a boy at the time. Maggie had suggested we take a leisurely honeymoon trip before facing the real world and we had planned an impromptu visit with the Stantons. We got to their farm just as Adolf was being buried. I guess it was a horrible sight when they found his body. When Adolf didn't come to the house in the evening his wife got concerned, of course. The next day his body was found lying next to a cold camp-fire at the south edge of their farm. I guess he wasn't just killed, but horribly beaten to death. The killer had bludgeoned his face until Adolf was almost unidentifiable. They found some scraps of a dead lamb, but no signs of the killer. Well, his death put an end to our honeymoon, that's for sure. We just couldn't consider spending the rest of the month travelling that back-country. It was partly because of the shock of Adolf's violent murder, of course, but we were also concerned that we were strangers there and we certainly felt isolated and at risk.

"Adolf Stanton and my father came from Germany about the same time. Adolf established a substantial farm near New Ulm, while my father, along with the children, continued on, ending up in Chippewa County. Our Heinrich family is well-represented around Montevideo. I guess you know that.

Tom wasn't sure where his conversation with Jack Heinrich was going but Jack seemed to have something he need to share. "As my own family grew, I became a Stone mason. I've created headstones for many families throughout the county. I guess there will always be a need for grave markers, although we always seem to believe our own won't be needed quite yet.

"We buried a daughter of our own, Maggie and me. Our other two children have made it to adulthood. Bessie is married and raising a brood of girls. Our son Clifford, Cliff we call him, is still single, but doing better. Cliff was in the Great War, saw a lot of death in France, and seems to still be bothered by it. I was afraid we would be needing a headstone for him. Turned my stomach in knots all the while he was over there, I can tell you. Even now, twenty years later, I see a haunted look in Cliff's eyes sometimes. For a long while I thought I could get Cliff to talk a bit about the war, get it out of his system, but after a while I decided the painful memories just had to stay hidden in the recesses of his mind and he would learn to live with them.

"Cliff was active in our congregation for a while, even had a short romance with one of the girls in the choir. Then, when the new pastor came, he just stopped coming to church... stopped believing, I guess. He said something about pastor Sherman bringing back memories of the war. I guess it was something the pastor said to Cliff, or something about body language when they met that made Cliff uneasy. So—he just stopped coming to church." Jack seemed to have cleared his mind of whatever problem he was struggling with. Tom thought maybe he just wanted to share something personal to show Tom he was welcome in the community.

Thirty-Six

WINTER LOOKED TO be just around the corner. Tom was beginning to get frustrated. Had he been a little more introspective, Tom would have recognized that he was always restless, and his restlessness was followed by the frustration he now felt. He wanted resolution of the mysterious deaths. When he came to Montevideo, he had no idea he would spend months looking for clues, questioning dozens of men and women. Farmers, businessmen, truck drivers, and travelling across the state but finding only hints, not answers. It was his unwillingness to stay inert that made him perfect for investigating such complicated puzzles as the one in Chippewa County. A quiet moment savoring a second cup of coffee was a moment to look at a problem from a new angle, think of another possible way to interpret some vague clue.

And then, there was Mary. She and Tom were now a couple. He was accepted wherever they went. *That guy from* Ohio who is looking for Bobbie Swan's murderer, or *the young Navy guy whose brother was killed up by Lac Qui Parle*, or *that handsome guy Mary has latched on to*, was now his description. More than that, in spite of— or perhaps because of—the gossip about him, Montevideo was beginning to feel like home to Tom. That came as a surprise. What would he do if—when—he solved the murders?

October had been replaced by November, and now as he and Mary walked the main street, looking at the Christmas decorations already filling store windows and watching excited families with children who couldn't wait for Santa to fulfill their wishes, or to make reality of their dreams, he was reminded of the last winter he spent here. Not until a mystery was solved, not until more brutal deaths had taken place, not until it was nearly spring when he boarded the train back to Ohio; not one day had he really considered giving up . He certainly would not give up this search any time soon.

As they walked, arm in arm, Tom remembered Jack Heinrich's comment. *"Something about pastor Sherman made Clifford Heinrich uncomfortable, perhaps reminded Cliff of the war, his father told me."*

"I wonder what that was," thought Tom. *"What was it in church that caught my own attention? Something the pastor said? Something in his body language? Maybe I should talk with Clifford Heinrich."*

Two days later, Tom and I were having coffee at the Stavos Café when Cliff and his cousin Billy came through the door. Both men were dressed in brown khaki trousers and jackets, their feet comfortable in lace-up Woodsman boots and their heads comfortably covered by hunting caps.

Although the men were unknown to Tom and me, Cliff had seen Tom at a distance numerous times and stopped to say hello. "My cousin Billy and I are on our way over toward Ortonville. Pheasants are thick as flies on a dead pig over there, and we thought it might be a good day for shooting a few."

"Join us for a cup of coffee," offered Tom.

The two hunters joined us, and as the waitress brought two steaming mugs of coffee, Tom went right to his point of interest. "Cliff, your father and I visited outside church the other day. He commented that although you had always been active in the congregation, for some reason you have dropped out."

Perhaps, thinking that Tom was going to give him a lecture about attending church or losing his soul if he spent too much time drinking with Billy, Cliff was at first defensive. "Oh, I believe in God, Tom. I'm a little surprised you might be the one to recruit me back into the congregation."

"No, no. I would be the last person to preach about church attendance or the hazards of drink and such, Cliff. I think he was just expressing his puzzlement over your dropping out of church activities. I only mentioned it because of you father's comment.

"I'm guessing you've heard that Mary and I spend a lot of time together and all that. We seem to be the focus of pastor Sherman's Sunday sermons; unless I'm just a bit paranoid. Thinking the pastor would give me and Mary any thought at all probably stretches credibility."

"I don't think I want to give up my hunting time to discuss religion, Tom, but Dad is right about my spending less time on religion than he would like. You may not know, but my parents and the MacGregors were the founders of the First Baptist Church here. I can see he might be self-conscious about his son not being in the congregation on Sundays."

"Cliff, I'm a Navy veteran, but not a combat vet like you. But, if there's anything you need to share about your time in France my time is yours. I can't think of anything worse than carrying a combat burden around your hometown might be."

Cousin Billy excused himself. "I'm going to the drugstore for some aspirin, Cliff. I'll pick you up in ten or fifteen minutes. We need to get out of here before the pheasants are all shot."

Left by himself now, Cliff leaned over his coffee. He didn't seem to be concerned by my presence.

"Let me share something with you Tom. I'd appreciate your discretion on this. I certainly don't want to cause a problem where one may not exist. I was raised here in Montevideo, and I'm related to half the town. Lutherans, Methodists, Catholics and Baptists; we all tend to be clannish, cloistered with people who believe the same as we do, so of course I know the Baptists just a little bit better than some of the others.

"I haven't lost my faith; it's nothing like that. When pastor Sherman showed up I was still pretty active in the church, even dated one of the Zaiser girls for a while. Sherman was a little nervous when he first arrived. I can understand that. He came to us from someplace in Iowa, he said… said he had been active in mission work there. Of course, that's different than dealing with our small congregation which has been here for a couple of decades.

"I thought I recognized pastor Sherman, but at first I couldn't put a finger on why I thought that. At the end of the war, after the battle of the Argonne, I got blasted from my foxhole by a Jerry howitzer. Between the howitzers, the snipers, and the constant shelling, we were all a mess. Sometimes our foxholes and the trenches were knee-deep in rotten water. There were dead soldiers and dead horses stacked three-deep in places. The smell of death was as bad as our fear of getting shot. Two of my buddies were killed right next to me and I ended up with a concussion. I think I was unconscious for a couple of days before I ended up in a hospital somewhere in France for a couple of weeks. After that, I was in and out of this world for quite a while.

"In the bed next to mine was another young guy. Actually, he was somewhat older than me. He might have been thirty-five or thirty-six years old for that matter. He was in worse shape than me. His head was bandaged from the top all the way to his neck; I never did see his face, except for around his eyes. He had a nurse taking care of his needs. He also had a broken arm and some ribs taped in place and compared to me he was a real mess."

"You must have felt lucky next to him I guess, Cliff."

"Well, Tom, the whole thing is this. We talked a lot. His voice was scratchy and sometimes garbled. Sometimes when he got really emotional he stuttered a little, even. But, I never saw his face, and that's what has left me uncertain of what I really experienced. You see, Tom, my head was really messed up. Sometimes I was loony, other times just as clear-headed as when we sit here today, I'm almost certain that guy's name was Sherman."

For a moment Tom was speechless. He put his coffee cup back in its saucer and leaned toward Cliff. He was not sure how to continue the conversation. "What else can you tell me, Cliff?" What else could he say?

"Well, one day while I was in the shower, the guy just disappeared. His nurse wrote a letter to me for him; he still had his arm in a cast. I had the letter in my duffel for a long time, but it disappeared somewhere along the way. I do remember that he told me in some strange way that he had found his God. He said he knew God had saved him on the battlefield for some greater purpose. Well, here's a fellow named William Sherman, a minister from somewhere, and I just can't put the two men together. As I said, my head was messed up, my vision screwy. I didn't need glasses before I was in the army, but now I'm nearly blind as a bat without these glasses.

"It's hard to believe in my own memory when I realize my brain was like a big mush ball. It's also confusing, since the pastor has never shown any recognition of me. That guy and I must have been bedmates for about two weeks. My head wasn't bandaged, I was just recovering from a giant head-banging. So, if our pastor was the guy in the next bed, he should remember me just a little, even if I'm not sure of him. On the other hand, it was about seven years from our hospital time until the pastor showed up in Montevideo. That's a whole life time. Maybe he also has some memory loss after all that time, or maybe my head was too messed up and my memory is faulty."

Thirty-Seven

TOM WAS CHASING a bit of egg yolk around his plate with his fork, seeming lost in thought. He and the judge had been eating a late breakfast at the Riverside Hotel, where the rich appointments and the quiet that surrounded them, made them feel at ease. A light snow was falling, and the solitude of the late breakfast made their conversations feel more intimate. Tom had eggs benedict, raspberry jam and a slice of toast slathered in the rich hollandaise sauce the chef was so proud of. Rightfully so, Tom thought.

Judge Chamberlin mused quietly over a single poached egg, then said to Tom, "You seem pre-occupied, Tom. I can only think of a dozen or so things that might occupy your thoughts. But, tell me, what's puzzling you this morning?"

Both men finished their eggs, folded their napkins, and at exactly the same time, reached for their coffee cups. They laughed for a moment, as they realized how similar their thoughts were.

Tom was not ready to share the conversation he'd had with Cliff Heinrich. There were still questions that needed answers. "I'm struggling, Judge. I've been here over three months. My short visit in August has gobbled up the entire summer and autumn. We're almost to Christmas and I can't believe I am still struggling to find more than some basic hints as to what has happened here in Chippewa County.

"I've chased all across the state trying to figure out this business. Once or twice I was sure I was making progress, but, as we sit here watching Christmas shoppers go by, I don't have one concrete thing I can report to you."

The judge responded, "My only truly positive observation so far, is your growing relationship with Mary. Oh, and don't worry. I have known for some time you and she are more than just friends. She was quite self-conscious when you first began spending nights together. When she confessed to me what you two were up to, I told her that I approved. She's not a child, but a grown woman who knows her own mind. You, of course, may leave when you wish, or you might in fact just find in Montevideo the home you've been looking for. That will be up to you. And, I wouldn't worry a bit if some of the blue-noses have those noses bent a bit. As a matter of fact, some of those with their noses bent the most have colorful pasts, if I remember correctly."

Both men laughed, then sat quietly, as the waitress refilled their cups and began to remove the soiled breakfast ware.

As they relaxed into their chairs and cradled the coffee cups, savoring both the coffee's aroma and the quiet moment in each other's company, Tom spotted movement at the restaurant entrance.

Turning to see what had distracted Tom, the judge saw Pastor Sherman moving in their direction. Coming in from the wintry street the pastor still wore his long top-coat, fully buttoned, the collar turned up, and a light dusting of snow covering his shoulders.

"Come join us, Bill. Tom and I are just relaxing before we head out into the festive crowd." The judge reached across to the adjoining table and snared a cup and saucer, then motioned the waitress.

Tom couldn't exactly identify the look on the pastor's face, but thought he looked chagrined, almost as if he had been slapped or insulted.

"Thank you, Your Honor." He gazed slowly at each of the sitting men, as if to determine their thoughts, almost as if questioning whether their private conversation was a threat to him, or to question if he had been the topic of their private talk.

"I really wish you would remember not to call me Bill in public, Judge. You know such familiarity makes me uncomfortable. I can't help but remember when you and I were young, when 'yes sir', or 'no madam' kept a certain social balance."

As the three men talked and savored their coffee, the conversation slowly shifted to Chippewa County's mysterious deaths.

One by one, they discussed Bobbie Swan, then Arne Thorson, and ultimately the mystery of George's death in his kitchen. Eventually, the discussion came back around to the death of Arne Thorson. For the first time, the judge mentioned the red shoe and woman in the red skirt.

Slowly, with just a bit of jocularity in his voice, Tom spoke of the beauty which had been described for him that afternoon at Buster's. He wondered aloud how she had escaped, voicing that she must have been close at hand when Arne was killed; so near, perhaps settling in the grass, both naked and unaware of the danger approaching them. "I can only assume, since Arne's body was found naked, that she had also shed her clothes, and that without warning the killer had charged in, crushing Arne's skull before disappearing in the night. What's a mystery to me is where the woman went. She just disappeared. Although Arne's clothes were strewn in the grass, the only sign of the woman is the single shoe that was found the next day. Somehow, she evaded the killer and grabbed most of her clothes before racing away. How could she have managed such a feat?"

The other two men sat in silence as Tom continued. "We have pretty well eliminated the woman as a suspect, whoever she is and wherever she might be today. It's unlikely she would willingly have wandered along the river with Arne, shed her clothes, then attacked him so violently .We know it was a single blow to the back of Arne's head which killed him. It is extremely unlikely she could have achieved that if she wanted to end their tryst at the last moment. Unfortunately, no one we have talked with had ever seen her before, or since. She may be the key to solving Arne's death. And," he continued, "I can't help but wonder why she never came forth."

As discussion of Arne's death dwindled, there was a pause while the three sipped their coffee. The pastor seemed a little non-plussed and fiddled with his coffee cup. Tom thought perhaps the discussion of the violent death was disturbing to him. As he set his cup into the saucer, Bill Sherman pushed his chair back a few inches. Now, he was Pastor William Tecumseh Sherman. He straightened his back, with his hands clasped together on the table.

"My whole congregation is talking about you, Tom. About you and Mary, actually. I suppose you know you are not only breaking God's commandments, but are ruining Mary's reputation, if not her entire life."

For a moment, the silence was palpable. Tom and the judge sat dumbfounded. How could either man respond to Sherman's flat statement snapped so sharply at Tom? There had been no warning of the impending rebuke. The two men looked at each other. Then, Tom turned in his chair as the pastor seemed about to continue.

"Bill, pay close attention," Tom began. There was no deference in his voice, no implied reverence for Bill Sherman's position in the community. "Don't get up! I'm going to explain something to you, even though you have no right to an explanation; no right whatsoever."

"You are the minister to your congregation because you have a piece of paper saying you are a minister. You are here in Montevideo because you have a letter asking you to come here for the benefit of the congregation. You do not have any right to judge Mary, nor to judge me. Your comment just now is so far out of line I am surprised you didn't slap yourself in the mouth to stop yourself from speaking. Mary and I are adults; consenting adults as a matter of fact, who are attracted to one another. How we conduct ourselves is no one's business but our own. Immerse yourself in your bible. Preach about sin and salvation all you want but stay the hell out of our lives."

"The wicked shall reap the rewards of God's vengeance," snapped the minister. That thought would haunt Tom the remainder of the day.

Without uttering another word, the pastor pushed his chair back so violently it almost tipped over as he left. After sitting in silence for a moment, Tom apologized to the judge. "I don't know what got into me. I was so surprised at his rebuke, I just exploded."

"Tom, it seems to me there might be more going on here than I understand. What is it?"

"I think I better not share my current thoughts, your Honor. What I am thinking is so outrageous I am afraid to even think it."

"You do what you think right, Tom. You know you have my support, but keep in mind, Bill Sherman is respected here, even if he's not always understood. It might also be that his congregation really is talking about you and Mary. But, you'll know best how you need to deal with that."

Tom left the dining room. In that exchange with Sherman, Tom had seen a new truth. The tone of the pastor's voice, the rebuke, the condemnation attached to the relationship of Tom and Mary, all added to Tom's certainty; it was something in the pastor's voice, the sharpness in the answer, the unexpected confluence of voice and body language that brought Tom to a new understanding. In that one minute, Tom saw the man before him in a new light. He had a clear image that had been cloudy just a moment before.

It was circumstantial, but there was no question in Tom's mind. He knew William Tecumseh Sherman, pastor of the meek Baptists, shepherd of their flock, the quiet and under-dressed man who hovered quietly in small crowds— Pastor Sherman was the serial killer. Deep in his gut, Tom knew Pastor Sherman was the man who had been wreaking havoc in this otherwise quiet rural community.

It made no real sense, of course. There was no reason on earth for Tom to connect Pastor Sherman to Max Bauer, or to the recent deaths in Chippewa County. It was foolhardy for Tom to jump to such conclusions. Just because the minister had rebuked him—just because Clifford Heinrich had some feeling of unease about the man. It made no sense, but in his gut Tom was certain William Tecumseh Sherman was the son born through incest and fathered by his own grandfather Maximillian Bauer. But, how could Tom prove such a fantastical theory—to himself, let alone in a court of law? What grand stretch of the imagination made Tom believe he could find a connection between the mild minister and a family vendetta stretching back nearly a hundred years?

Who could think, let alone believe, that the meek pastor with his threadbare clothes and bad haircut could have survived in the undeveloped Minnesota wilderness as a child, then wreaked death across half a state over who knew how many years? Nothing in Bill Sherman's demeanor gave the slightest indication he could have survived in the wilderness as a child. Until the outburst at coffee this morning, Tom had never seen or heard anything that might indicate the minister had even a single violent gene in his entire body.

This man who stood before his congregation, and before God, could not possibly be the conscious-less killer who had crushed Arne Thorson's skull, had attacked Art Iverson and Inga Clauson, had shot Bobbie Swan in the motel room, and so recently killed George Stavopolis. Could he?

Could this mild pastor also be responsible for the death of the sheep farmer? That thought alone was a wild and demented theory. That violent death had occurred some forty years ago. Could Pastor Sherman really have viciously killed his own mother and grandmother by nailing shut their cabin door before he set it afire nearly fifty years ago, then disappearing to heaven-knows-where for decades before showing up in Montevideo, Minnesota as a Baptist minister?

"The wicked shall reap the reward of God's vengeance," he had snapped. Pastor Sherman had visibly reddened when Tom had spoken of Arne's death. The pastor's jaw had clenched at that comment. Then, unconsciously, without any apparent thought, he had taken a packet of gum from his pocket as he had stood and started to leave. With small motions he tore the gum from the wrapper, crushing the frail foil into a tight ball. He began to throw it into the wastebasket, but had second thoughts, putting it instead into his pocket before storming from the restaurant.

As he recalled the earlier encounter, that simple innocent move—changing his mind about the scrap of paper, the momentary flash of his eyes—had been the catalyst that made Tom jump to his wild conclusion. In that one moment Tom recognized the look of an animal, barely escaping a trap. It was a look that should never been expressed by a mild-mannered minister. Although it was completely illogical, Tom no longer had any doubt about the pastor's guilt. He did have one new and very serious concern, however. Did Pastor Sherman suspect that Tom had discovered his horrible secret? If so, what might the pastor do to protect himself?

Tom's encounter with the Baptist minister had begun innocently enough. Now, his mind raced as he thought about the encounter in the restaurant. He certainly had not expected his breakfast with the judge to erupt in a conflict with the pastor. At least on the surface there was no reason to think of Bill Sherman as anything other than a small-town minister. In his subconscious however, Tom had developed some questions about pastor Sherman. What had attracted Tom's attention to the pastor? Was it that momentary look of panic? What had he said and what other mannerisms set Tom on this path of questions? How did the pastor of this small congregation spend his time, Tom now wondered? The only times he saw the pastor was when Tom met with Judge Chamberlin. It seemed an unusual coincidence that the pastor apparently had no social life, had no friends, male or female. How could it be that the pastor had no social life whatsoever?

When recalling pastor Sherman's sermons, Tom thought there was a narrow and often repeated pattern: the sin of adultery, the sin of dishonesty, the sin of pride, the sin of greed, God's retribution when sins went unrepented. Was this pattern typical in the retinue of Baptist liturgy? *Sin, sin, sin, repent, repent, repent, retribution, always retribution.* Tom thought not.

In addition, Tom felt certain the sermons were directed not just to the congregation in general, but to certain individuals in the audience. Hard looks, frowns and tightened jaws impacted the pastor's speech as he gazed across his congregation on Sunday morning. And, recently he was sure he himself had been the target of comments about fornication, pride and retribution. *What was that about?*

As Tom had excused himself, the judge continued to sit over his coffee, staring into the room, with no apparent thoughts on his mind, but with several questions forming there.

Now, with his thoughts reeling, Tom walked slowly along Main Street. Past Tomhave Drug with its windows alive with small glittering Christmas lights, then Ekbergs', the men's furnishings store, which always seemed to Tom to be a little high priced. He paused a moment in front of the huge Montgomery Ward store, with its two floors of merchandise, containing everything a family might want or need, then he continued down the street. He was walking toward the train depot with no purpose in mind, but he felt a need to reach out and touch Mary, who at this moment would be collecting mail from the morning train.

He passed the Coast-to-Coast store, then waved as young Dickie Canton emerged from the J.C. Penny store across the street. Dickie had recovered from his shove off the college ski jump last year, but still favored the broken arm he had gotten from Timmy Coyle's shove.

The light powdering of snow should have cheered Tom, but his new revelation weighed heavily on his mind. *"How in the world do I deal with this? I know I need to tell Mary, but how do I explain my belief? Oh, my God!"* he thought, *"If Bill Sherman really is Boyd Bauer, does that mean Mary might be in danger?"* The over-riding question now, Tom knew, was whether Bill/Boyd knew of Tom's suspicion. *"Time would tell, he knew; but would it tell in time?"*

Thirty-Eight

TOM HAD TO talk to Mary. He knew that was going to be complicated. How do you say, *"I think the pastor of your church is a murderer. I think your pastor is an imposter. Well, no, I do not have any proof, but I feel certain Bill Sherman and Boyd Bauer are the same person. And, yes, I know how ridiculous that sounds, but what if I am right?"*

On the other hand, what if I'm wrong? Think of the hornets' nest I will have stirred up. Imagine a whole congregation startled by the accusation, then told, *"never mind; guess I was wrong. I just jumped to that conclusion because of"...of what? What made me so certain of his guilt that I would accuse an innocent, if somewhat strange acting man of leading a double life and of being a serial killer?"*

Tom continued his trek down Main Street, smiling and greeting shoppers he met, lapsing into his thoughts in quiet moments. The world around him seemed wrapped in Christmas spirit, but at the moment Tom could not quite embrace the holiday season. He was worried about the mystery of Boyd Bauer and Bill Sherman. As Tom was about to open the depot door a gust of wind drove a blanket of icy snow intro his face. All of a sudden, he thought, *"how like my winter here to retrieve Ernie's body. I never expected another deadly winter in Montevideo, Minnesota."*

This time it could be worse, Tom thought. If Bill Sherman really is Boyd Bauer, he is a real threat; not just to the community, but to me personally. If Bill is really Boyd, he cannot allow me to continue probing like I have been. But, maybe I am wrong.

And, what about Mary; is she in danger? If Bill Sherman sees me as a threat he might also feel threatened by my relationship with Mary. Not just that I might confide in her; his comments about our living a sinful life might just be the surface of his anger and his need to seek God's retribution.

Tom kept his concerns to himself as he and Mary walked back up the street. Mary bubbled, laughed, and waved to everyone she knew, and she knew many, many shoppers. He thought it best to keep his concerns to himself for the moment and decided not to share his concerns with Mary or the judge for the time being. Risky, he knew, if he was correct. But, he was developing a plan. He believed Mary was safe from harm for the time being.

As they walked arm in arm, Tom shared his plan. "I'm going to Minneapolis tomorrow. No, I'm not driving. The weather and the roads are too unpredictable, so I'm going to take the train."

"Will you be gone long, Tom? I miss you, when you're gone for even a day. And, Christmas is so close. I just want to share it all with you."

"I won't be more than a couple of days," Tom answered. "I'll drive to Benson and take the train straight into Minneapolis. I can stay at the Minnesota Hotel, just a few blocks away, and take a streetcar any place I need to go. I just have to confirm a couple of things that have been bothering me."

"You be careful, Tom. And, don't forget, the Christmas program at the church is Sunday evening. I'd love to go, and of course, I want you to be there with me."

Tom gave a little shudder. Would the mystery be solved by then? Probably not, he thought. And, was the congregation really abuzz over Tom and Mary's relationship? Would there be polite smiles on Sunday, or would the Baptists shut them out, frowning and scolding Mary by turning their backs as she and Tom tried to join the festivities?"

"Listen, Mary, I have to do this. I'll get back as soon as I can. I'm sure I'll be back before Sunday."

Mary turned and looked into Tom's eyes. Was that worry she saw? Probably not, she thought. That would be so unlike him. She stepped in close, slid her arms around him. The snow was now heavier but floating softly onto them. It was just as it should be, right before Christmas. She tilted her head upward. There was a twinkle in her eyes, and she smiled. "Let's get your car and sneak off to my place. Lunch can wait."

Tom was easily convinced. A few minutes later he guided the little Ford coupe out of its parking space, then turned up Main Street. There was just enough snow to make the tires crunch but not enough to make the drive difficult. Tom's problem was that Mary could not keep her hands off him. She leaned up and kissed his ear, ran her fingers through his hair, tickled him by sliding her hand inside his warm winter coat. The car moved easily up Main Street, then Tom turned up Second Street hill, turned on Black Oak Avenue, and followed it to the edge of town, A left turn, a right turn, and another right turn, brought them to Mary's driveway.

By the time Tom stopped the car they were laughing and poking each other's ribs. They ran into the house, tracking snow as they ran. It took only moments to drop their coats on the floor and kick off shoes that were wet from the ankle-deep snow. They never got past the living room. Kissing and clutching at each other they fell to the floor. Piece by piece, without regard for anything but each other, they shed their clothes and threw themselves into a frantic embrace.

Neither Tom nor Mary knew if it was minutes or hours later that they lay wrapped in each other's arms. They snuggled comfortably on the floor for a few minutes more, then Tom rose, picked Mary up in his arms and carried her to the huge soft bed at the end of the hall, where they made love for a second, more gentle time.

They missed lunch. They missed supper, they laid in the now darkened bedroom, touching, nuzzling and kissing for hours, each thinking only of how wonderful it was to be in love. In their ardor they also missed the shadow thrown alongside the house, cast by a somber figure who watched them, then moved stealthily down the driveway.

Thirty-Nine

BILL SHERMAN HAD not always been in the ministry. His life had been ordinary he thought, but in the war he had found new meaning to life. With death and agony on all sides he thought frequently of God. He came to God, when under a heavy barrage of German artillery, his life was spared. All around him the trenches were littered with mangled corpses, men who watched their lives drain into the pools of their own blood. Corporal Sherman was spared, while he was surrounded by gore and mayhem.

Bill Sherman was not unscathed, however. He would spend two weeks in the hospital. He would leave a small part of himself in a muddy trench somewhere in France, but he would surely live.

When one of the last German barrages was fired, Sherman would be hospitalized with shrapnel in his right arm. The last section of two fingers of that hand were missing as a result of a six-inch long piece of fiery steel shrapnel that would have taken his life if its trajectory had been just a few inches left. A nasty laceration along the crown of his head, although nicely repaired, would leave a faint scar. When he awoke in the hospital, his arm—minus the fingers—was suspended from an overhead cradle and his head was wrapped in gauze from crown to neck. It was then he recognized that only God could have saved him, and that God surely had a mission for him to fulfill.

In the bed to his left another corporal, Clifford Heinrich, lay with a severe concussion. He had a plethora of bruises from being thrown into the air from another explosion, but no other apparent damages. The two soldiers were bed neighbors for the next two weeks. Heinrich was in and out of consciousness for several days before he began to hear and see again, and there was a constant roar in his ears.

Each nurse seemed to be two women, slipping into focus for brief moments.

Corporal Sherman was cared for by a no-nonsense nurse who fed him and steadied him through his daily ablutions. In their moments of shared lucidity, Heinrich and Sherman exchanged whispered stories, or croaked their joy at being alive, even though somewhat damaged. They spoke softly of their homes; somewhere in Kansas for Sherman, while Heinrich aspired only to get home to Minnesota. Sherman was effusive in declaring his love for God and his plan to dedicate his life to singing God's praises. Occasionally Sherman's voice would falter as he praised his savior, a slight stutter that perhaps came from the explosion that put him in the hospital.

When Corporal Heinrich returned from his shower one morning, Corporal Sherman was gone. The nurse had written a note from him to Heinrich, thanking him and offering God's blessing in his future life.

After recovering from his battlefield wounds, the zealous Bill Sherman had been transported across the English Channel, then after another week in a British hospital, he hobbled up the gangway of a troop ship for the final voyage back to the United States.

At first, he drifted across Kansas and Nebraska, and then northward into Iowa. With no surviving family, there was no need to return to his roots. He went where God called him. He spent a week here and a month there, assisting small parish leaders as they offered what help was available to their communities. Months became years. As he travelled, he formed the habit of keeping a diary.

Nights which might have been lonely, instead became moments of reflection, as he sang God's praises and recorded the experiences of his life in his journal. Bill Sherman found peace as he recalled small Christian victories. In the moments of pleasant reflection he made occasional notes of his hours in battle and gave thanks that God spared his humble life. From time to time he reflected on his wounds, his hospitalization, and the short-lived friendship of corporal Clifford Heinrich.

By the time he arrived in Sioux City, Iowa his status had risen from friendly volunteer to pastor's assistant, and then to lay minister. He never sought or received official recognition in the ministry, but always served God in the best ways he could achieve. Academics and documentation seemed unnecessary in a world where God's servants could be counted on without some official recognition.

Bill Sherman gloried in his role as lay minister. He assisted in church services, offering communion as the local pastor spoke comforting words of love and redemption. Eventually, the congregation and the staff at the Mission just called him Pastor Sherman or Reverend Sherman, and other respectful titles. The Mission was, in fact, just a warehouse on the east side of the military road paralleling the Missouri River, and was just one among a dozen buildings going to ruin. With the war's end, manufacturing war equipment ceased but was slowly being replaced by the need to provide machinery for America's burgeoning farm economy. Unfortunately, the middle years of the 1920's were seeing the beginnings of drought in many prairie states.

It was at the Mission Bill Sherman found his true calling. This spring the Missouri River roared out of the north, splitting Iowa from South Dakota and Nebraska as the raging water flowed over its banks before winding its way across Kansas, on the way to joining the Mississippi River. The Missouri River had been the highway used by traders, trappers, and explorers for a hundred years. As it moved across the plains now, it carried silt, gigantic trees and commerce, both upstream and down.

The river and the adjoining lands also provided opportunities for travelers seeking new lives for themselves. River-trade was mostly seasonal, and it was hard labor for little gain during the best of times. Because of the economic crash and the drought which devastated the plains states for a decade, even those opportunities were becoming hard to find. History would play up the 1929 stock market crash, but the hard times began on the prairie and the northern states of Iowa and Minnesota as early as 1921.

As the Great War was ending, America's farmers were reaping the rewards from lands turned from native grasses into thousands of acres of shallow-ground crops such as oats, corn, flax and corn. The factories which had been producing machinery at a record pace by the end of the war were not so lucky. There was no demand for war implements, and for those manufacturers cash flows declined. When uncommon dry years engulfed the prairie states, the farmers who had so recently enjoyed prosperity, were finding they could no longer pay for new equipment. Ultimately, they could not even pay the taxes on their farms.

By the 1930s, nearly one-half of America still lived on farms. As the dust bowl spread and the economy weakened, whole families found themselves homeless, indigent, and desperate. In all directions the future looked dim. The Missouri River turned to the northwest just north of Sioux City. Because the developing riverside highway reached a bottleneck right in the heart of Sioux City, the city was also a collecting point for a rough and tumble scattering of men who had little regard for local citizens, for the law, or even the rules of God-like behavior.

It was there, in that slum of humanity, that Bill Sherman saw the greatest need for his love of mankind. He spent uncounted days and nights among the roughest and most undisciplined men, trying to quell fights and soothe violent tempers. He brought warm coats and blankets, he brought produce he had begged from local merchants, and most important to him—he brought the word and love of God to those in need.

By March of 1927, Bill Sherman was an integral part of the Mission in Sioux City. His love for his fellow man kept him busy, either in the mission or in the hobo camps along the river. Some days he wondered how he could continue being cheerful when he was not cheered by his surroundings. Some nights he railed, wailed of God's great love for humanity, even though there was so much misery around him. In spite of his zeal, he wondered at times if God did really exist.

For nearly two weeks Bill Sherman had come every day to the miserable camp along the Missouri River. Some of the men cried in thanks when he came with a coat or a blanket to make their night a little more bearable as they prayed together for salvation in any form. Bill Sherman knew he was doing good. He knew that as he preached God's love he sometimes got through to an occasional man, who only an hour before had seemed to be losing all hope.

One man in particular had attracted Bill's attention. In this camp of despairing humanity, there was one man who seemed to be seeking God's word, seeking understanding of how God worked. This new relationship kept Bill's morale just a bit above abysmal. The two men were of the same age and both were veterans of the Great War. When Bill gave the other man his attention late at night, when all the others had retreated to their shelters, these two huddled around the fire, caught up in discussing God.

Some nights this vagrant traveler was cheerful and receptive to God's word. Other nights he seemed on the edge of violence. On those nights his response to Bill's guidance then was thrown back with violent expletives. "Why has God not shown me mercy and grace? How long must I live in the wilderness, scratching for food and shelter, when so many others have riches and refinements?"

Bill tried his best to make the unhappy man understand his plight was only temporary and throughout the bible men had questioned God's love, only to find it did indeed exist if they would just continue to have faith. He felt particularly good this night. It was going to be the last time he would visit the hobo camp. Tomorrow he would begin a new life. As an example of the rewards that come with having faith, he took from his coat pocket the letter he had received only days before.

"I have been wandering the prairie since the end of the Great War," Sherman began. "At times I lost faith and cried out to God for some sign that I was worthy, that my wandering might cease. I love God, and I love bringing his word to men like you, but some days I found it nearly impossible to continue." He took the letter from the envelope and slowly unfolded it. He leaned toward the fire and read it aloud. It was a gift from God he wanted to share with his new companion.

"I received this letter last week. Tomorrow I will be on my way to a new life. I thought my good news might give you hope that your own troubles might soon find an end."

"Dear Bill," the hand-written letter began. *"I am attaching a letter of recommendation for your use. Today I responded to Avery Kohr, an acquaintance from Montevideo, Minnesota, inquiring if I could assist in their search for a minister to replace their recently deceased pastor. Avery had contacted me a week ago and I immediately thought of you. Your zeal and your willingness to dedicate your life to God, in spite of your own hardships, has left no question in my mind as to whether you are the right choice for their community. I have taken the liberty of assuring Avery that you will make the journey to Minnesota, even though you and I have not discussed that decision.*

"Our Mission here has been blessed to have you for so long, But, this is a move you must make, so I am leaving you no other option than to accept their offer. The Sisters of Mercy and I wish you God's blessing as you continue to serve God."

Bill Sherman leaned back, sitting quietly as he folded the letter and returned it to his inner pocket. In spite of the chill of the late night he felt a warm glow. Yes, he was happy and even proud of his good fortune. And yes, he knew it might have been slightly sinful to boast of his good fortune, but he was certain the man across from him would find the letter inspiring, find in Bill's good fortune the possibility that he also would be blessed with some good fortune.

Bill continued to talk, enjoying the opportunity to let his hair down, to speak of his own dreams for his future. In his excitement, he did not notice that his companion was no longer responding but was shrinking into his heavy coat. In the darkness he did not see the fire building in the other man's eyes, or the clenching of his fists. He did not know that the more he spoke of his good fortune, the harder it was for the other man to listen.

It was unfair, thought Sherman's companion. It was another insult put on a man who deserved so much more. If he—instead of the pious shit of a country pastor—had gotten that letter, there would be some justice in the world. If he had gotten the recommendation to move from this decrepit hobo jungle, he could smile and ramble on just as Bill Sherman was doing. But no, God had not yet given him a sign, or a blessing, or any hope for a future. He was going to be left here in this cluster of trees beside the raging Missouri River. He would have another day, or another month, or even another year of wandering aimlessly, with no hope for the good fortune of a letter from some stranger offering him a new and better life. This prissy minister, with his simpering smile, would go off in the morning to a new life, while he would once again disappear, as if he had never existed.

The revelation came slowly. It began with the anger that Bill Sherman would be gone to a new life the next morning, while he would still be cold and damp in the camp along the river. In addition to the anger, there came jealousy. He could just as well have been chosen, couldn't he? Bill Sherman was a war veteran, but so was he. Bill Sherman had moved from town to town before coming to Sioux City, Iowa; so had he. In only a few days Bill Sherman would arrive in Montevideo, Minnesota, and although a stranger, he would be welcomed. He would leave his past behind and start a new life.

Now his brain was afire. The plan jumped into his mind, became a reality in only a few moments. "I can't believe your good fortune, Bill. You deserve it, of course. Just think how it will change your life." He was suddenly cheerful, wishing Bill the best of luck. "Do you think I could see your letter?"

After hesitating for only a moment, Bill offered him the envelope and the letter which was going to change his life. It actually made Bill feel a little better as he watched the other man slowly unfold the letter and begin reading it aloud. After holding it and thoughtfully gazing into the fire, the letter was replaced in the envelope and offered to Bill.

Bill leaned forward, stretching to his right in order to avoid the fire between the two men. As he was about to take the envelope there was a sudden rush. The other man lunged forward, withdrawing the envelope as he swung a gritty rock the size of a small muskmelon into the side of Bill's head. One blow was all that was needed. Bill's temple was no challenge for the rock that left him lifeless in just that split second.

The plan that developed was simple. Bill Sherman would be stripped naked, his body slid into the raging Missouri River. With any luck, by morning the current would have carried him well past Sioux City. To be sure there would be no recognition, his face was given a half-dozen additional blows, removing any trace of facial expressions. A quick and stealthy trip to the mission would retrieve Bill Sherman's briefcase and suitcase, so handily ready for travel. Everything needed to become Bill Sherman was right there. By morning, a dozen or more miles north of Rapid City, there would be a train that would spirit him out of Iowa. He would find a quiet town, spend a few days while he became familiar with Bill Sherman's trappings, then continue on to Montevideo, Minnesota.

From this moment, the pastor travelling to Minnesota would be known as reverend William Tecumseh Sherman, not Bill Sherman. An unidentifiable body tumbling in the raging Missouri River would remain a mystery forever. Boyd Bauer, veteran, itinerant traveler, murderer of his own family, would also disappear.

Forty

REVEREND WILLIAM TECUMSEH Sherman, pastor, spiritual leader to a doting congregation. It felt good, it even felt right. "*I have been a good leader here,*" he thought out loud.

Pastor Sherman should have been preparing his Sunday sermon, but instead he sat staring into the darkened room. His thoughts flashed from anger, to fear, to unexplained elation. In the decade he had been pastor in Montevideo no one had spoken to him as Tom Hall had done today. As the leader of his congregation, he knew he was responsible for protecting their souls from evil. It was his responsibility to correct those who strayed, to reprimand, slap on the fingers as it were, parishioners who were putting their eternal souls in jeopardy.

As pastor, he had offered a sympathetic ear many times. He had offered guidance to a wife whose husband had strayed and to more than one husband who drank the family's grocery money instead of bringing it home at the end of an unrewarding week of mindless or underappreciated labors.

It had taken some time for Reverend William Tecumseh Sherman to meld with the Montevideo congregation. He had arrived a stranger, with no wife, in a community where single adults were rare. He came with the sparest wardrobe, but in fact looked the part of a middle-aged Baptist missionary, a man who had foregone wealth for a life serving God.

Life as a small-town minister was not bad, the pastor thought. His first weeks in Montevideo had been a little shaky, but his nervousness and his mistakes had been attributed to shyness and the discomfort of a new life in a new community. They knew the rough edges would wear smooth as the new pastor settled into his new routine.

Reverend William Tecumseh Sherman; he occasionally had to remind himself he was no longer Boyd Bauer. That man was as dead as the body he had pushed over the bank and into the Missouri River. He knew it would be only a matter of time before he became comfortable, reading aloud from a bible in front of the congregation, making analogies that made sense of some scriptures. He was now a leader, after all. When he spoke, his shy demeanor made his words all the more believable. "Blessed are the meek," was all the more believable because this new minister was meek. "Thou shall not covet," could not be questioned, because the pastor never showed signs of envy. Meek conservative Pastor William Tecumseh Sherman soon fit in very well.

In his large leather brief case, the pastor's notebook had provided an entire year's celebrations and sermons conveniently scheduled by the notebook's previous owner. Every Sunday was described. The motivations, the homilies that would draw the congregation together were all there. Songs to be sung were listed, as were the motivations needed for symmetry and for the mutual comfort of pastor and congregation. The notebook and other contents of the briefcase had provided all that had been needed to guide him in his new career. It had all had been carefully and lovingly laid out by the man he had replaced.

Also in the briefcase was the diary, carefully recording a life in the service of God. Was diary-keeping unmanly? No. God's shepherd should document days of joy, nights of fear, or hours when life was uncertain. Bill Sherman's life in the Great War was clearly noted, along with his travels, his moments of joy and the frequently lonely nights. Now, ten years later, the pastor read and re-read the diary, reminding himself who he was, and how he had become pastor of Montevideo's First Baptist Church.

The journey for Boyd Bauer, now the Reverend William Tecumseh Sherman, had been long and fraught with anxiety. It was not the miles between Sioux City, Iowa, and Montevideo, which were not that many. It was the transition he had to make; from being a vagrant living outside the law, to the man of God, who would soon be judged by a close community of Christians. One day, he was a vagrant with no history and no hope for the future—the next day, he had to become a new man. There was no training period, as there had been when he enlisted in the army. The new day had to begin with a new man.

By sunrise, the newly imagined pastor was hunkered down in the corner of a freight car in a train heading north and eventually, far from Sioux City. The train's destination was not important; he just needed to get away from Sioux City and the potential problems waiting there. His destination was less than two hundred miles away but may as well have been on another continent. Before arriving in Montevideo he needed a long-overdue shave and bath. He needed to be presentable when he introduced himself to Avery Kohr. More important than anything, however, he had to become William Tecumseh Sherman. In the suitcase and the large briefcase were all the tools and trappings to help make the change. In those bags were the only props available to make the change real and correct.

The locomotive lurched its way north, never achieving great speed, but never stopping, as it passed through the small prairie towns. At mid-day, as the train was leaving a small town, he threw his bags to the right-of-way and dropped to the gravel, then retrieved the bags and walked back the way he had come. There was a nondescript hotel just across form the depot and for two dollars he took a room. Fortunately, the previous Reverend Sherman had saved some money, which the new and current pastor needed to use judiciously.

Fortunately, during his time with Alice Bevins, years ago, Boyd had learned to read and write with reasonable skill. It was a skill he had seldom used, but for the next twenty-four hours he read and re-read every document and note in the two bags. He used the notepad in the briefcase to practice writing. It was the single skill that needed the most improvement. The shower and shave right after checking in made him feel like the new man he was to become; the shower and shave he took just before checking out confirmed his new role and gave him confidence that this ruse might work. He took a late-in-the day Trailways bus to Watertown, South Dakota, where he would spend another night studying and fretting over the great lie he was going to perpetuate.

He also prayed to God—several times—practicing contriteness. After all, how could that hurt if he was going to immerse himself in this new life? He prayed for guidance, not forgiveness. He believed nothing he had done in his previous life could have been considered sinful. The food and clothing he had stolen were needed more by him than the previous owners; the violence and the deaths he had perpetuated were necessary for his survival. Amen to that.

Surely, those actions were not sins. His wretched mother and grandmother were already living in sin when they died. Hadn't they killed his father for no reason at all? The stupid sheep farmer should have just kept his mouth shut and let Boyd enjoy the tender lamb, instead of ragging-on about what a bad person Boyd was. And, that couple in the woods, the unfortunate loss he suffered when his opponent proved too strong for him to overcome. Well, she would have been an enjoyable diversion and she obviously was inclined to commit the sin of adultery, so where was the sin?

He prayed for strength and for wisdom to make good decisions. He still felt anger when he thought of the fiasco along the river, when that naked red-head had tossed him into the rocks, knocking him unconscious. He knew she would have enjoyed sex with him as well as the stupid guy she was with. Sometimes, however, the best laid plans go amiss, he thought.

He had a whole new life to live now, and all of that unpleasantness was behind him. In closing his prayers he made one last request of God. Now that he was a new man, surely God could find a way to punish those miserable, self-serving Iverson's for all the grief and tribulation he had to bear for his entire life. *"Just see that they are punished, God. That's all I ask."*

William Tecumseh Sherman's transition into his new life and into the fabric of the community was shaky in the beginning, but the small community seemed to like their new minister. He met all the important citizens and learned in short order who was not really a good Christian. After all, who better to recognize that, than a man with his own experience?

In his zeal to reach Montevideo, he had not noticed that he was close to the scenes of his previous violence. The unsuccessful encounter with the couple in the farm grove was already more than twenty years in the past. The eighteen miles from Montevideo to Milan was still a long journey when he arrived in Chippewa County in 1927. New Ulm was still further, in both miles and time. The decades spent wandering the countryside, just trying to survive, were now only vague memories which had retreated into the recesses of his mind. Even his encounter with the army recruiter in Benson was twenty years in the past. The memories of those years erased by war and more wandering in the wilderness. As he made the journey north, the pastor had visions of his wandering that were like those of Moses wandering the desert. The pastor was certain his old life was far away from his new home.

The violence had been left behind. Pastor Sherman gained respect in his new community. He was proud, not too proud he hoped, but proud to gain the trust of his congregation. He dressed simply and he was well-groomed. He became the guiding light in the First Baptist Church in Montevideo. He never heard a bad phrase uttered about him or his ability; he preached against sin, offered communion, and offered guidance to those in need.

Forty-One

LIFE IN MONTEVIDEO was relatively uneventful for Reverend Sherman. His needs were simple, inexpensive, easily achieved. He occasionally thought of Alice Bevins, of the love and the carnal pleasure she brought into his life. He certainly had to thank her for extending his reading and writing skills. There were some days and—some nights—he was overcome by a loneliness he had not known in all the years he skulked in the shadows.

Perhaps the loneliness came from being so close to all the congregation and observing their family lives, seeing the intimacy that they did not try to hide, and which left him with a hollow feeling. It was now 1937 and he had now been in Montevideo ten years. Boyd Bauer no longer inhabited the minister's body; he was Reverend William Tecumseh Sherman now. But, sometimes the pastor missed the soft curves Alice had shared with the man he used to be.

From time to time he met a woman who attracted his attention. He did not know how a man of the cloth was supposed to approach a religious woman. He had no idea how a Baptist minister might suggest they enter into a relationship that ultimately would lead to carnal relations. His social skills had been retarded by the years of solitude. Ten years in the ministry had not resolved that problem. Alice had come to him, not just suggesting they co-habit, but seducing him on their very first night together. They had enjoyed each other's bodies and had found joy; not just working together, but also in bed, where she had taught Boyd things he had never imagined.

But the bible did not explain how a man might broach that subject. What if the woman rejected him? Would she tell the community of his carnal desires? Would she and her friends laugh at his amateurish attempt at seduction? In the end, he fought back his desires, kept lustful thoughts under control, even though his anger and frustration grew greater as he saw others surrendering to their desires.

By 1930 the depression and drought were taking a toll on the country; Minnesota was no exception. At first he thought he might be sent away. The congregation tightened its communal belt as times grew more difficult. Tithing not-withstanding, the weekly collection dwindled from a rustle to a tinkle. The church council, however, assured their pastor that he was needed by the flock and his needs would be met until the quality of life improved. In 1932 the council provided him with a year-old Chevrolet sedan. He was needed, and that transportation would help him reach out to the rural members of the congregation.

The pastor nursed his automobile through the summers and winters as he made calls around the county on a limited basis. Until now, he had not realized how big the county was. During quiet Tuesdays, or Wednesdays, as he thought about the coming sermon, he visited Milan, Watson, Wegdahl and Clara City.

It was a Saturday, however, when he made the drive to Benson. Something, some bit of nostalgia, drew him the thirty miles north to revisit the place he had enlisted in the army. In Benson, he was at first nervous. It was here he had leapt from a train and within hours was in the U.S. Army. He laughed nervously to himself as he realized it had been nearly fourteen years ago he last visited here. His entire life had changed that day. For a moment, he remembered the farm with the dog, and the Clauson farm with its pretentious sign by the road. And, he remembered the luscious young woman in the grove, just out of his reach, as it turned out.

Visions of Inga Clauson still flooded his brain as he decided to have lunch in Benson. Oh, how long ago that night seemed, how luscious she would have been, if he had been successful in defeating the man with her. Art *Something*, he remembered now. But, that was all in the past.

The Corner Café was just across the street from the train depot. It seemed like the place a minister could have lunch without spending too much money. He took a booth against the wall, nearer the kitchen than the front door. Maybe it was an old habit carried from his past life. He liked to see who came through the door. His own cooking was mediocre at best, and he decided to splurge on a roast beef dinner, with mashed potatoes, green beans, whole wheat bread, coffee and apple pie. There had been months and years when such extravagance would have been unthinkable. Even today, he gave serious thought to the decision.

Perhaps he had expected a motherly woman to take his order, maybe even a grandmotherly woman. What he got, however, was an eyeful of voluptuous red-haired beauty. The young woman who waited on him, obviously in her twenties, dressed more like a movie star than a country waitress. She smiled a gigantic toothy smile and as she asked for his order she threw one hip to the side, which exaggerated the luscious shape of her figure and her flat stomach. When she waited for him to order the pastor wanted to forget the roast beef and tell her he wanted her. He wanted just her, right in the booth, or if necessary, on the table. Even the floor in front of the booth would be a perfect place for them to share the rest of their lives as he ravaged her and shared with her the secrets he had been taught by Alice, so long ago.

Instead, he mumbled his desire for roast beef, beans, coffee and pie. She seemed to not notice him blush. Instead, she just murmured in a throaty near-whisper, "I'll get that for you right away. My name is Laura, if there's anything else you want, just call my name." As she turned to the kitchen, Reverend William Tecumseh Sherman became, for just a moment, Boyd Bauer. He imagined he could see her creamy skin right through the tight skirt she wore, he could feel her firm breasts, which threatened to burst from her blouse. He could hear her moaning, just like Alice Bevins had as he made love to her, thrusting himself time after time until they both collapsed, their passion satiated.

It turned out to be just the roast beef dinner, however. Although she smiled warmly as she placed his dinner in front of him, and although her breasts, obviously unencumbered by anything other than the blouse, pushed hear his face for a dangerous moment, his only desert was the pie. As good as it tasted, Boyd Bauer needed more than pie.

As he nursed his way through the roast beef, the potatoes, the beans and the pie, he overheard laughter and joyous talk from the kitchen. Laura was saying, "I have a date with Arne tonight. God, he is so hot. I just love being with him." More laughing, whispering and giggling kept him distracted as he ate. "We're going to Busters, that place by Watson—where they built the new dam." More whispers and giggles. "…some band; farmers from Milan, I guess. Arne says they're spectacular. I really don't care as long as we have a… good time." Boyd could imagine what the pause meant.

Eventually, he knew he had to leave, walk out the door and forget her. He left a quarter tip. Twenty-five cents was plenty, he knew. Highway 29 was a straight drive back to Montevideo, just over an hour away. *"I have to go home and polish my sermon for tomorrow. Forget the woman, forget the carnal pleasure she might have promised."*

His dreary little house on Fourth Street, just a block from the church didn't welcome him today. Its faded paint, worn linoleum, and shabby furniture, screamed out at his poverty and his confinement to the norms of the small town. In the ice box, he found a partial quart of milk and drank as if it was his last drink before being crucified, just as Jesus had been crucified. Stale bread waited in the breadbox on the dingy kitchen counter. His supper was bologna, just on the verge of turning green, and mustard generously applied on the stale bread helped him choke down the miserable meal. Desert tonight would not be another piece of the rich pie, but a handful of dried prunes, kept in a jar in the cupboard next to the sink.

He ate as he sat on the threadbare mohair couch with its springs just starting to poke through. He cried, then laughed, then screamed to God to help him through another miserable night. "Just let me be loved somewhere, by someone, God! I deserve more than this miserable lonely life." It was the first time since coming to Montevideo that he had looked into his dark soul. He cried some more.

He fell asleep with the bologna sandwich only half eaten and woke again just as the sun was setting. The house was stifling hot. It was a hot August night and there was no such thing as air conditioning in a small rural town. He thought perhaps a drive around town might at make him feel cooler.

He didn't know exactly how he got there, but an hour later his drab Chevrolet was parked alongside the road, just above Buster's Roadhouse .The pastor just sat there for an hour as cars passed by. Buster's was no place for a man of God to be seen. In fact, it was no place for any man, or any woman for that matter. Everyone knew sin just fermented in places like Buster's, but he thought perhaps he could look in a window, see if Arne had really brought the beautiful young woman here. The roadhouse was a sinful place and could only lead to more sin if they actually came here. The noise was terrifying. The fiddles, the guitar strumming a steady beat, and the redhaired drunk with the harmonica, blasted tune after tune, while men and women whirled around the room.

He spotted her, held tightly against a tall good-looking man with a deep suntan and curly hair that just reached his collar. During slow dances, they were almost obscene, as they clenched each other in vulgar gyrations. When a polka or schottische played, they swung wildly across the floor, laughing and whispering what were obviously obscene words in each other's ears. They seemed to never stop. When would they stop? He couldn't take his eyes off the couple. Somewhere, during their last dance and just before midnight, Reverend Sherman disappeared. In his place outside Buster's stood an angry Boyd Bauer, with no other thought than to possess the sinful, carnal-inducing, red haired harlot in Arne Thorson's arms. The one with the innocent-sounding name. Laura.

Forty-Two

BOYD BAUER STAYED in the shadows as Arne and Laura left the roadhouse. Anyone who recognized him, would have wondered why Reverend Sherman was loitering outside Buster's. Had they seen the expression on the man's face they would have been very confused. That face belonged to Boyd Bauer, a man unknown in Chippewa County. It was a face distorted in anger. It took the amorous couple several minutes to get in the car. First, there was kissing and hugging, Arne pressing Laura's body hard against the side of the car. Their temperatures were up, and their sweaty bodies attracted each other like metal filings to a magnet. Then, by mutual consent, they slid into Arne's car. With some additional pawing at each other, they laughed as Arne drove from the parking area.

Boyd had no actual plan. He could force Arne's car off the road, kill Arne and attack Laura right there, but the danger to himself was too great. Arne, younger and obviously in better shape than he, might just win in a fight. In addition, his own automobile might be damaged in such an attack; obviously it was not a plan that guaranteed a good result for himself. He followed Arne's car at a distance, sometimes a half-mile behind, sometimes they were completely out of sight. They were easy to keep track of but following them was maddening. Arne's car weaved all over the road, certainly caused by Arne's lack of concentration as he and Laura pawed at each other.

As Boyd's car descended the grade ending in the Watson Sag, he saw the brake lights from Arne's car, bright for just a moment before all the car's lights went black. At the bottom of the hill, Boyd turned his own car lights off and coasted slowly, until he was a hundred yards from the darkened car he had been following. He edged his car onto a field approach road and sat quietly for several minutes before easing his door open, then quietly closing it when he was outside.

Although he could have just walked purposefully along the paved roadway, he chose to take quiet steps, pausing frequently as he padded through the summer grass on the road's shoulder. His years of living off the land, stalking game, easing into a back yard to steal what he needed to survive, made this an easy maneuver. His prey would soon be overcome, his demands met, even if he had to kill them both. Arne was going to end up dead for sure. Probably Laura as well. She was no longer the gorgeous woman in the café, the sultry seductress in the roadhouse; she was just the solution to his carnal needs, and she would be his—no matter the circumstances.

When he was alongside Arne's car, Boyd stopped. The car was still parked partly on the road. Its front wheels were tilted nearly over the road's shoulder, and the passenger-side door hung open. Boyd guessed the couple were too intent on their forthcoming sin to close it.

He followed the faint path along the river, carefully stepping over rocks jutting up in places. A short way along the path he crouched and looked for the couple who had disappeared into the night. There was enough light from the stars to make the small river glisten. The path alongside the stream disappeared just before the grove of trees where the river curved. Just ahead of him, Boyd could just make out the couple as they fell to the ground. They were naked as jays, they were frantic in their need to couple. Laura reached up to draw Arne to her, and as he settled to the grass above her, Boyd struck.

With a rock he had picked up along the trail, Boyd took Arne's life in a single blow. The couple had no idea Boyd was there. Why would they? Arne dropped heavily on top of Laura. Boyd began to roll the lifeless body aside, certain he would take his place before the woman beneath him could react. As he leaned forward to throw Arne's body aside, things went wrong for Boyd. Laura, not really knowing what was taking place, lurched to her feet and drove her shoulder into Boyd's side. He was thrown back towards the river, where he landed violently and smashed his head on a rock, then fell unconscious.

When he awoke, Boyd was alone with Arne's body. Laura was nowhere in sight. The man was dead, there was no question about it. In a panic, Boyd tried to think of his best move and decided to throw the body and the clothing into the river. Maybe, if his body were found, and it probably would be within days, it would be assumed he had come for a swim, removed his clothes, and died as a result of hitting a rock when he dived into the river. Yes, he thought, that makes sense.

Boyd was back in his car and heading for Montevideo in just minutes. He was sure the welt on his head would be gone by morning, or at least unnoticeable. Church service would be held as usual. He was sure the woman who had caused this had not seen his face. She was gone; Boyd was home free. As he drove, he worked extra hard to put lustful thoughts from his mind and concentrated on being the kind of man the congregation expected him to be.

Unfortunately, for Boyd, Laura had left a shoe in the grass and Tom Hall got lucky when he waited for the train in Benson a year and a half later.

Forty-Three

TOM WAS STRUGGLING with his new belief about the minister. He was not quite sure what to do next. Although he was certain that William Sherman and Boyd Bauer were one and the same, he hadn't figured out how to prove it. He was also concerned that if his suspicions were correct, there were new and possibly immediate concerns to worry about. Just believing that gum wrappers led to complicity, and just because the mild-mannered minister had become agitated over his relationship with Mary, was not enough to accuse a possibly innocent man of multiple murders.

Train service to Minneapolis was provided from Benson, just a thirty-three-mile drive from Montevideo and was a better option than driving more than one hundred miles on wintry roads. When Tom arrived at the Benson depot he found himself an hour and a half early for his departure. After purchasing a ticket, he wandered across the street, where he saw a ladies fashion store, a shoe store, a drug store, and a café on the corner. It was aptly named The Corner Café.

Since he could think of no reason to wander into any of the retailers, he thought a cup of coffee might be just the thing to consume some time. He took the booth next to the street-side windows. Winter looked better from in here, he thought. "I'm going to have just a coffee and a piece of that chocolate cake in the case," he began, without looking up, even before the waitress could ask for his order.

The waitress chuckled and responded, "You didn't waste any time thinking about that." She spun around and headed for the coffee pot. A minute later she set a steaming cup of coffee in front of Tom, who was absent-mindedly looking through the notebook he had taken from his jacket pocket.

When the waitress returned with his cake, Tom looked up for the first time. He almost jumped out of the booth. He stammered and stuttered; the waitress almost laughed aloud. Undoubtedly, she had experienced Tom's reaction from other men. Her response might have been caustic: "*what are you looking at?*" It might have been any number of things, but she just smiled and put the cake in front of Tom.

"I'm sorry to have been rude." He paused, then continued, "I'm not sure I have any way to explain my surprise, except to ask you a simple question."

She continued to smile but took a step back before responding. "No, I don't own the café. No, I'm not a movie star hiding from the press; and no, I'm not looking for a date. Are there really any other questions? Because, I can tell you I have heard most of them, as well as comments on my great smile, how efficient I am at being a waitress, and are those real?" She just threw a hip out, putting her weight on one leg and continued to smile.

"It's going to take me a moment to recover from my surprise," Tom started. "I don't deny you are very attractive, and you might even be a movie star. I'm not looking for a date, either. But, I have to ask you something so strange and you might take offense. Please, let me explain."

When Tom first began his explanation, the young woman visibly blanched. Tom was afraid she was going to bolt for the door. He introduced himself, explaining only the minimum of what he guessed. When it looked like she was going to leave, he asked, "is your name Laura, or Lorna, and do you know Arne Thorson? I'm no threat, believe me. I'm trying to find anyone who might have known him, and you fit the description I was given of a woman seen with him the night he was murdered."

At first the young woman paused, shuffled her feet, looking around the room, as if seeking an escape route. When Tom assured her again that he was not a threat, even took out his identification, she became less agitated. "Please, sit with me for a moment if you can. I am supposed to catch the train to Minneapolis in a little while, but if you're the woman I think you are, I need to stay here. It might help solve a horrible crime. It may even be that you are in danger, and by helping me you can help yourself."

"Yes," she began. She was shaking all over. Tears welled up in her eyes. She could hardly sit still in the booth . They were alone in the café. Whoever was in the kitchen stayed out of sight. For ten minutes Laura and Tom exchanged bits and pieces of Arne's last night on earth, and a little at a time Laura calmed down.

"Do you have any idea who attacked you and Arne? Had you ever seen the man, can you tell me anything about how he looked, or anything he said?" Tom knew he was putting a lot of pressure on the young woman. "Believe me, I am not judging you or Arne. We— Judge Chamberlin and I—are trying to find out if the attack on you and Arne is connected to some other violence in the area. Anything you can tell me might help find a murderer."

"Like I said, it's not unusual for strange men to fall apart when they first see me. Oh, sure, I know I dress a little extravagant for a small town. Some people think of me as striking, I guess, but a girl can't help what she looks like. Arne stopped here for lunch a lot, and after a while he got used to me, just saw me as Laura, from the café in Benson. By the time he asked me to go dancing at Buster's we were almost old friends. I will admit though that we sure had a big physical attraction! But no, I can't think of anyone who ever gave me trouble—other than the high school boys who were still trying to figure out what tits are all about." She laughed so hard Tom couldn't help but join her.

"There was a guy in here earlier that day, however. I guess he was kind of strange, as I think about it. He looked somewhere between lonely and messianic; I mean, he had a look in his eyes like he was on some kind of a mission, looking for something to complete his life." Although she was less nervous than before, she continued to glance around the café, as if expecting someone to jump from the shadows. "Do you know what I mean? He was just a plain looking guy, wearing slacks and a shirt with a worn collar. My guess is he was about fifty, maybe a little more. He didn't look like he really worked. Do you know what I mean?"

"Did you happen to see his car? Even that might help, because I can tell you, we have no idea where to look. I know that Saturday was a long time ago, but anything..." he paused. "I have been questioning people all over Chippewa County, looking for even a little clue. It never dawned on me to go just a little farther. Benson is not that far from Montevideo, but it just didn't enter my mind to come here, since it's in another county."

"You know, there is one thing. I never gave it any thought, since guys are always staring at me, it just slipped my mind. Keep in mind, it's been a year, maybe more by now since Arne and I... well, you know what I mean. My life got so messed up that night I haven't even wanted to think about it. But, after the guy finished his pie he just sat there, watching me as I cleared the booth and went about my business. Before he left, he took a pack of gum from his pocket, sat chewing the gum for maybe five minutes; maybe longer. Then, he put the wrapper in his pocket and walked out. That's strange, because he could have left it in the booth like most guys do, and I would have thrown it out for him."

Tom frowned as he absorbed what Laura had just told him. Although the vague description could fit a hundred men, two comments fit the pastor. *Somewhere between lonely and messianic.* It sure could be a description of Bill Sherman; thinking of him as William Tecumseh seemed a little out of his current reality. And, *the gum*, the gum and the way he crushed the wrapper; Tom could see it in his mind. It fit. Now, how should he proceed? Even with this description, there was still no real connection between the pastor and the crimes Tom was investigating. By now, it was too late go to Minneapolis. He had missed the daily train and driving there was out of the question; at least for today.

Tom and Laura exchanged contact information, with a warning from Tom that she should probably not think of going to Montevideo or to Buster's until she heard from Tom that there was no danger. Tom's only choice seemed to be returning to Montevideo. It was obviously time to share his thoughts and concerns with the judge and Mary. Maybe, where his lone vision was just stymied, three minds could find a path forward.

Forty-Four

THERE WAS LITTLE Tom could do but return to Montevideo. The daily train to Minneapolis was long gone, and now, Tom needed to seek some help. Mary and the judge needed to hear everything he had learned today. The drive back to Montevideo should have given him time to make a plan. With so much new information but still no proof, what could he actually do? This new information still did not really implicate Bill Sherman.

Tom decided he should pick Mary up from work, then the two of them, unannounced, just stop at the judge's office. From there they could make a plan. The day had been gray and overcast. It was not a problem yet, but heavy snow had been predicted by the weatherman at WCCO, in Minneapolis. Snow and bad roads would reach Minneapolis by morning. That meant southwestern Minnesota could expect the same by evening. If the prediction was correct, Montevideo would be a winter wonderland by morning, with fresh sparkling snow from horizon to horizon. It would also mean the small town's streets would be impassable for hours, maybe even a day. It would be a small problem for Tom, but Mary still needed to get to the depot; train schedules were not adjusted for just a local snow storm. Tom and Mary would worry about that later.

Mary was surprised to see Tom. "You are supposed to be in the Cities," she remarked. "But, I'm glad you're here. We're supposed to get a storm tonight, and I'd like you next to me in a warm bed rather than off in some dreary old hotel."

Tom agreed; it sounded much better. When she began inquiring why his plan had changed, he put her off. "Let's just go visit the judge before he goes home. I think there are some serious things to discuss and I 'd like to do it just once."

"Oh, my; that sounds cryptic!" She couldn't decide if the comment warranted a smile or a frown. Whichever, she would just have to wait him out.

They found the judge just preparing to leave his office. "I usually work just a little later than this but thought I would get a bite of supper at the hotel before I head home. Why aren't you in Minneapolis? I didn't expect to see you for a couple of days." Tom began to give the judge a brief explanation but was stopped with a raised hand. "You two join me. The restaurant will be quiet tonight, with the storm warning we got. We'll probably have the room to ourselves and we can take all the time we want."

It was dinner, desert, and coffee, before Tom began to tell them about the day's revelations. The judge was right. By the time they began eating desert the dining room was deserted. The judge beckoned the waitress. "Just leave us a pot of coffee on the burner and head on home. We want to visit for a while, but there's no need for you to stay."

An hour later the judge and Mary sat wide-eyed, trying to make sense of Tom's story. A dozen times Mary had exclaimed, "My God! I don't believe it." A dozen times the judge murmured, "Now some of my own concerns make sense." And a dozen times Tom repeated, "I still have no proof, but I am certain Reverend Sherman is actually Boyd Bauer."

"I had planned my trip to the Cities to learn if there were any military records we could search, and to visit with a contact at the State Bureau of Criminal Investigation. I can still phone them. Maybe that's a better option anyway. In any case, it's too late for the trip this week, and I can still go to Minneapolis next week." "For now, let's just sit on all this information. I can't imagine there is any immediate danger of new violence. The pastor is unlikely to have any idea that I spoke with Laura today. He obviously has never returned to Benson in the last year and a half, so we have no reason to believe he will go there this week. Let's let the weekend play out. Mary and I can go to the Church Christmas pageant Sunday night and just act as if we have no concerns other than to enjoy Christmas. While we do that, I'll keep thinking of how to proceed. Your Honor, if you have any thoughts on this, you know how to reach me. Let's just enjoy the coming snow-day. And, let's all just be careful."

Forty-Five

WHEN DAYBREAK CAME on Friday morning it came snarling and howling across the prairie. What began as a gentle dusting of snow, with huge flakes just drifting over the countryside, changed. By midnight, the Minnesota River valley temperature plunged to ten degrees. Soft friendly snowflakes became hard pellets of snow, driven by winds that gusted to nearly forty-miles per hour. Valley residents needed to be where they intended to stay; by morning the entire region would be frozen in place.

Pastor Sherman woke slowly. Several times during the night he was awakened as the wind blew a particularly strong gust against the house. The oil burning furnace, which most nights kept the house comfortable, was incapable of competing with the wind and the dropping temperature. He wanted to stay in his bed, rolled into a ball. He tucked his head beneath the blanket and the heavy quilt he had expected to keep him warm; but to no avail. In spite of the storm, he had to leave his bed. He turned up the control on the furnace, hoping against hope that the house would warm up. Then, he would drink some coffee, shave and do all the things civilized people did before confronting the world.

There were still many things to be accomplished before Sunday. The sermon was ready to be delivered; just review it one or two more times to be sure he had his inflections just right. He felt certain the storm would clear before Sunday. The custodian of the month would shovel the sidewalk to the church entry, turn up the heat, and make certain God's children would be comfortable when they came to worship Sunday morning.

The pageant Sunday night would be just like the one last year, and just like the year before that. There would be songs and Psalms.

There would be words of encouragement for those still suffering from drought, depression, and the tribulations of life in general. The pastor would repeat the annual liturgy, the story of the wisemen, the inn without room for Mary and Joseph, the stable, the manger, and all the rest. It would be a wonderful story. It would send everyone home feeling good that God had brought His son into the world. He wondered if Christmas in Jerusalem had been as cold and miserable as it was going to be in Minnesota.

Then, after his evening eulogy, it would be time for the children of the congregation to perform their pageant. They would wear home-made robes, dish towels draped over their heads as they tried to look wise; *they would wear mittens if the chapel did not get warm*, he thought with a smile. The Cole, Baker, MacGregor, and Morehouse children would perform nervously for their parents and grandparents, becoming Joseph, Mary and the wisemen for a few minutes. Then, with applause for the annual performance, mothers would pass out small bags containing curly sugar candy, lemon drops, peanuts, and a small toy like they would find in Cracker Jax. Adults would linger, drinking hot cider or hot chocolate while they wished each other Merry Christmas, even though Christmas was still days away. Then, they would shepherd their respective families home and enjoy the warm glow of righteousness. Everyone, except Reverend Sherman.

When Sunday came, his expectations were proven correct. The morning service went well. All the pews were full. He went home and ate a small lunch after the service, then returned to the church to be certain all was in order for the evening festivities, which also progressed just as expected. The regulars were all here; the Morehouses, the Coles and Iversons, the Shultzs, except for Clifford. Relatives from far away and people the pastor never knew existed, filled the church. Judge Chamberlin and his wife sat right in front, as they always did; next to them were Tom Hall and Mary. *How could they even think of entering God's house?*

"What is going on with Tom Hall," he wondered. *"I smell trouble there. I cannot believe he spoke to me like that, and now here*

he is right down front in the church. " While adults and children were having their refreshments, the pastor wandered from group to group. He smiled and wished everyone Christmas greetings. *Did Tom Hall and the judge change the subject as he approached?* He could not be sure. His better judgement told him to avoid Tom Hall; no sense sparking a needless confrontation in front of the congregation.

As he moved around the room, the pastor's thoughts wandered back over his tenure in Montevideo. He had arrived with the serious belief he could put his entire past life behind him. It should be easy, he thought, to just become a minister. How difficult could it be to become pastor to a rural congregation which probably had low expectations of a new minister from Iowa. On what worldly experiences could they base their judgements of him? *"I can do this,"* he told himself. For the most part Boyd, now Reverend William Tecumseh Sherman, was successful.

His memories of life in the wilderness faded. He told himself the death of the sheep farmer was justified; in any case, who in this town even knew about that death, so many miles away and so many years ago. No; just be their pastor and enjoy their friendship. *"Was it friendship,"* he wondered, *"or just politeness?"*

The weeks, months and years had passed without incident for the new pastor. From time to time, however, a strange paranoia clawed its way to the surface, but each passing week put his deprivations further to the back of his mind. The ministry gave him a stress-free life. It brought recognition and respect he had never experienced. Then, when he had seen that woman in Benson, his carefully structured life fell apart.

He felt lustful for the first time since leaving the wilderness. Oh, yes, there had been moments when he thought he sensed lustful thoughts toward him from some woman of the congregation. He immediately banished such thoughts. Life as this congregation's minister was all he needed to complete his life. But, something in him snapped as he had watched that woman move back and forth in the café. It was unfortunate that he had given in, but the entire episode was put out of his mind. He told himself it never happened, it had been Boyd who committed the atrocities in those earlier days. It had been Boyd who killed Arne Thorson. Besides—Thorson had it coming to him.

There had been days recently when that the pastor's mind raced, uncontrollably jumping from one lucid thought or vision to another. He sometimes experienced mood swings that were totally foreign to him. Sometimes, lately, he found himself places without any recollection of how he got there.

He was used to living alone, used to being his own confidant. He told himself he was comfortable, walking the streets at night, alone with his thoughts as he planned another Sunday performance. He walked through the park, around the swimming beach, and along the wooded path to visit the family of bears, the elk and the wounded eagle, which was forced to live off scraps while inside its big cage. Then, there had come the afternoon he discovered Roberta Swan's infidelity.

The trail he had followed so many times along the river ended in a cluster of willow trees near Highway 212, just fifty yards from the Swan's guest cabins. As he was about to leave the shelter of the trees, he was shocked to see Mrs. Swan leave one of the cabins. It was not the sight of her exiting one of her own buildings—it was the moment she turned and in a deep embrace kissed a man who was not her husband. For a moment, as the stranger fondled Bobbie's breast, he was afraid he was going to be forced to watch them couple right there in the doorway.

It would have been both improper and embarrassing to step into the clearing at that moment, so he faded back into the woods. The couple parted with lusty, almost vulgar, laughter and the man drove off. Mrs. Swan disappeared into the cabin and a short time later left with an armload of linens. No doubt, to dispose of the evidence of her infidelity, he thought.

Bill Sherman found himself taking the path along the river more frequently after that experience, sometimes waiting in the shelter of the trees, sometimes seeing Mrs. Swan's immoral activities. It was always during the daytime, of course. She needed to be an obedient wife by suppertime. One day, he stealthily moved closer to the cabin. It was there he discovered that if he stood in just the right place he could see into the cabin and view the activity as it was reflected in a huge mirror. From that moment, he was no longer just a spectator. He could hear and see what was happening, as Roberta seduced one man after another.

There came a day when the pastor and Bobbie Swan met on Main Street. Of course, he could not confront the woman about her infidelity. Instead, he greeted her. They casually spoke of the weather, the summer, all sort of inane subjects. He hinted—very carefully he thought—that he thought her to be a beautiful young woman, that although he didn't want to seem forward, or out of line, they might find time to spend together.

To say the woman was shocked would be to say a tornado was only a passing thunderstorm, but she handled it well. She had fended off men since she was fourteen—when she wanted to. "Why Pastor Sherman, that's a very strange thing to hear, especially from my own minister." Yes, she was a member of the congregation, but recently she had been drifting away. She was seldom seen in church on Sundays anymore.

They continued their conversation, each sparring, each protecting their true thoughts. Although Bobbie could not see the subtle shift, the man before her changed. He looked the same, but Pastor William Tecumseh Sherman slowly was replaced by Boyd Bauer. Boyd Bauer did not like the way he was being treated, spoken to as if he were some insect, to be ignored—or crushed—if she wished. He continued to sound like the pastor, but the eyes that had coveted her now saw only Bobbie the harlot, Bobbie the sinner, who should not be allowed to seduce innocent man, not be allowed to destroy their families and put their souls in danger. He realized he had made a huge mistake, but also realized he had a task which needed to be completed. This needed to be corrected soon.

It was a strange dichotomy. Reverend Sherman walked the streets and prayed for the souls of his congregation and gently tended to his Baptist flock, while Boyd Bauer seethed. Boyd ranted in private, swore violent oaths at all who, in his imagination, had maligned him. Vengeance, retribution, more vengeance. He fell asleep in his lonely bed at night, thinking of how Hans Iverson had caused the downward spiral of his life.

From one minute to the next he was a tormented and God-guided soul, without sin in his mind, or in his heart; in the next, he was a parentless child, without a moral compass. One thing had changed, which was noticed by no one. He disappeared nearly every afternoon. Who would care where he spent his time? Boyd Bauer knew the parish only used him for their own salvation. Why should he care about them? He would just use the small community and the security it provided until he solved this temporary problem. Maybe it would all blow over; maybe his anger would just disappear. If not, he could just leave, disappear again, become a wilderness traveler once more. Moses in the wilderness—or Jesus suffering for the world—what did it matter?

He waited in the willow grove day after day. Then, the day he had waited, for arrived. Today he would answer Roberta Swan's insult. It was hot, sweaty, oppressive. When the harlot and the young heathen closed the door of the cabin, Boyd moved up to the big tree where he had found cover for his observation of Bobbie's sins. Through the window, he saw their reflections in the wall mirror.

He watched as they coupled. Against his every wish, he listened to their moans of passion. Then, he watched as the man paraded his nakedness into the bathroom. Now was the time to act. Quickly, but quietly, he left his shelter, went to the cabin door, slowly pushed it open. As Bobbie arched her back, luxuriating in the afterglow of her sin, he removed the gun from the pocket of his well-worn suit coat. The gun had had lain, unused, in a drawer for a decade. Occasionally, he would remove it, fondle the hard grips, and slowly rotate the revolver's cylinder, never considering that he might someday use it in this manner to take a life. The nine-millimeter Walther had been taken from a dead German officer who had died at Corporal Bauer's feet. As the officer's eyes glazed over, Bauer had smiled and softly whispered in German, "Go slowly to hell, Herr Captain." Although it was forbidden to loot the enemy, he had taken the revolver, slipped it inside his tunic, and spat on the dead man's face.

Now, Boyd quickly pointed the gun and fired one shot, closed the door and disappeared into the willow grove. When he was safely in his home, he sat on the thread-bare couch and shook violently as he recalled the deed, then rushed to the toilet, where he threw up. He washed his face with cold water, then lay down again on the couch. When he woke an hour later, Bill Sherman was famished.

Forty-Six

I HAD COME to Montevideo to look for my ancestors. I had wandered around town: meeting cousins, near cousins, people who were married to cousins. I made notes and graphs, trying to find that important marriage someplace in the past that might lead back to a king or a duke or some important political figure. So far, all I had found was more cousins; and occasionally someone who knew one of my great great-grand-parents. What was I to really expect? My family had lived in a small midwestern town. Some of that family farmed near that small midwestern town. What part of a royal family would leave the luxury of European royalty for this?

From time to time, I had lunch with Tom or Mary. I had discussions with them and others, not just about family, but also events taking place around us. I was no longer quite the stranger as when I first arrived. Although people shared information about my family, I had no idea of how close Tom Hall was coming to resolving at least one of the recent killings.

Christmas was almost upon us. We had survived the snow storm that left a foot of sparkling snow covering the prairie and left drifts half as high as a grown man in many places. We had enjoyed the Baptist Christmas pageant on Sunday night, in spite of some roads being unpassable. Our local snowstorm left Mary and Joseph with only two of the three wise men looking into the manger. I knew Tom had turned back from his train trip to Minneapolis, but I had no idea why his trip had been cut short.

Because of the impending storm and Mary's need to be at the depot in the morning, regardless of the weather, Mary chose to stay with Tom at the Riverside Hotel on Friday night. Saturday morning she trudged the length of Main Street to open the depot and clear the deck for any stranger who might wish to detrain later in the day.

Tom walked with her as far as the Stavos Café, where he was nearly alone with his breakfast and coffee. Since George's death, Howard Logan had come in to cook nearly every morning. The exception was Sundays; church time for the family on Sunday came first. As a sailor with a lot of kitchen-duty experience and being the father of five rambunctious girls, Howard knew how to cook for a group. Howard had come in long before the sun rose, and now he and Tom sat looking out on the snow-covered scene.

As Tom was enjoying a third cup of coffee, he and Howard were joined by Cliff Heinrich. "A couple of eggs over easy and a slab of ham big enough to carry me 'til supper, Howard. I'm only going to make this trip once today, and I'm such a horrible cook I might starve to death, if not for George's place, here."

A minute later, Howard was thrashing in the kitchen. The cast iron frying pan sizzled on the stove. He came out with ham and eggs for Cliff and a pan of caramel rolls, still steaming hot. "Be right back," he popped, then disappeared again.

Tom was just beginning to speak to Cliff, when the front door of the café opened, letting in a blast of snow and cold air. Tom looked up at the new arrival and snapped his head toward the kitchen. "Howard, where did you come from? I just saw you go to the kitchen."

"Why, I went out through the pantry. I felt a draft I thought was coming from the apartment entry and went out that way to see if a door was left open."

"You mean there's another way out of the kitchen? I thought the alley door was the only access, except to Main Street. Can you show me that entrance?"

They left Cliff with his ham and eggs and headed to the kitchen. Sure enough, another door. Tom had not known the pantry, along the north wall of the kitchen, had a door to the hall which served the apartment upstairs. The door wasn't used often and was nearly invisible. It was cluttered by shelving and boxes of the stuff that gets in the cook's way if left in the open. Tom walked up the stairs; a dead end with a locked door. He and Howard went out onto the street. While Howard returned to the café, Tom stood looking up, down, and across the street, for a minute before rejoining the other two men.

The three sat and visited, as men will do on a snowy Saturday morning. Howard offered, "Tom, you probably don't know I am married to Cliff's sister Bess."

It was actually not news to Tom, but he let Howard continue. Although Cliff's father Jack had talked of him at the church, there had been no mention of Howard and Bess. He recalled Jack had mentioning something about his son, wondering if his withdrawal from church activity was connected to his military service, but Tom could not quite put his finger on Jack's inference. His recent visit with Cliff over coffee however, had given him new insights about Cliff's withdrawal. It was unfortunate that Cliff was not clear about whether his hospital recollections were real or imagined. Although those questions were to be unanswered for the time being, Tom was about to get a lesson on country genealogy.

Cliff had a sparkle in his eyes he said, "I've been hearing quite a bit about you, Tom."

Tom was a bit puzzled. "You've got me, Cliff. I have only met Howard a couple of times and there was no discussion of his family. But, I suppose with all the snooping I've been doing, someone might just talk about me as well."

"That was unfair of me." Cliff laughed aloud, then continued, "That sweet girl you like so much is my niece. Well, not directly. But her mother is my niece. Her grandmother is a MacGregor. I don't have any children of my own of course, and she's almost like a daughter to me. She stops to see me every so often. Naturally, she talks about you and what you two are up to. The Heinrichs and MacGregors have been here longer than Montevideo has been a town, so we're also related to half the county." He laughed again, and the other two men joined in. Tom had some new questions to ask.

What Cliff had not stated was that Jack and Maggie Heinrich's daughter Bess had married Howard Logan, which Tom knew, and their eldest daughter Margaret, obviously named after her grandmother Maggie, had married Harlan, the eldest son of Art and Inga Iverson. The MacGregors truly were related to most of Chippewa County and the loop was tightening.

Forty-Seven

IT SHOULD HAVE been a perfect Christmas morning. It was a sunny Sunday, neither too cold, nor too warm for a December day. Saturday night, December 24th the congregation had left their homes for a short Christmas Eve spiritual enlightenment. All the right words came from the bible. Joseph and Mary, the bright star in the east, spending the night with the animals in the stable when the hotel was booked. Children in the audience were hugged and had received nurturing kisses from loving parents who, once again, felt the glow of their Savior's birth and could not help but pass it on. All the churches around Montevideo were aglow with Christmas spirit, and small congregations around the county made certain all was well.

Reverend William Tecumseh Sherman cooed and murmured all the loving accolades that were appropriate for Christmas, and the next morning Christmas arrived with snow that sparkled like crystals. There were no clouds in the sky, no blustering winds to drive the congregation into their shelters. The pews of the First Baptist Church were filled. Extra chairs were brought from the Sunday School room. When the congregation sang *Joy to The World,* the building literally vibrated with love.

The only thing that tempted discord from the pastor was un-noticed by the congregation. The front rows on the left were filled with Charles and Lucinda MacGregor, nine of their ten children—and their children. On the left were the John and Maggie Heinrichs, their son Clifford, and Bessie with her husband Howard. Crowded behind them were the five Logan girls, including eldest daughter Margaret holding her year-old son, and her husband Harlan, whom the pastor did not recognize. The eldest Logan daughter and her family only showed up at the Baptist church on special holidays. Clifford had not been inside the church in more than a year. Squeezed in next to Margaret and her husband and baby were Mary Collins and Tom Hall.

Somewhere in his lower brain the pastor knew he should show joy that so many had filled his church this morning. God's love should prevail, of course. But, he felt Tom Hall's presence in the front pews was like a spear jabbed into his gut. Sinners, fornicators, sacrilegious heathens—Tom and Mary should not be there. He kept his anger in check by not looking at them, gazing instead, across the room at those who deserved his attention.

Although the sun shone brightly through the colored glass windows, there was a dark shadow bearing down on the pulpit. The hymns were sung, the birth of baby Jesus was celebrated, the joy of family shared and encouraged. The final blessings for a spiritual new year was murmured with a smile. There was no rush for the congregation to leave. Christmas dinner was an hour away; perhaps more, if a family had driven from the country.

Pastor Sherman took his place near the church entrance, flanked by the church board president Morehouse, and Jack Heinrich. Love and mercy were to be equally shared with all who attended this special day, and one by one, the families were greeted and sent on their way. Since the Heinrich, Logan and MacGregor families had been in the front pews, they were among the last to leave the church.

Jack Heinrich proudly threw an arm around his granddaughter, hugged her close while being careful to not squeeze the infant to closely. He announced proudly, "Pastor, I don't think you have met my granddaughter Margaret and her husband Harlan Iverson. Of course, you know my niece Mary Collins and Tom Hall."

If anyone had been looking closely at the pastor, had someone been watching for a reaction, they would have seen him flinch and go tense for a moment before he collected himself. "Of course; hello Mary, Tom. And, no I haven't met this great looking couple. Welcome to our little family."

When the church had emptied, the pastor sat in a front pew as he collected his thoughts. His brain swirled as he analyzed the morning's activities. It had been a great service; he was proud of himself. *Just think, not many years ago, I was living in the woods, wandering aimlessly, without a mission of any kind. Then, I found my salvation in God and my new home in Montevideo, Minnesota.* Oh sure, he countered to himself, *some improvement. Now you live in a crappy little house. You're still alone at night, and your only friends are the stupid rabble who come into the church on Sunday. You never eat with friends, you never sit and laugh over the stupid things they obviously think are humorous. The only woman who even smiled at you despised you and you killed her just to get even. What makes you think this is such a good life?*

He wandered across the chapel, mumbling to himself, stopping occasionally to yell to the empty room. On one pass of the small tree, placed in a corner, he grabbed a shiny ornament and crushed it between his hands. *And, an Iverson. Right here in my church. I should have known there was something wrong with Mary and Tom. Of course; she's another Iverson. Oh sure, not directly, but they are all related; Iversons, Heinrichs, MacGregors, the whole town are part of this conspiracy to keep me from having a happy life. How could I be so stupid?*

Forty-Eight

MONDAY ARRIVED, JUST like Mondays always did. Howard Flynn's drivers delivered fuel oil and coal. Ziaser's drivers were all out in their vans, delivering milk and cream around town. Swift and Company was slaughtering chickens and processing butter, while the drivers made the rounds on the snowy roads to Watson, Clarkfield, Dawson, and a half-dozen other county locations, to collect the fresh milk brought in by farmers who worked every day of the year. By nine a.m. the stores were all open for business. Every merchant was hoping for a flurry of after-Christmas shoppers to eliminate unwanted inventory by the year's end.

On the hill above Main Street, the Baptist church congregation would rely on the same congregants as always to clean up after the Sunday Christmas program. Bruce and Ester Morehouse, Hazel Coyle, and others, who would straggle in for a few minutes of labors before slipping away, would take ornaments from the tree and sweep up the mess left by all the needles which now cluttered the floor. Hazel would mumble something to herself about the pretty tree ornament she found scattered across the floor.

They were somewhat surprised that pastor Sherman was not the first person there, with his lop-sided smile, to open the front doors and welcome them. Before long, he joined them in their happy chores. His eyes were a bit swollen and bloodshot and his face was puffy. He explained it away by confessing an oncoming cold. There was a lot of that in the congregation this week.

The pastor and Hazel Coyle retreated to the small office in a back corner of the church to count the proceeds from Sunday's collection baskets, while the others cleaned and reorganized the chapel. At a later time Hazel recalled that the pastor seemed withdrawn, which was unusual for him, especially when the baskets were so generously filled.

While the church chores were being addressed, Tom and Mary were spending a leisurely morning in her large comfortable bed. Tom had risen early, poached two eggs, made coffee and toast, then gently wakened Mary, who was curled deeply under the down-filled comforter. The breakfast was followed by an hour of snuggling, smooching, and fondling, which led to a moment of gentle coupling, followed by a nap for each of them.

Mary was needed to open the depot and deal with the day's mail. The light powdering of snow on the depot platform would be shoveled and broomed away by Bill Olson, the maintenance man. Tom decided he would spend the day making and deciphering his notes about the mysteries. Then, on Tuesday he would make the trip he had previously postponed. While Mary was out, he made several calls, just to make sure Minneapolitans did not take the holiday week off. By the end of the day, Tom had developed a plan. He hoped he could make it work.

Forty-Nine

IT WAS WEDNESDAY before the highway to Benson was cleared enough for Tom to feel comfortable about making the journey to there. He left his car next to the Swift County court house and walked the two blocks back to the depot, plodding through snow, sometimes knee-deep, but always above his shoe tops. In places he balanced precariously as he slipped on icy spots or over tire ruts. When the eastbound train arrived, it was fifteen minutes late. Snow had drifted six feet high just east of Morris and a clean-up crew had been called to free the tracks from winter's grip.

Two days later, Tom stepped back off the train in Benson. His trip left him with both a feeling of satisfaction and a feeling of unease. Although he knew he had been too optimistic, he had hoped to find answers, and with those answers a path to resolve the questions about Boyd Bauer. He had, instead, been assured of answers to his questions, but was given no promise as to how soon the answers would arrive.

Tom had three deaths on his list of problems to be solved. While on the train returning to Benson he had listed questions, answers, and guesses, as to possible paths to follow: the death of Arne Thorson was apparently tied to Laura, although her conclusion that Pastor Sherman's meal in Benson tied him to the murder later that night was not very provable. If Bauer were arrested at some future date Tom had no doubt Laura would identify him —it would still take more than that to prove the minister guilty of murder. The connection between the minister and the death of Roberta Swan was only connected by the discovery of the chewing gum wrappers found in the area of the tourist cabin; that hardly led to a legitimate conclusion. The death of George Stavopolis had no obvious connection to the pastor, so Tom's next step in *that* mystery was to question anyone who might have been near the Stavos Café that Saturday morning.

The belief that Pastor Sherman and Boyd Bauer were the same person was such a wild hypothesis as to be unimaginable. That question could soon be answered, however. Tom's belief that Sunday sermons were directed at him and Mary and their relationship could very well just be his own embarrassment regarding their relationship. Except that Reverend Sherman's verbal attack at the restaurant was very pointed and nearly violent, and for no apparent reason. Tom was unsure how he could explore the minister's attitude toward his relationship with Mary. He was equally uncertain if that attitude had any connection to anything connected to the overall mystery of the deaths he was investigating.

Tom decided that to lessen his own confusion he should look at each death individually but theorize that all were also connected. Each circumstance should also include the possibility that Bill Sherman was the perpetrator without visibly accusing him; just let the facts fall into place. Clifford Heinrich's uneasiness about Sherman seemed to be a question without an answer. Perhaps, with the expected communication from Minneapolis, that question might be resolved. Yes, the question of whether Sherman and Bauer were the same person would answer itself in time, possibly accelerated by his recent trip to Minneapolis.

Fifty

SATURDAY MORNING FOUND Tom at a table in the Stavros Café again. He thought that by sitting in the same place as he had the morning George was murdered he might resurrect an image of that morning's activity. Mary was taking care of business at the depot and planning to join Tom for lunch.

That morning, I was visiting the Heinrichs in their home on Fifth Street. Maggie, she apparently disliked being called Margaret, was my main connection to the Heinrich and MacGregor history. Maggie was a tiny woman, perhaps five feet tall if she stood very straight, and perhaps weighing a solid one hundred pounds. I could see how Jack had been attracted to her. She and her four sisters had married into the full spectrum of Chippewa County's society, but Maggie and Jack were the most visible couple in the family. In addition, Maggie was the go-to person for the Avon Company, a New York firm manufacturing personal products that women were finding it difficult to live without.

Every week, Maggie visited the women around Montevideo, sharing Avon's newest and most desirable products. She was a natural for the task; perky, well-spoken, well-connected, not only through Avon, but as an officer in Daughters of the American Revolution, and, of course, to the extended family offered by her siblings' marriages.

Maggie's husband Jack was a stone mason, specializing in decorative carvings for cemetery headstones. Although the family were at first farmers in Chippewa County, Jack had seen creative opportunity with chisel and maul. When he would later lose his eyesight as a result of stone chips being cast into his eyes for a decade, it was Maggie and Avon who would support the couple.

On this Saturday we were in their comfortable living room, mostly discussing MacGregors, and occasionally talking about some member of the Heinrich clan when Cliff joined us. With his high forehead and his hair buzzed short, he looked like an imp. Short, going a little large around the middle, Cliff showed little of his experience in the Great War. When you looked into his intense and sad brown eyes however, there was another man staring back at you who hardly seemed an imp.

Cliff's parents gave him nurturing smiles and asked of his well-being. I could see they tread carefully, perhaps thinking an inopportune comment could send their son to some mental place they did not want him to go.

We were all surprised when Cliff said, "I've had some time to think about our discussion at the café, Tom. As much as I try not to think about the war, you did me a favor. When I spoke about being in the hospital, I think it gave me some release. I've always realized I was lucky to have gotten home with just that concussion. I have just pushed all that out of my mind for a long while."

Maggie looked apprehensive. "Cliff, you don't have to talk about it if you don't want to."

"No, Mom. I think this is a good time for me to say a few things. Tom is trying so hard to solve Bobbie's murder and as I've watched him chasing all over the county and to the Twin Cities I have realized how lucky I am. When he and I talked about my hospitalization I got some new insights into my life. But, that's not what I wanted to clear up."

He turned to me, then back to his parents. "I sort of dropped out of the church some years ago, Tom. Actually, it was right after Reverend Sherman came. I was still struggling with the war and something about him made me uncomfortable. I have always had the feeling that he should have been the man in the next bed, but I couldn't make it fit. Oh, my head was fuzzy, but I wanted to ask the pastor if it had been him there in the hospital. Then, as I was thinking about it this it dawned on me why I was uncomfortable. I realized

Pastor Sherman couldn't be the guy from the hospital. That guy shot up as he was, and all wrapped around his head, couldn't be corporal Sherman. Besides having his head all wrapped up and his arm in a sling over his head, Corporal Sherman had a couple of fingers shot off, or blown off—or something. So, it looks like after all this time I was just plain wrong about him."

Jack, Maggie, and I, chuckled nervously at Cliff's confession. I could see their relief that Cliff had found some new peace with his war experience. As we continued our visit, Maggie brewed a pot of black tea, which she served with a plate of sugar cookies. Maggie could hardly contain her joy and rubbed Cliff's head every time she passed by.

I wasn't sure if this new information would be of interest to Tom. At that point in time I was unaware of much of the information Tom had collected, or what secrets he was trying to uncover.

Fifty-One

TOM EXPECTED THAT by Monday morning, or at the latest sometime Tuesday, his trip to Minneapolis should start bearing fruit. He had asked a simple question and therefore should get a simple answer in the shortest time possible. *Were there records of U.S. Army service for William T. Sherman and Boyd N.M.I. (no middle initial) Bauer?* Although, by itself, the answer to that question would not solve any mysteries, knowing if either, or both men had served during the war might point him in the right direction.

The query could take some time, however. Tom had not been able to provide any pertinent information for the search. He had no birth dates or locations, and no other historical information on either man. He was quite certain there would be no record of Bauer's birth; that man had just disappeared sometime in the nineteenth century. Sherman had just appeared in Montevideo in 1927, and Tom was unaware any discussion of possible military service had ever happened after he arrived in Montevideo. Tom thought this was not a good time to start a local inquiry.

In the meantime he was thinking of George Stavopolis's death and how the killer could possibly have gotten away so fast. If Sherman was Bauer, how could it be that Sherman and the Methodist minister were seen together as they came into the café? That seemed to be a strike against Tom's theory about Sherman. It was a question which could possibly be answered by the Methodist minister, but also a question that needed to be carefully asked.

And, Tom thought, his reaction to the pastor's outburst in the Riverside Restaurant really could be his own guilty feelings about his relationship with Mary. Was he just taking advantage of her? Was he subconsciously planning to leave her behind when this mystery was solved? And what was Mary expecting from him? They certainly enjoyed each other, but she had expressed no concern for permanence. How did women deal with these things, he wondered?

As Tom mused over these things, reading the holiday edition of the Montevideo American newspaper, he decided to just let the mystery slide until he heard from the people in Minneapolis. It was a holiday, after all and he would just put it out of his mind.

Fifty-Two

IT WAS NEW Year's Eve, the last Saturday, of the last week in December, and the final day of 1938. Reverend William Tecumseh Sherman sat alone at his kitchen table. To anyone passing by the pastor's house, it seemed like any other home in Montevideo. The paint was a little shabby but didn't need immediate attention. The shingles should last another few years before being replaced. It would be a stretch to call the yard landscaped; a couple of bushes at one corner of the yard couldn't be considered real landscaping. In the spring, dandelions bloomed faster than they could be chopped out of the ground. If not for the helping hands of parish members, the grass may have been left un-mowed. It was just another ordinary home in an ordinary town. It was a house which had not had a visitor through its door since the pastor arrived in 1927.

As his eyes wandered around the room, there were no signs of a home maker's loving care, no pictures hung on the faded wall paper, no potted plants or bouquets in vases. The counter top was worn and chipped linoleum, almost a match to the dreary tabletop on its spindly chrome legs. In a corner near the sink, a soggy grocery bag collected refuse from the week's meals.

The pastor stared at the bible on the table but did not actually see the text. When he opened the tattered book, he had expected to find solace, some twig of wisdom to raise his spirits. Unfortunately, as he thumbed through the journal, words of joy, consolation, or forgiveness eluded him. Finally, he gave up and sat with his head bowed and his hands draped limply on his lap.

For a few minutes he closed his eyes, trying in vain to recall some moment of joy. His mood spiraled down, tears flowed, and he sobbed without control. He could find no memory of joy in his entire life . The memory of a well-delivered sermon was tarnished by the memory of Tom Hall staring at him. Where he might have found a moment of pleasure, he recalled only pain or anger. He thought of the beautiful woman in the red dress, only to have that memory destroyed by the image of Arne Thorson about to defile her. As he thought of Laura he sobbed aloud, remembering the night the image of her purity died as she lay naked and welcoming along the river bank. Bobbie Swan had deceived him with her seductive looks, only to scorn him later. With each memory recalled, he sunk into deeper depression.

His arrival in Montevideo had come with a small amount of fanfare. For several weeks he had been dinner guest to church celebrities, had dined in homes both large and small. Eventually, the dinners stopped. He was not a great conversationalist or entertainer; he chose to keep his earlier life private. "How could my simple past be of any interest," he would respond when questioned. "I was born to a poor farm family. My parents died while I was still very young."

Of his church experience he could only say, "I found God while I served my country. I was just dodging bullets, like so many others. Then, as I travelled the country I got involved with the Mission in Sioux City, and now here I am." What more was there he could say about his life?

As he sat at his table, he watched the snow swirling across his yard. Gusts of wind blew up great clouds of snow dust and rattled the storm window above the sink, sending a chill up his back. It was just another day; another lonely day of being unappreciated and not included. The good memories were the memories of fishing from the shore of the Missouri River and memories of roasting the lamb over an open fire near New Ulm. Even those memories were tainted, however. The old fool who ranted about his lost lamb; and then there was the strange banker who thought to take advantage of him so many years ago. Did he just attract encounters such as those? Was he being tested by God?

By four-thirty the sun was below the horizon. The wind still kicked up clouds of fine snow, but the temperature, at 24 degrees, was not bone-chilling. A couple of hours later, Bill Sherman pushed his feet into the four-buckle overshoes needed to keep winter out of his shoes, took his heavy woolen mackinaw from the hook, shirked into its heavy warmth, then wrapped his only winter scarf around his neck and pulled the cap with its earflaps tightly onto his head.

He wandered aimlessly about the quiet town. The streets were mostly not plowed yet; probably would not receive any attention until sometime Monday. Sidewalks, where they existed, were snow-covered. Some of them would not have the concrete exposed to daylight until the spring thaw. As he wandered in the darkness, he occasionally could see families, reading in a comfortable chair, putting a puzzle together on a dining room table, a father showing some mystery in a book to a son, or a mother and daughter hovered over a Singer sewing machine.

An hour passed, perhaps more. With some surprise, he found he had come to the furthest end of town. He had followed no path he recognized, turning left here, right there, perhaps motivated by a sudden gust of wind that caused him to turn away from its snow-filled blast. He was standing in the protection of a cluster of evergreen trees carefully planted many years earlier by the forward-thinking property owner. On nights such as this, they offered welcome protection from the cold wind. The road here, leading northward and out of town, was intersected by the driveway, which followed the slightly undulating roll of the land into a neatly organized set of buildings. The driveway and buildings were surrounded by more evergreens, mixed with several large and now-barren oak trees. The scene before him, with moonlight shining on the tidy house, the garage, and the now unused outbuildings, could have been found on a Christmas card sent to some far away friend or a distant family member.

It was as if he was being drawn by a magnet, or an invisible elastic band constricting and drawing him into the yard. The house was nearly dark inside. A single rosy light emanated from the center of the house. Just audible, was the sound of some big-band music, a piano, a trombone and other sounds quietly filled the night, probably being played on a phonograph or even coming across the airwaves from a radio. He cautiously made his way to a window and peered into the living room. The fireplace along the south wall glowed and crackled. The fire was safely contained behind a screen. On the floor, just a safe distance from the fire, a jumble of blankets, or quilts, thrust up like a giant mouse nest. A decorated tray to one side held three or four brown crackers, joined by a block of cheese and a wine bottle, now empty and resting on its side.

In the midst of the blankets two naked people cuddled together, each holding a glass tumbler that still contained a small amount of wine. Tom Hall rested his head on a large pillow, obviously taken from the nearby bedroom. Mary Collins lay tightly against Tom's hip, rocking her wine glass back and forth over his stomach, as she whispered some words heard only by Tom. Although their voices could not be heard, it was obvious they were unaware of anything in the world other than themselves.

Bill Sherman did not think of himself as a voyeur—or a peeping Tom—as people might have considered him at that moment. He was unsure why he had been drawn here tonight. When he left his house he had no intention of ending up outside this house. Some thought of God's will drifted through his brain, but there was more to it than that. He would not have said he was lonely and certainly could not have admitted Mary Collins held a carnal attraction for him. No, that could not be it.

As he watched, the couple emptied their glasses and set them aside. Their onlooker could not take his eyes off Mary as she turned and moved still closer to Tom. The upward curve of her hip was hypnotic and as she slid her leg over Tom's abdomen, the hidden observer was tantalized when her breasts were pushed to a new shape before disappearing between the couple. When Mary lifted herself upright, then straddled Tom's hips, it became unbearable to the dark figure outside the window, who turned and ran. He had to put the unholy scene behind him. His mind screamed: *"Fornicators, harlots, sinners, deceivers!"* His brain was afire with carnal thoughts mixed with biblical admonitions, with violent anger, and thoughts of how he had again been betrayed by someone related to the Iversons; the bane of his life.

Fifty-Three

THE INFANT YEAR of 1939 arrived on Sunday. Across the country, men and women awoke with feelings of joy and feelings of anticipation, or fear of unknown dangers. Some woke with the recognition of new-found love. In some homes men or women woke with violent stirrings of hate.

In the small and untidy house around the corner from Montevideo's First Baptist Church, a man lay in his bed, unsure of the course he should take. The man who was to give the first sermon of the new year was struggling with the man who had a barely controllable desire to commit murder. Boyd Bauer and Reverend William Tecumseh Sherman were in a life or death struggle. The pastor's seemingly comfortable life of the past eleven years had been challenged, disrupted by Boyd Bauer and the violence he had lived with from the day of his first memory.

In three hours the pastor was expected to bring a message of hope to his flock. They needed his guidance for the coming year. Yes, there had been dark days for some of his flock, and of course, some members of his parish would have to deal with strife in the coming days. But, their pastor must tell them that with God's love and with guidance from the church, everything would eventually be alright.

If only it were that simple, chided Boyd to himself. All around him there was irrefutable sin. Those appearing most innocent were frequently the ones most deeply involved in—and controlled by— sins of the flesh. *"Did they not understand the sinfulness of their actions?"* he asked out loud. Or, were they really innocent, just needing counseling and guidance? Moreover, and now he was thinking of Tom Hall and Mary Collins, were they flaunting their sin in his face, tormenting the pastor because they knew he was helpless to change them?

The struggle for control over the tormented man continued as he rose from the bed, showered, and with shaky hands shaved. While the pastor made and ate a bowl of bland oatmeal, Boyd screamed for attention. *"They cannot be allowed to torment you. It has always been like this and you know it! Arne Thorson and that slut he was with deserved to die, just as Roberta Swan needed to be stopped. Laura, and the banker, and that stupid farmer, were all living in sin and you were absolutely right when you did what you did. Even Bullshit Sherman was living a lie, trying to make you believe he was your friend. All the while, he was just basking in the perceived righteousness of his ministry."*

As the minutes ticked by, the mental battle continued. As Bauer's torment raged, Sherman's anguish left him wringing his hands. *"Why can't I just let all this confusion drift away? Surely, if I can just act as if nothing is wrong, that none of the mystery is connected to me, the whole thing will just blow over and disappear."* Part of him wanted and needed the simple and safe life of his ministry, *"Maybe Tom Hall will just give up his search and leave Montevideo. When that happens my life will be normal again."* Today was going to determine the future of the man Montevideo knew as Reverend William Tecumseh Sherman.

Fifty-Four

AT 10:02 PASTOR Sherman walked calmly to the lectern as the congregation rose in respect. He was freshly showered and shaved, his hair neatly parted on the left. He had gotten a fresh haircut on New Year's Eve. His slightly worn brown suit jacket hung comfortably, as it always did. As he crossed the room, the baptismal tank beneath the floor echoed just slightly. It was a good reminder of the path to salvation.

The pastor smiled confidently as he welcomed his congregation to the new year. They all bowed their heads for an opening prayer. *Onward Christian Soldiers*, *Hallelujah to the King*—they all sang with gusto. The minister was in good form. He smiled at every row of onlookers as he brought words of hope and joy. Smiles for the Heinrichs, Morehouses and Coles; smiles for Tom and Mary, and for Clifford Shultz, whom he was surprised to see in the congregation this morning.

It was New Year's Day, the first Sunday of a new year, and the first Sunday of the month. Communion, with its cracker and grape juice replacing the body and blood of the Savior. All seemed right with the world. Although Christmas was now past, the congregation sang *Joy to the World* one more time before filing slowly out of the church.

At the door, each congregant was greeted by name, hands were shook, pleasantries given to the children who were anxious to be outside jumping in the snow. Tom and Mary were greeted. "I must apologize for my outburst at the Riverside, Tom. I know some days I over-react."

Tom didn't know what to say, so said nothing.

"We three should meet someday soon; maybe talk about your plans and get to know each other." The expression on the minister's face was benign, forgiving even.

When Cliff Heinrich, flanked by his parents, stopped, the pastor smiled and reached for Clifford's hand. "It has really been a long time since you joined us, Cliff. I'm so happy to see you back."

"I guess I have been struggling with old demons, Pastor." He could not help but look at the minister's right hand as the exchanged their pleasantries. The minister had all his fingers. "Some days I am overwhelmed by the war memories, the days I spent in the hospital, and all the death I saw in France. I can't quite remember it all, of course. My head was pretty messed up; I guess I hallucinated some. I have just been confused about the whole mess. When you arrived in Montevideo, I... well, I don't know. I just got disturbed by old memories."

The pastor gazed into Cliff's eyes, searching for any hidden meaning. "I know what you mean, Cliff. There was a lot of awful stuff that happened in that war. It was my own war experience that led me to God." He continued, "You and I should have coffee or lunch someday soon. It might help us both." William Tecumseh Sherman seemed to be in control of his life.

Fifty-Five

TO A CASUAL observer, Pastor Sherman would have appeared to be at peace with the world, just as he should be. What concerns could a small-town Baptist minister have? His congregation listened to his rather bland sermons on Sundays, and Wednesday, the bible studies were just comfortable social gatherings, where talk wandered to children and weather, often as not. The church council had provided him with an automobile, albeit a somewhat worn version of luxury. They mowed his lawn and pruned shrubs for him with no prompting. It was a good Christian thing to do.

The pastor was welcomed into any home he chose to visit. When a member of the congregation and he passed on the street, there was always a pleasant exchange—a *"lovely morning,"* or *"you look like you're on a mission today."* For reasons not even considered, none in the congregation recognized that the pastor never opened the door of his own home to guests.

And so it was; the first Sunday of the new year, the first Sunday of a new month. Just another Sunday, with parish members dining with family or friends, as they often did. On those same Sundays, Reverend William Tecumseh Sherman walked the short distance to his home, where he would have a lonely lunch and sit alone in his shabby living room.

He paused now at his front door before going inside. Snow had drifted across the step and he kicked at it, then scuffed the entire step clear. "Clean enough," he mumbled, to no one in particular. Of course, the door was not locked. Who would break into a pastor's house?

Once again, he drank the nearly sour milk from the refrigerator. He spun the metal band off a can of Spam and made a cold sandwich on bread that would be moldy in another two days. Spam; it was new on the market just a year ago. Some genius from Iowa had found a way to use the horrible shoulder-cut of pork and thought to make it popular by calling it "Spiced Ham." The sandwich would carry him through the day.

As he slouched on his shabby couch, tears welled up in his eyes. He had said a three-word prayer, *"Bless this food."* But, he wasn't sure who he was praying to. These sad moods had held him more frequently of late. He was suddenly very unhappy with his life as a pastor. The glow was gone. He was jealous of men who had wives to care for them, fix their meals, do their laundry, love them after a hard day doing whatever men do.

He sobbed softly as memories of all his hard years flashed in his brain. The excitement, mixed with the fear he felt as a ten-year-old, when he set fire to the cabin. The memory of the winter with Anna and Johan. That might have been a great opportunity to led a normal life, if not for the pervert banker. He could not escape the past. As he looked back at his life, the pattern was there. No escape—a promise of hope, followed by some unsought or unavoidable catastrophe, which sent him back to a life in the wilderness. Whenever he found a woman who attracted him, he met defeat again. Always the same; *rejection, rejection, rejection*! And, why was there always someone named Iverson lurking there, just waiting to destroy his normal life? In his fitful dream, he had visions of the war, hunkering down in a water-filled trench. In his mind he saw wide-eyed German soldiers trying to kill him before he could take their lives. Then even that small pleasure was stolen when the war was declared over.

The lonely pastor dozed and dreamed of the good days in his past. There were too few good days when compared with the pain and loneliness he was feeling again today. In his fitful sleep, he saw Mary. Voluptuous Mary, tall and shapely, her short hair flicked provocatively when she laughed. Mary—who had seemed so virginal before Tom Hall showed on the scene. She was turning out to be as much a harlot as Roberta Swan. And now he understood; although she was just a cousin, she was another person related to the damnable Iverson clan. They seemed to be everywhere he turned. For a moment, he wondered how he came to be here among these people, then he recalled the night he became William Tecumseh Sherman. Maybe life as Boyd Bauer was not so bad, after all, he thought.

"What am I going to do?" he questioned himself. *"I should just get out of here. I can take my meager possessions and take a train, go to California, or to Arizona. The whole world is closing in on me."* By now he was pacing the floor, turning abruptly, spinning from room to room as his thoughts began to become clear. *"A plan; I need a plan."*

Fifty-Six

WHILE BILL SHERMAN was considering his life as Boyd Bauer, Tom was reclining on a bench in Smith Park. Later, he was going to meet Mary. They were going to spend the evening with Judge Chamberlin and have dinner with the judge and his wife. By now the judge seemed almost like a father to Tom. At the moment however, Tom was wrapped in his mackinaw and he wore a thick soft woolen scarf, which Mary had given him for Christmas, wrapped around his neck. In spite of the cold afternoon he wore only his snap-brim fedora.

He was in deep thought, with his hands folded together and his fingers pressed against his lips. Ten feet away from him was the huge cage confining the symbol of America. The eagle, which Tom thought should be perched on a branch high on some mountain peak and should be casting his eye over some wide valley below, was instead hunkered down, just like Tom. *"He looks dejected,"* thought Tom, *"and why not?"*

Tom had left Mary at her home. She had some housekeeping she wanted to catch up on. Tom just needed some solitude while he tried to sort out his options. He was caught in a game of strategy, a waiting game, that he didn't fully control. His every instinct told him the Baptist pastor was Boyd Bauer. The problem was that he did not have any real proof of that hypothesis. He was unsure how to gather the proof. He certainly could not confront the pastor; *"I think you are a fraud, Boyd. You're not really Bill Sherman, but Boyd Bauer, the killer."* Sherman's reaction was likely to be either ribald laughter, or a turn to violence with some horrible consequence.

No, it was not yet time to confront him. Another day, maybe even two, or at the most three days, should get Tom the information he now felt was so important to solving the mystery. Bill Wilhelmson promised to give this problem his full attention, and Harold Conrad, from the Minnesota Criminal Investigation office, was certain he could provide answers to the questions Tom had laid on him. There was no way to determine if military records he asked for would answer any questions, and in spite of explaining how critical that information might be, Tom knew government wheels turned slowly.

As he sat exchanging stares with the eagle, Tom decided there were some logical paths he could follow: he needed to talk with the people who had been on Main Street the morning George was murdered; he needed to talk to Cliff Heinrich again. Cliff might have some information for him, which had just slipped Cliff's mind.

The eagle shuddered and fluffed its wings just as Tom had a chill and shivered in his mackinaw. Both looked over their shoulders, as if feeling some premonition. Tom looked past the eagle, through the park, and across the river. The cluster of scrub willows, with the path where he had discovered the first chewing gum wrappers stood like a mob of tall skinny cadavers. They seemed to be staring at him and demanding Tom solve the convoluted mystery before spring, when they wanted to spread their leafy green wings.

Tom rose from the bench, mumbled some words of encouragement to the eagle as he left the park. "How peaceful," he thought as he made his way along the trail toward the river. He walked through the small drifts accumulated between the trees and wondered aloud, *"Why did the pastor seem so calm and almost repentant when he greeted Mary and me this morning? Have I so completely mis-judged the man?"* He dismissed that thought as wishful thinking.

The afternoon light was fading as Tom crossed the bridge above the river and the rocky spillway just below it. Ice had formed around some of the rocks. The water looked black and menacing, gurgling for a short distance before disappearing beneath the ice. Tom stopped and watched for a moment as the image of his brother Ernie rose in his mind. *"It's been two years since my brother died. How strange, that I'm here again and trying to solve another murder."* Somehow, the thought of Ernie gave Tom a moment of peace.

Fifteen minutes later Tom was on his way to Mary's house. He had stopped at the hotel to retrieve some personal items, then guided his car up the slippery Second Street hill. As he pushed through small snow drifts in the sheltered areas of Black Oak Avenue he told himself that, in spite of the mysteries surrounding this community, he was quite at peace with the world. *"It's a new year, after all."*

Tom navigated the wintery street. There were drifts here and there, an occasional icy spot, but certainly no problems Tom couldn't handle in the little Ford coupe. Although the Sunday evening church service had been called off because of the weather, Tom thought it seemed like a pleasant evening.

Tom parked near the house, then sat quietly for a moment as he contemplated the life that seemed to be enveloping him. The calm feeling he had when thinking of Ernie just a while before came back. There was no doubt about it; he was in love with Mary. That thought did surprise him, as he acknowledged the fact for the first time. Over the past five months they spent more and more time together. Together, they made plans for a day, or for a week; they considered each other's needs as they talked. She was a joy to be with. It was no longer just lust and sex. *"The sex was good, though,"* he thought with a smile. *"Maybe we should talk about marriage."*

Fifty-Seven

CLIFFORD HEINRICH SPENT a quiet New Year's Eve and day at home. He and his parents spent the evening reading; he with a unique premise by Buckminster Fuller, detailing how, if all the humans on earth were stacked one upon the other, they would reach the moon and back nine times. Cliff found that to be a laughable waste of paper. At other moments he was intrigued at how even Fuller could compile such a theory.

While Maggie slowly made her way through Margaret Mitchell's *Gone with the Wind,* Jack sat quietly, listening on the radio to Glen Miller's orchestra bring the year to a close. At one point, just before indicating she would not stay awake to usher in the new year, she commented, "I understand they are going to make a motion picture out of this book." Jack grunted something unintelligible and continued to smoke his pipe while he calmly rocked in his leather-covered chair.

At about ten 0'clock Jack and Maggie excused themselves. With a cautioning comment to Cliff to not stay up too late, they wished him Happy New Year. They pushed aside the heavy brocade drape which separated the living room from the bedroom, leaving their son alone in the living room. Then, once in their night clothes, they sat together on the edge of the bed and held hands for a moment while they prayed for a safe, successful, and joyous new year. As they had done every night since Cliff returned from the Great War, they thanked God for their son's safe return, before sliding deeply beneath the heavy quilts covering their bed.

Cliff turned off the light over his father's rocking chair a short time later, then returned to his place on the couch. A small table lamp gave just enough light to read by, but he did not reopen his book.

Instead, he put his head back and let his thoughts wander. New Year's Eve was a good night to reminisce, he thought. It came as a bit of a surprise when he realized he had been home from the war for seventeen years. Where had the time gone? He had been hospitalized nearly a year before being discharged from the Army, then came back to Montevideo with a small disability pension. In some ways, it felt like the war had just ended.

Something in his head had not been right since his concussion. He had some memory loss. Sometimes he just seemed to fade out of whatever discussion he was having. For a while, he had dated one of the girls from church; Mildred, he thought her name was, but she had needed more excitement in her life than Cliff offered. When she was not in church one Sunday, he asked about her and was told Mildred had gone to St. Paul with Tommy Thompson. Tommy had been a big star on Windom College's football and baseball teams. With his college degree in hand, he went to work as a salesman in Ekberg Clothing store for a while. Cliff thought he was just a self-centered prick, but now Mildred and he were gone; and that was that.

Cliff joined his parents for church New Year's morning. Although his mother asked him to join them for church nearly every Sunday, Cliff had usually said no. He thought she offered out of habit, rather than with the expectation that he would actually join them. But, this day he responded, "Maybe it's time I changed some old habits, Mom. I think I will."

The church service was bland, which did not surprise Cliff. Singing *Joy to The World* seemed a little mis-placed, but Cliff thought an extra moment or two of joy couldn't hurt anything. After the Heinrichs shared pleasantries with friends, followed by a minute or so with the minister, they went home for lunch. As they sat together, sharing a cup of soup and a sandwich, Cliff wondered to himself what the pastor had meant; *"...the war is where I found God."* Why would he share that thought with Cliff? And, what was, *"We should get to know each other..."* about? The question faded from Cliff's thoughts.

He thought of calling cousin Billy to suggest they go out to Carlton Lake. He momentarily thought they might chop a hole in the ice and hope to catch a fish or two. Instead, he decided to spend the afternoon folding his laundry and re-arranging his bedroom closet.

Most of the closet space was taken up by plaid flannel shirts and gabardine trousers. He owned a few sweaters, but they were seldom taken from their hangers. He had worn his brown pin-stripe suit to church today, and it now hung in its usual place. It had been a long while since it had left the closet, and now it was returned there, perhaps to be worn again next Sunday. At the far end of the closet he paused, then removed the heavy hanger-bag holding his Army uniform. It had hung there since he came home nearly two decades ago. He had worn the heavy woolen trousers during his first two winters back in Minnesota. They had been just right for hunting and fishing, but they had disappeared somewhere along the way.

He slid his tunic from the canvas bag. It smelled just a little musty but looked just as if he might be expected to wear it again. The round black buttons with eagles clutching arrows shown as if new. The campaign ribbons, with the purple heart and the one awarded by the Queen of England, hung crisply above the left pocket. He sat on the bed for a moment, and with his head bowed, visions of the war flashed through his mind. Somehow, it was not a bad feeling this time, even as he rubbed his fingers across the ribbons. For so many years he had been afraid to look back. The trenches, the serpentine wire, and the death and chaos of battle, had always lurked too near the surface of his memory. He ran his fingers over the corporal chevron on the sleeve, recalling the last time he wore the uniform. His homecoming had been both joyful and tearful. The pain and the fear of dying had slowly gone away. Today, those distant times no longer had their chains wrapped around his heart.

As he shrugged his way into the tunic, Cliff heard the crinkle of paper from one of the buttoned pockets. He watched his reflection in the mirror over the bedside commode as he removed a wrinkled and yellowed note, wondering what scrap of paper might have spent so many years there. He noticed the uniform, although snugger than he remembered, still fit fairly well; it was a little tight through the shoulders, but he felt just a bit of pride to still be so trim. Satisfied with his look, Cliff sat again on the bed and unfolded the mystery note.

Tears welled up in Cliff's eyes as he recognized the note which had been written by Corporal Sherman's nurse and left at his bed side. He took a deep breath and swiped the back of his hand across his cheek, then continued to unfold the note, before reading it aloud.

Corporal Sherman has been transferred to a military hospital in the States, where he will be undergoing rehabilitation. He asked me to thank you on his behalf for being a great buddy and bed-mate, and to wish you well in your own recovery. I feel certain his recovery will go well, although it will take some time to get used to the missing fingers.

Fifty-Eight

TOM SMILED AS he listened to Mary humming some tune he could not quite understand. It had taken him much less time dressing for the evening than it was taking Mary. *"I suppose I'll have to get used to that if... well, whatever."* His thoughts wandered as he sipped on a drink. Perhaps, when they returned from the judge's home this evening, they could talk about their future. In the meantime, he decided he should just enjoy the evening ahead.

Mary had changed her mind about her evening's attire several times. She wasn't satisfied that her sweater matched her skirt. Then, after changing the sweater, she decided the skirt wasn't just right. Being so indecisive was unlike her. Mary's life had been filled with decision-making; she had no problem deciding right or left, blue or gray, more or less of something. When Tom Hall had entered her life it somehow changed.

Day by day, she was becoming a different woman. Instead of spontaneous decisions, she found herself asking Tom's opinion about her daily activities. Should I do this, or should I do that? What do you think, Tom? Little choices that had once been made without hesitation now required some thought. More and more, she needed some show of approval from Tom. She smiled as she stood in front of her mirror, thinking how nice her life had become.

The woman who stared back from the mirror surprised Mary. Had she ever really looked at that person? She now thought maybe at five-foot- ten she was taller than her female friends; hmmm, never gave that a thought before. *"And, I suppose my figure is adequate."* The woman in the mirror stared back as she raised her hands and cupped her breasts. She turned slightly, her gaze wandering down to the curve of hip, then onward to slender, nice looking legs. *"Yes,"* she smiled back; *"I guess I am not too bad."*

She was wearing new undergarments Tom had never seen. Just before Christmas, Mary had used the Montgomery Ward catalog to buy Tom a scarf, which she would never have found in the store here in town. Then, as she paged through the women's section, she came upon the scandalously tiny underpants. *Bikini*, the description said, white or pink, with a delicate lace fringe across the top and around the leg openings. She was a grown woman but had never before considered wearing such frilly underwear. The photograph next to the bikinis showed a young woman, skinny, Mary thought, wearing a brassier that was almost nothing at all. Mary knew her own bosom was much larger than the girl in the picture. Could she even get away with wearing such skimpy underwear? Would she just topple out of that nearly invisible bit of lace?

Yes. She might topple out if she was not careful. She had laughed aloud at the mere thought of herself in such provocative underwear. And she ordered both items. Delivered unopened and a secret to everyone but herself.

Now, it was a new day and a new year. Perhaps it was time for a new woman to emerge. The logical thing to do would be put her slip back on and choose another sweater and skirt. Instead, she turned and walked to the living room door. "Tom, will you come here and help me with something?" Dinner with the Chamberlins could wait just a bit.

Without giving Mary's request much thought Tom put his glass on the floor next to the couch, then turned, expecting that Mary perhaps wanted his help moving some piece of furniture, or zipping a zipper on the back of a dress. Instead, he found himself staring at the backlit image of the tall owner of the house, wearing next-to-nothing, as she smiled and beckoned him.

Tom's momentary pause was not to question whether he should continue across the room but was because he believed he had never seen such a beautiful and ravishing woman in his life. At that moment, he was glad he had put his drink on the floor. Had he been holding it, he was afraid he would have dropped the glass at the sight of her.

Mary held Tom at arm's length. Of course, he had wanted to rush into the bedroom and crush her tightly against him. "I actually bought this outfit for your Christmas present," she cooed. "Then, I thought I would unwrap it for New Year's Eve, but something got in our way and I just never thought about clothing." She spun around once before Tom wrapped his arms tightly around her and buried his face in her neck.

They both laughed and twirled toward the bed. The lamp on the night stand shed just enough light to cast their elongated shadows across the bed. Dinner would have to wait once again. Tom could not pull his gaze from Mary. The chestnut hair, which had moments before been pulled into an efficient bun, was now flowing across her shoulders. Mary tugged Tom's sweater up and over his head, laughing as he struggled with having to choose between shedding he sweater or continuing to hold her against him.

The decision of what to do next was made for them. Just as Tom's head cleared the sweater, he was thrown violently past Mary, as a single shot from Boyd Bauer's 9 mm Walther crashed into his shoulder. His inertia threw Mary to the bed. As Tom spun from the gunshot, he tipped the small lamp, sending it to the floor as he careened backward, slamming into the night stand and falling unconscious to the floor.

Mary raised up from the bed. Her ears rang from the gunshot an. In confusion she wondered why Pastor Sherman would be standing in her living room. As she came to terms with what was happening, she recognized it was not the pastor who came at her, but Boyd Bauer. William Tecumseh Sherman had left town, disappeared into the night and into the recesses of Bauer's memory.

The man coming toward her was wild-eyed. He waved the gun back and forth across the room and was shouting something unintelligible. As Mary tried to rise from the bed, he lashed out and struck a heavy blow with the pistol at Mary's head, causing her to fall back onto the bed.

He shrugged out of his topcoat, flinging it to the side of the room as he continued to scream. Some of his words were in English, some in German, but that did not matter. He was screaming about redemption, about adultery, fornication, and sins that must be paid for in full.

He pointed the gun at Mary's head, then it wavered, pointing toward her ample chest. He screamed again and turned the gun toward Tom once more. His next shot went wild, grazing Tom's temple. Then, he laid the Walther on the night stand and turned again to Mary. He grabbed her by the hair, twisting her body backward until she screamed in pain. He grabbed the lacy undergarment covering her breasts and tore it viciously from her body.

"I should have known the first time I saw you that you were a Jezebel! You are nothing but a whore and a blasphemy to the name Mary… the sacred mother of Jesus!"

"Don't do this, Pastor!" she screamed. "Why are you here?"

The man's eyes were ablaze as he continued screaming at Mary. "Your entire clan should be removed from the face of the earth! I can see it all now. All of you Heinrichs and MacGregors are in cahoots with the Iversons. Every place I turn there are more of you, and you just corrupt everything and everyone you come in contact with.

"I have been trying with all my heart to live a good life, and what good has it done me? I've been a good minister all the while I have been in this puky little town; I *am* a good minister! Why can't any of you see that? Now, I'm going to put this all behind me. But, first, you have to pay God's price for your sins. And Tom Hall, who thinks he is so wonderful, he is going to die right in this room. Before he does, however, he will get to see how God treats whores."

Mary had stopped screaming. She knew It would be to no avail. Tom lay unconscious, or possibly dead, beside her bed. There were no homes or streets nearby; no one to hear her screams or the gun shots. She was left alone to confront the madman in her bedroom. His only thought now was to violate her.

As she tried to cover her naked breasts, the red-haired man hovering over her was struggling, still holding her by her hair as he tried to undo the belt around his waist. He screamed in frustration as he tried to free himself from his trousers, only to be tangled in the thread-worn suitcoat he was always so proud of. He slapped Mary viciously again, knocking her to the bed, then grabbed at the delicate bikinis Tom had so recently admired.

Mary's brain was ablaze as she struggled with what was happening to her. She stared up at the maniac hovering over her, whose hair was now a wild tangle. He struggled with the shirt, necktie and at the jacket that hung from his shoulders and confined his movements. His trousers were now around his knees. Mary could not bear to look at his nakedness as she kicked out in self-defense.

Bauer now had his hand around Mary's neck, squeezing so tightly that she could not scream, as he forced her back on the bed. Then, with a knee on the bed, he began to lean over her.

At that moment, the chaos in the bedroom took a tumultuous turn at the violent eruption of another gun shot. Standing in the doorway was Clifford Heinrich. The .45 caliber pistol in his hand was still pointed at Bauer. The 230-grain lead bullet had left the gun's barrel travelling at 830 feet per second, meaning Bauer had lived less than one-one-hundredth of a second after Cliff pulled the trigger. The lead slug entered near Bauer's lowest rib and destroyed his heart and both lungs before exiting just beneath his clavicle and finally coming to rest lodged in Mary's flowered wall paper.

Mary had no idea what was happening. She screamed at the unmentionable penetration she was expecting as Bauer's body fell with full force on her now-naked body. Her next recollection was seeing Cliff, as he wiped the residue of Bauer's life from her face. Her nakedness was now covered by the bedspread Cliff had thoughtfully pulled over her. "Little cousin," he whispered, "I hope you will forgive me for making such a mess of your bedroom."

Fifty-Nine

I'M NOT SURE what I had expected when I came to Montevideo. I thought to learn some family history of course, and to meet some of those relatives for the first time. Fortunately, my business and my investments gave me the freedom to stay in Minnesota longer than I could have possibly considered. Now, January 2, 1939, I found myself included in the quiet gathering taking place in Judge Chamberlin's office. I was joined there by the judge, Cliff Heinrich, William Smith, M.D .Also in the room was Montevideo's chief of police, and the judge's secretary, who was quietly taking notes. Missing from the meeting were Mary Collins and Tom Hall. I supposed I was there as surrogate for the two of them.

Mary was receiving the tender care of Maggie, the aunt who seemed more like a mother to her. The two women were talking quietly in the suite Judge Chamberlin had arranged at the Riverside Hotel, to be available as long as she needed it. It was going to be some time before Mary's house was available; even longer perhaps, before she would be comfortable there.

Tom was yelling at the nurses and doctors that he was certainly well enough to get out of the hospital, but Doctor Smith had taken no chances and ordered him to stay in the hospital for at least another day. Boyd Bauer's first nine-millimeter slug had torn through the little gap between Tom's shoulder blade and spine. That bullet-track missed certain death for him. Although the concussion of the bullet was itself dramatic, it was the fall against the night stand and wall which left him unconscious. Bauer's second shot had removed a strip of hair along Tom's crown that now looked like his hair had been parted with a spoon. He would have a scar when his head healed, but the doctor had smiled when he said, "At least your brains are still on the inside, Tom."

Tom was expected to be released from the hospital later in the day, or on Tuesday at the latest. We were gathered in the judges office to give Cliff a chance to relieve his stress by sharing Sunday's events.

Sixty

THE JUDGE HAD begun the meeting with a simple statement. "Well, this is a hell of a way to start the new year!"

One by one, everyone had an opportunity to voice their surprise and concerns. We all looked at Cliff, knowing or at least hoping, he had the answer to our real question; *what happened that brought Cliff to Mary's house?*

"Cliff, bring us up to speed on this." The judge leaned across his desk. Although he had a freshly sharpened pencil in hand, it seemed more like a tension release tool than a writing instrument at the moment. "I have a ton of questions. Can you just tell us what sent you out to Mary's house? You're the last person in the world I would expect to rush into someone's home with his gun blazing. We have been trying for months to find a killer living amongst us, then bang; all of a sudden you show up with this."

"I'm not sure how to even start this, Your Honor." Cliff began. "I discovered something that afternoon and just jumped forward. Lord; I can't believe it all happened just yesterday."

"Cliff, Avis here is going to take notes on all this. We can put it into some logical form later, but why don't you just start talking. Let your thoughts go where they may."

"Well, I think you all know I served in Europe during the Great War. When I came back to Montevideo, I was at something of a loss. While I was in the trenches in France I got caught by a huge bombardment. I had a pretty bad concussion, was unconscious for several days, and then in and out of it for a long while. I spent quite a while in hospitals before I was discharged.

"While I was in the hospital in England, I was bed-mate with a guy who was all bandaged up from his wounds. He had an arm in a sling and trussed over his head. I never did see his face. His head was covered with bandages all the way down to his neck. Just his eyes and mouth were exposed. He had gotten it worse than me. He also had his right hand bandaged; he lost a couple of fingers, I was told.

"Like me, he was a corporal. He was soft-spoken, stuttered a bit when he got agitated. I never found out where he was from. Maybe I should say, if he told me where his home was, I have just forgotten. What I do remember however, was he said his experience in France, being saved when so many around him were being blown to bits, had brought him to God. Somehow, I was left with the impression he thought he would become a minister or a missionary.

"One morning, while I was getting my own therapy down the hall, he disappeared. When I came back to our ward there was a note on my bed, written for him by his nurse. The guy's name was Bill Sherman, the same name as our pastor.

"I had forgotten his name until Sunday. Yesterday. I guess it was just party of my fuzzy brain for all these years."

"Cliff, are you saying our pastor was the guy next to you in the hospital?"

"No, I don't think that is what I am saying at all. When the new pastor showed up in Montevideo in 1927, I had been attending church pretty regular. Since my parents were part of the founding group I could hardly not attend their church. Well, after the new pastor had been here a few weeks, I got this uneasy feeling. I'm not sure how to describe it, but something about him left me uncomfortable. Of course, at that time my memory of being in the hospital with a man of the same first and last name just wasn't there. I guess that old memory was just rattling around, trying to find daylight. The new pastor never said anything about recognizing me or being in my ward at the hospital. I guess that's because he was never there. I just had this fuzzy memory of corporal Sherman in my head.

"On Sunday—New Year's Day—I was straightening my closet. I had thought of calling my cousin Billy about going ice fishing out at Carlton Lake, but decided I would rather just have a quiet day at home. Mom and Dad and I spent the previous evening together and I was just feeling in a homebody kind of mood. Well, that isn't important. As I was hanging some shirts in the closet, I came across the bag where I have kept my uniform since returning from the army. I was curious how it fit; maybe a little nostalgic about being younger and being shot at I guess. Anyway, I put on my dress uniform jacket and found a paper folded in one of the pockets. It was the nurse's note from the hospital."

Our eyes were all riveted on Cliff as he told his story. I couldn't help myself. "What did it say?" I blurted. "Do you have it with you?" a hundred other questions raced through my brain, but the judge interrupted.

"Cliff, I need to see the note. If you don't have it with you, we need you to get it, or send someone to you house for it."

"No; no… I have it right here, but I'm not sure what value that might be."

The judge read it slowly, then the note was passed to each of us, who read it and finally gave it back to the judge. "It's interesting, Cliff. But I don't see anything here that might have sent you rushing out to Mary's house."

"Well, it wasn't just the note. After church on Sunday, the pastor was visiting with the congregation, of course. Before we left, he commented that he and I should get to know each other better. The other thing he said was, 'the war is where I found God'." That little comment triggered something in my memory. I wondered at the familiarity of the phrase, then thought that like me, maybe the pastor just had memory loss.

"After I recovered my composure at seeing myself in my old uniform, and after staring at that old note, I decided that since it was a new year and since the pastor had reached out to me, I should just go visit him. It being New Year's Day and all that, you know.

"It was a pleasant enough afternoon. I just guessed the minister would be home. There wasn't going to be an evening service. I suppose I was just motivated to reach out. Our homes are only about six blocks apart. I suppose I could have walked, but with the fresh snow I decided to drive over there.

"When I got to his home, I didn't see his car, but I noticed the door was ajar. I thought maybe he had left his car around the corner at the church, so I parked and went to the house. I knocked, then hollered his name; politely of course. And… well, there was no answer. Since the door was open, I thought I would just leave a note to let him know I had stopped by, maybe encouraging him to get in touch with me.

"I have to say, I have never seen a house in such a mess. I'm single, so I understand men aren't always great housekeepers, but his house was worse than just unkempt. There were clothes strewn throughout the house, In the kitchen I found part of a bottle of sour milk and some moldy food that looked to have been there for days. My first inclination was to shut the door and get away as fast as I could. I might have done just that, but when I passed by his desk with all its own clutter, I stopped in my tracks.

"In the midst of the clutter I saw three things I couldn't ignore. That stuff on the desk changed my entire view of what I was supposed to do."

If any of the others in the room had thoughts of interrupting Cliff, they clamped their jaws as tight, as I did my own.

"I might have just looked past the book on the desk if not for the two other things which seemed completely out of place. I picked up the book, which had been open and lying face-down. The book was old and looked like it had been around a long time. The cover was like the army olive drab; the kind of journal I kept for a while in France. Although it was faded, I could make out the hand-written note on its cover. It stated simply, 'This is Bill Sherman's Diary'."

"I felt guilty as I turned it in my hand, randomly looking at pages. The notes went back many years. My guilt got the best of me and I started to put it back on the desk. That's when I saw his last entry. It was made Sunday—New Year's Day. I had seen notes the pastor had written, and this looked nothing like his handwriting. The scrawl was so terrible I couldn't make out some of the words. What I saw looked like the scribbling of a madman. I suppose in the end that is what the pastor was.

" As I stared at the diary, my eyes were again attracted to the other two items that were so obviously out of place there. A partial box of 9 mm ammunition lay on its side, some of the shells strewn randomly in the clutter. It definitely was not the look of someone just caring for his weapon. Next to the box was an oil-soaked rag. It looked much like the cloth I wrapped around my own service pistol.

"I reached out to touch the rag as I read the final notes in the book I held. You can read for yourselves what was written there, but in essence it said, 'Tom and Mary were going to be punished for their sins'.

"I didn't have to think twice about what I needed to do. Without really thinking, I jammed the book in my jacket pocket and ran for my car. When I got to my home, I left the engine running and the door wide open. My mother screamed as I rushed past her. I didn't answer when she asked what I was doing but shouted that she needed to call the police and get them to Mary's house as quick as possible; and, that with any luck, I would be there.

"I've kept my service pistol in my dresser for sixteen years. On a few occasions Billy and I shot at tree stumps, or at a skunk, but since the war I have never needed to kill anything—until that afternoon. I'm sure I took the steps two or three at a time as I rushed back past my mother."

There was a pitcher of water and a half-dozen glasses on the desk, and Cliff took the time to half-fill one, and drink it in a single large swallow. We were all staring at Cliff. The judge's secretary had stopped taking notes long before.

My guess is that there was enough electricity in the air to spark a fire if we moved. We exchanged looks, then returned our gazes toward Cliff, as he continued.

"I almost lost control of the darn car several times on the way to Mary's. It's less than a mile of course, but I took the corners way too fast. It was late in the afternoon by now, almost dark, I guess. I should have had my headlights on, but never gave a thought to it. All I could think of was Mary having to face a madman with a gun. I didn't know Tom was with her, but they seem to be together all the time these days; I never gave that a second thought. I was just thinking about Mary.

"I think the snow-cover on the driveway kept my arrival from being heard. As I pulled into the driveway, I saw Tom's car parked next to the house, but there was no other car in sight. Then, I spotted the pastor's car—the one our congregation had bought for him— parked over by the evergreens. It was nearly out of sight. The first sound I heard was a gun-shot, coming from someplace in the house. My brain must have just reverted to my time in the war. I leapt from the car and headed for the front door of the house.

"As I entered, I could hear Mary screaming. I could hear other yelling but couldn't make out what was being said. There was a second shot. That's when I charged to the bedroom and saw Bauer attacking Mary. His pants were around his ankles. He looked like a madman—I guess he actually was. Well, he had Mary by the neck and was just climbing on to the bed when I fired. He fell on top of Mary, knocked the wind out of her, I guess. She stopped screaming. Only then did I realize I might have shot her.

"Well, anyway, the pastor—I mean Bauer—was dead; parts of him were spread across the bed and wall. Mary was unconscious, so I threw Bauer to the floor and covered Mary with her bedspread.

"I turned to Tom, expecting the worst. He was bleeding from his scalp, and there was a lot of blood around his shoulder. I saw a lot of nasty wounds in the war of course, so I just grabbed the doily from the overturned dressing table and slapped in over Tom's wounded shoulder. I'm not sure what it was I took from the dresser drawer to stop his head from bleeding, but I'm sure I won't be blamed for the loss of whatever it was.

"About that time, Mary was coming-to, and then the police pulled into the yard. I helped find Mary some clothes. I guess the rest is history."

We spent the next two hours discussing the mystery surrounding Boyd Bauer. Not the least of the unanswered questions was, what had happened to the real Bill Sherman? I questioned whether the newly-discovered diary might shed light on the deaths of Bobbie Swan and Arne Thorson. Tthe judge just answered that the diary would be reviewed in good time. "With any luck," he commented, "our counterfeit minister might have kept a better diary than a criminal should have."

As the meeting drew to an end, I asked for a few minutes with the judge. "My genealogical expedition has been successful," I told him, " although not nearly producing the exciting results I had hoped for." I explained that I would probably leave Montevideo in the next several days.

"Yes," I told the judge, "I think I'll head for Alpena, Michigan, to see if I could learn how the Logan family had made their trip from Normandy to America. Then, unless I find a king or queen in my ancestry in France, I should get back to tending to my businesses. I think I'll leave the Iverson history for Tom and Mary to solve. On the other hand," I continued, "maybe I'll go to Norway; there might be royalty waiting for me there."

Sixty-One

WEDNESDAY MORNING TOM was released from the hospital. His head ached, his shoulder and chest hurt from the damage done by the 9 mm bullet that had torn its way through his body on the way to being imbedded in the wall. And Tom's pride was hurt. He couldn't forgive himself for putting Mary in such danger.

I met Tom at the hospital's reception desk. In the car which had been loaned for his use, I drove him to the Riverside Hotel, then left him as I went to the Stavos Café for lunch.

There was no pressure now to get the results from Tom's queries. All the information in the world would—at best—just confirm or deny what was now known. Those of us involved in the Chippewa County murders decided to just let Tom rest until he was absolutely ready to get re-involved.

Mary left her aunt Maggie at the hotel entry, then met Tom in the lobby. The couple slowly made their way to her suite on the third floor. The well-appointed set of rooms had a huge window looking out over Smith Park. Just out of sight on the right was the Chippewa River spillway. They were too far removed from it to hear the pleasant gurgling as the cold water sunk beneath the ice. The path leading alongside the stream was snow-covered. The chilly new year had not enticed anyone into taking a secluded walk through the park, so the captive eagle was left to himself.

The couple were almost shy in each other's presence, each concerned that the other might need delicate treatment. For several minutes they stood together, looking down on the river and park. As Tom looked into Mary's eyes now, he thought she seemed tinier than he remembered, a more delicate flower than just two days before;

perhaps a damaged soul who might need to be treated with special care.

As he turned toward her and started to speak, Mary put her fingers to his lips. "Don't talk," she whispered, then took his hand and led him toward the bed. "I would really like you to just hold me for a minute."

The bed was huge and soft. More pillows than a person could use for sleep were piled beneath a huge carved headboard. Although they were both fully clothed, Mary pulled the down comforter from the bed's foot and covered them to their necks. In only minutes they were both asleep in each other's arms.

When Tom opened his eyes some time later, Mary was staring at him. "I have a wonderful idea," Tom whispered. Mary's brow furrowed as she ran her fingers carefully along the wound in his hair and tried to hear him as he whispered, "I think you and I should get married. To each other, of course," he continued with a quiet laugh. "I have never been happier than I am with you, and I cannot imagine how I could have continued if Bauer had taken your life but not mine." He kissed her lightly, then continued, "We should get married, get on the train, and just go and go, until we're tired of traveling."

They were like two children, hiding from the world and letting their imaginations carry them far away. This was a world apart from everything that could cause them concern. They cuddled and kissed, gently holding on to their solitude.

"Tomorrow morning," Mary whispered, "I think we should drive to the courthouse. If you haven't changed your mind by then, we'll get a marriage license. On Saturday we'll meet here in the lobby and have Judge Chamberlin marry us," Tom took that to mean she agreed to his proposal. "There is one problem, my darling. I have a job which will give us groceries, but little else. You have been wandering around Chippewa County without any income since August. Do you have some secret cache of wealth you are hiding from me?"

"I have a little surprise regarding that problem." Tom smiled, then sat up against the headboard. "While I was waiting for Doc

Smith to release me this morning I had a phone call. No, that is not the surprise. A book publisher in Chicago has offered me a nice advance to write about all this madness. It seems Maximillian Bauer's legacy of hate and murder has sparked some interest around the country. The advance will keep us very nicely for nearly a year, while I ferret out the truth of Boyd Bauer. There is little doubt he was insane. Maybe his insanity grew slowly over years. Maybe the pressure of knowing I was looking so deeply into the lives of all the people he had affected just drove him over the edge. In any case, he was never the man he portrayed himself to be.

"As I research the book, I can take all the time needed to get to the truth. We can travel to those places the Iversons and Heinrichs came from. Maybe, even the MacGregors. We might finally get to know the truth about Max Bauer. You can work or not. Of course, if you keep your job, I may have to travel alone. What do you think?"

In response, Mary took one of the huge pillows and playfully beat Tom until they both collapsed with laughter.

m m m

About the Author

Minnesota native Arthur Norby has spent more than our decades devoted to the arts. Since beginning his formal career in1976, at the age of thirty-eight, he has created more than six hundred sculptures, including more than a dozen life-size and heroic sculptures in public places. He opened his first of eight galleries in 1979 and has represented more than one-hundred-fifty artists.

Although well-known as the creator of the Minnesota Korean War Veterans Memorial, which was dedicated in 1998, his personal-size bronze and terra cotta sculptures continue to be sought by collectors across the U.S. His sculptures can be found in collections in Canada, Europe and South America.

Still active in his eighties, Arthur Norby accepts sculpture commissions, while concentrating on oil paintings of vibrant skies which he is universally well-known.